Test of the Professionals – Part I:

The Adventure
of the
Flying Blue Pidgeon

Test of the Professionals – Part I:

The Adventure
of the
Flying Blue Pidgeon

Sherlock Holmes and
His London
Through the Eyes
of Scotland Yard

by Marcia Wilson

Edited by David Marcum

MX Publishing

ISBN Paperback 978-1-80424-638-2
ISBN AUK ePub 978-1-80424-639-9
ISBN AUK PDF 978-1-80424-640-5

Published by
MX Publishing
335 Princess Park Manor, Royal Drive,
London, N11 3GX
www.mxpublishing.co.uk

David Marcum can be reached at:
thepapersofsherlockholmes@gmail.com

Cover Design by Awan
Illustration of The Yarders by Marcia Wilson

Sherlock Holmes and
the Scotland Yarders
by Marcia Wilson

1. *You Buy Bones*
2. *Test of the Professionals: The Adventure of the Flying Blue Pidgeon*
3. *Test of the Professionals: The Peaceful Night Poisonings*
4. *Test of the Professionals: Leap Year*
5. *The MoonCursers*
6. *A Sword for Defense*
7. *The Narrow Path: The First Storm*
8. *The End of All Things*
9. *A Fanged and Bitter Thing*

Further adventures forthcoming . . . .

Foreword
by Marcia Wilson

Looking back, it was a strange time. High school in the late 1980's meant Tolkien, King, Christie, and Poe were always checked out of the school library, but we had multiple copies of Sherlock Holmes on the shelf. If students were going to apply for English-oriented scholarships, by gosh, we were going to read the good stuff, and that meant short stories with murder and mayhem. In emulation of the masters, our choices were usually ACD or . . . Hemingway. It wasn't much of a contest. Hemingway didn't have a demon glowing Death Hound on the moors.

High school segued into college, but we had *Mystery!* re-runs on PBS, even if we had to visit people to watch it, and besides Jeremy Brett, we had Christopher Plummer's compassionate Holmes against Jack the Ripper, a role that shattered the domination of Rathbone and Bruce. Our classmates swore it was necessary for our sincerity as fans of Sir Arthur to see it.

If that sounds like pithy stuff for high schoolers, my generation had a flexible relationship with media – or even power grids. Even if they existed, they weren't exactly as reliable as the sun coming up every morning. The further into the West Virginia panhandle you got, the bigger the library room in the house. Even the poorest of houses, be they on blocks or wheels, had at least one shelf of sanity to rely on when the power was out, or the brownouts made hash of anything but AM radio. When a flood took out the local libraries, it was devastation.

There was media, but there wasn't enough – there's never enough – but as far as the books printed in the wake of Sir Arthur . . . it really was never enough. You were lucky to find something in a thrift store or library sale, and your odds were no worse than combing the bookstores in the mall. Oh, for the days when there was more than one bookstore in a mall. If something was found, readers had to buy it on faith that it wasn't a waste of their time.

Look, our standards weren't low, they were desperate. We made a lot of poor book-buying choices, which were hastily returned to the ecosystem of flea market sales for some other poor shmuck to buy up. One girl, bless her, would donate the books after carefully penciling in every sin the authors made against Canon, history, plot contrivance, and attempts to pair Holmes up with a romantic partner. I like to think she cackled as she returned the much-improved dreck to the public. She always cited her sources . . . .

It shouldn't be a surprise when we wound up obsessing, ever so slightly, with what little we could find that wasn't terrible, and (*Hooray!*) didn't go against The Canon. I wonder if anyone has ever tried to list all the knockoffs and illicit print runs out there. Probably not – I'd like to think nobody could be that crazy.

Fan fiction was the outlet for a crying need that had hit breaking point. Paper fanzines of decent quality were even harder to find than a decent paperback on the shelf – you have never bought a pig in a poke until you've combed through a hand-printed zine catalog, squinted at the type, and decided to spend your allowance on what sounded the most promising – and too bad the cover art was rarely as good on the inside.

Fanzine editors lived in the twilight, trying to put out their passion projects between the obligations of home, family, and keeping a roof over their head, as well as hanging on to entire drawers of receipts to make sure a rival 'ziner didn't get spiteful and report them to the IRS. (That actually happened.) Zines were non-profit only, which is partly why the zines we could afford were always shipped Media Mail on whatever paper was on sale. If you were very lucky, you got your order in three weeks.

Maybe we shouldn't talk about the pastichery in animation . . . .

The Internet found its feet and bloomed with forums and places to hide and talk about the lack of stories, and that led to posting paper zines online, and people began writing fresh stuff, online, and showing it for reading and/or critiquing. Almost overnight there were clubs, groups, and social organizations that could get their fix on the stories between the boom-and-bust world of conventions and newsletters.

There were friendships made that I miss to this very day. The sheer power of a small number of people who were intelligent, thoughtful, and mindful of Canon encouraged so many of us. They helped with research, knew how to spell, and learned different languages in this world. They reviewed books, scrounged supplies, and let us know if someone was copying our plots just a little too much for comfort. Plagiarism and how to address it was a real eye-opener when it came to intellectual property that wasn't yours to begin with, but you could claim the OC's (Original Characters) were yours, and debatably, your unique perspective on the people, places, and things created under the pen of Sir Arthur.

I was a fan of these fans. They were amazing and – honestly – damn good writers. *Damn* good. They were role models. They read the whole Canon, and they kept track of everything, and they led us to places like *fanfiction.net*, where we could post with a minimum of fussing.

I could write about anyone I wanted, but it was partially out of respect for these writers that I began to veer away from making just one more story about Sherlock Holmes and Dr. Watson. I loved the stories, but part of their appeal was their world. And there was a lot to that world that was relevant today. Methods may alter crime, but motives rarely do.

At the time, there was a pretty well-represented group that was pro-Watson, and they wrote some of those "damn good stories" with Watson as the protagonist – or at least, a powerful, equal voice. The Granada series was a huge influence, as well as the Russian series, and throw in some of "the radio show" for good measure.

These fan writers may have loved the tight scripts and drama of the Rathbone and Bruce approach, but as they grew up, they said, collectively, "Man, that was bad for Watson!" There were other words, much less polite. Burke and Hardwicke were a positive force for the shift in the thinking that pointed out Watson was *not* an idiot and we couldn't do a decent job showing how smart Holmes was by surrounding him by idiots. This had already been tried, during Classic Dr Who, and nobody had been left happy about it. Nobody blamed the actors for doing their job too well.

Fine, I thought, *there are a lot of really good writers writing for Watson. I can do that.* But I also caught on that if Watson illuminated Holmes by writing of the man from his point-of-view, *maybe I could write about Watson through other people's eyes.* The question was: *Who?*

Enter a re-visit to the Granada Series, and "The Norwood Builder".

I make no secret of the fact that I am heavily synesthetic. Face blindness comes with its own challenge, and I have to train myself to recognize people. With an irony that approaches opera-grade comedy, I literally could not tell Holmes from Lestrade in Granada's "The Norwood Builder". Also, Lestrade made me angry when I was a hero-worshipping teenager watching the show with other hero-

3

worshipping teenagers. *How dare Lestrade challenge Holmes? Couldn't anyone see Holmes was the smartest man in the room?*

Older adult me revisited that part of my life and went *Oops!* because there were some of those Fanfiction Demigods that rather liked Lestrade and had plenty of backup reasons. I wish I could remember the name of the one who mused, *"Colin Jeavons is the only actor who could be bulldog-like and also ferrety."* I was doing a lot of research at my job, and that included the Victorian era and law enforcement. Somehow it all started clicking together, piece by piece.

A writer whom I regret losing (her entire message board went the way of LiveJournal – only, it vanished for good. Poof. No trace) challenged me on whether or not Lestrade was stupid. He knew more than he let on, she said, and I . . . kind of said, *"Oh? Prove it."*

Ouch. She did, lining out events in "The Boscombe Valley Mystery" and "The Second Stain" and a few other bits and pieces, and I ate crow. A lot of it. I was wrong. Still, I could at least write with this new perspective. Bad as it was to be wrong, it would be worse to stay with it.

Add to this a sleep disorder that can politely be called *insomnia*, and a marriage turning into a nightmare of violence, and no health insurance – but writing was the cheapest therapy out there . . . Lestrade slowly woke up and came to life. I'll blame Colin Jeavons for knowing what the writers wanted out of the scripts. It's on him.

"Trust your characters," my old English teacher would say, sternly, so I did. I wrote short stories that could connect with others to make a fuller piece. A necklace is made one bead at a time. I wrote at night. I had to. I needed to stay awake, listening to any sounds that might be my ex-husband's return to stalk us – tampering with my car, crawling under the house, draining the well his own children needed to drink from, and taunts to the police that tried their best, but could only work within the limits of the system. They failed, but it was the system that failed. They cared, and they shared my rage that when the ex was finally brought to justice, it was too late for one of his victims.

There is only so much a policeman can do against so much collective injustice out there. If Sherlock Holmes had existed on that force, they would have begged for his help against my ex-husband. They knew he could go where they couldn't, and they would know when not to ask the awkward questions about how information was collected. They would have sniffed and said, "Well, that's a pity," and shrugged and did things according to the law – *their* law – but not expecting civilians to follow the same oaths they swore.

I empathized with Gregson's ability to buck the rules, and I empathized for Lestrade's inability to do so. The Yarders took on their own lives and, without knowing it, the job had changed. I was now sitting back and watching the stories unfold, writing them as fast as they told them. They had a lot to say. They still do, but the stories are whispering now. We are safer, there is no need to listen for danger. I am learning how to sleep.

More years ago than I'd like to recollect, I received an email so startling I forwarded it to my sister before a family dinner at the pizza parlour. It wasn't a fantastic day. Before long I would be needing their help to flee across the country in the middle of a winter snowstorm. The mood was glum. We were subdued.

My sister looked at me over the table and said with uncharacteristic bluntness, "You impressed that man."

That man was David Marcum.

Marcia Wilson
February 2025

Scotland Yard's Story
Editor Foreword
by David Marcum

Back in 2008, it was still a different Sherlockian world from today.

In those days, the quest for more excellent Holmes adventures beyond the pitifully few sixty Canonical adventures was still quite difficult. Each year, only a few slipped through the needle's-eye clutch of the moribund major publisher model. (In fact, if one is still publishing by that route, then this fact remains true.) But there were many Holmes adventures waiting to be revealed, and they just needed an outlet. Is it any wonder that the Internet was that path?

Holmes pastiches have been around since William Gillette's 1899 play, *Sherlock Holmes*, showing that Our Heroes' adventures did *not* have to pass across the first Literary Agent's desk. Some amazing and accurate adventures appeared on the radio in the 1930's, courtesy of visionary Edith Meiser. And the door kept getting wider, with more radio shows, films, and the occasional book giving us more traditional, authentic, and Canonical Holmes.

But it was not enough.

In 1998, *fanfiction.net* was created, allowing another outlet for sharing Holmes's adventures, wherein those who had discovered them could get them directly to starving readers immediately, without facing the impossible discouragement of the faceless soul-dead major publishing model. I was fortunate to discover the site a few years after that, and began to visit regularly to read and print and archive stories about the True Holmes. There are thousands of Holmes stories located there, but many are parodies, or anachronistic, or related to modernized and offensive simulacrums, or with incorrect ghost-busting leanings. Others were clearly written by individuals who have no clue about Sherlock Holmes, or have hijacked him for their own agendas. These stories may be ignored, even if they have to be waded through – for buried in the muck of this backyard goose lot, for those who take time to look, are some true and rare jewels.

And in April 2008, the beginning of a couple of stories were posted, "An Ordinary Meeting" on the tenth, and "Truth is the Critic" the next day, both as written by an author going under the curious sobriquet of *aragonite*.

"An Ordinary Meeting" gives details of Lestrade's first consultation with Sherlock Holmes, and "Truth is the Critic" is written from the perspective of the Scotland Yard inspectors as they read *A Study in Scarlet* – and providing their reactions when see how Watson has described them. These were well written and interesting, and this approach really hadn't been attempted before.

(To be accurate, there had been some stories about the Yarders, but they were inconsistent. For instance, M.J. Trow's long Lestrade series veers wildly from legitimate mysteries to unreadable parodies, with particularly bogus attacks on Sherlock Holmes, and Trow inexplicably gives Inspector G. Lestrade the first name of "Sholto".

In "Truth is the Critic", *aragonite* was already painting the Yarders – Inspectors Lestrade, Gregson, Bradstreet, and Hopkins in particular – in well-rounded and respectful ways that hadn't been seen before. They had their own life stories beyond The Canon, and weren't just the inspector *du jour* appearing in this-or-that Canonical tale. Who knew then that this new author, slipping quietly onto the scene, had such an overall vision for these individuals, with fully realized details about their personal lives, their backgrounds and histories . . . and a plan for a massive overarching adventure that would span decades in their lives?

Over the next few months, more stories quickly followed – "A Cookout in Cornwall", "Route to Madness", and "Just Inspector Will Do" (my all-time favorite of these works, relating the events on the Paddington platform when Mary Watson awaits her husband's return from the Continent in mid-May 1891. I re-read it every year on Reichenbach Day.) But on April 17th, 2008, *aragonite* raised the stakes, publishing the first chapter of a novel, *A Sword for Defense*, the first of a massive story arc relating what Watson and Lestrade and the other Yarders faced in the months after Holmes's supposed death at the Reichenbach Falls.

While keeping one story going would overwhelm many authors, *aragonite* – whomever he or she was – had even greater ambitions. New stories and chapters began to be posted at a feverish pace. A week after *Sword* started, another serialized novel began, *You Buy Bones*, telling how Watson, in early 1882 and fresh from his first year living with Holmes in Baker Street, comes across a monstrous crime that directly and personally affects the Scotland Yard inspectors. And a few months after that, *aragonite* started another novel that served as a prequel leading to *Sword* called *The MoonCursers*, telling of Lestrade's own terrifying adventures in late April and early May 1891, occurring at the same time Holmes and Watson were playing cat-and-mouse with Moriarty, on their way to a fateful encounter in Meiringen.

Over the course of that summer, nearly every day brought some new chapter: Sometimes another episode in *A Sword for Defense* or *You Buy Bones* or *The MoonCursers*, and at other times a seemingly stand-alone story that that filled in some crucial and interesting aspect about the Scotland Yarders that only made the overall painting richer and deeper.

Imagine if Charles Dickens were writing and publishing three serialized novels at once, and adding in short stories too. And they were going straight from being written to being posted for public consumption as soon as they were complete. And clearly the overall storyline wasn't being generated along the way – there was a *plan*, for little threads mentioned here and there about Lestrade's boyhood or Bradstreet's family had massive importance much later.

Over many months during this time, *aragonite* was also constructing another massive work, *Test of the Professionals*, which related the events after *You Buy Bones* and served as a set-up for *A Sword for Defense*, telling us much more about Lestrade's past, his unfortunate and dangerous life-long connection with Professor Moriarty's agent, the truly evil Jethro Quimper, and the escalating and terrifying events surrounding his courtship with Clea Cheatham.

In August 2008, with all of this going on, *aragonite* started another brilliant novella, *A Secondary Stain*, the *other* events of "The Second Stain", in which Lestrade was not as clueless as he appears in Watson's manuscript, actually working behind the scenes to assist Holmes's investigation. It was the brilliance of this story that finally prompted me to write a fan letter.

Using the fan fiction website's messenger feature, I emailed an extensive message to *aragonite* in October 2008, and soon received a wonderful and informative reply.

First, I learned that *aragonite* was really Marcia Wilson. In subsequent communications, I learned that *aragonite* – which curiously I'd never looked up before then – is calcium carbonate used by marine organisms to build their shells and skeletons. Since aragonite can be found in cave formations, and since Marcy is a caver – the evidence of which can be found in some of her stories brilliantly dealing with caverns and London's Lost Rivers – I suspect that's why she chose the unusual pen-name.

Over many emails over many years, Marcy has explained to me that she wrote so prolifically in those early years because she had insomnia, and that was a very productive time to write. She also could *see* all of these scenes, and almost couldn't write fast enough to convey them. In her very first reply to me in October 2008, she explained, how she approached telling the Yarders' story, and why she named Inspector G. Lestrade *Geoffrey:*

> *I've never liked the playing down of characters. It's a lazy way to pump up the character in your mind. I have to be very careful not to wander into the Fangirlyverse. Usually I deal with it by giving a character a name I dislike, and for some reason, I dislike Geoffrey so naturally I stuck it on the poor guy.*

She also explained that:

> *I was so bleeding tired of writing against another person's notions on Holmes and Watson that I just went to another character that I rather liked. (When I was younger, I hated Lestrade. He should have been kowtowing to Holmes' genius like all of us!) Later on, I realized that it took a pretty remarkable man to refuse to see Holmes in a reverent light. [The] clues about Lestrade were subtle and interesting. There had to be a reason for someone who was supposed to be such a good cop to stay a police inspector after his initial promotion. I made him a Celtic Breton out of a half-thought. I was seeing Colin Jeavons in my head, and he's so Welsh he's probably half-Neanderthal! Being a Breton or a Channel Islander would have made [Lestrade] an English citizen, but he would not have been accepted as an equal in race or status by many people.*

Our communications continued, as did her writing. By early 2009, *A Sword for Defense* was complete, and the next book in the ongoing saga, *The Narrow Path* had commenced. Those were great days to be a Sherlockian and to be reading *fanfiction.net*, as there were other great authors there as well – *Westron Wynde* and *KCS* among them, all with powerful and correct understandings of the *True Holmes*. These authors were writing for the fans, and also for each other, and I was privileged to be in contact with many of them. In a few years, Marcy and *Westron*

Wynde – who turned out to be amazing pasticheur Sarah Bennett, whose works are slowly being made available from Belanger Books – began to take down their online works and publish them in real books. (It was at this time that I let Marcy and Sarah read my first Sherlock Holmes pastiches, written in 2008 and at that point seen by no one but my wife, and with their encouragement I started publicly publishing my stories too.)

Marcy initially published *You Buy Bones*, along with some related short stories, in 2010 (from Lulu Publishing. That version is now out of print.) Next came *Test of the Professionals: Leap Year* (2013, also from Lulu and out of print), also collecting the original online novel and working in some supplementary material.

In 2015, I came up with the idea of *The MX Book of New Sherlock Holmes Stories*, and of course Marcy was in the initial list of invitees. Since then, much of her writing has been turned to contributing stories to these anthologies, having submitted nearly two-dozen. Through these books, she became associated with MX Publishing, who issued a new edition of *You Buy Bones* in 2015, as well as splitting *Test of the Professionals: Leap Year* into three planned smaller volumes. The first two, *The Adventure of the Flying Blue Pidgeon* and *The Peaceful Night Poisonings*, were published by MX in 2016 and 2017, respectively. Unfortunately, due to a combination of events, the third part of *Test* – the much larger piece called *Leap Year* that relates the exciting conclusion to that narrative – was not published.

So for the wider public, those who were never able to read Marcy's massive *ouvré* on *fanfiction.net*, her available works consisted of these three novels, and her well-respected stories in the MX anthologies. (Unfortunately, Marcy, Sarah Bennett, and several others were forced to pull their Sherlockian content from *fanfiction.net* several years ago after some of their works were stolen – copied-and-pasted and then republished under other author names by way of Amazon's self-publishing program.)

In late 2024, I was in the process of working toward assembling and editing the final volumes, Parts 49, 50, 51, and 52 of the MX anthologies, a process which would continue into early 2025. While looking around in my computer files, I found something I'd forgotten: Years earlier, I had saved and formatted the files for five of Marcy's novels – those relating to Watson and Lestrade's adventures during The Great Hiatus. Since the late 1990's, I've printed and archived every traditional Canonical Holmes adventure that I've found online –

thousands of them – and I have over 175 binders of pure Holmes adventures – including all of Marcy's now-withdrawn stories. But luckily I had these novels as Word files. And I had an idea . . . .

I contacted Marcy, who hadn't had time in several years to think about publishing more of her works, and asked if I could shepherd these five novels to publication – *pro-bono*, just because I was passionate about other people reading these incredible stories. Marcy was willing, and so I started editing with great enthusiasm – even as I was supposed to be editing the final MX volumes, stories for which were rolling in every day.

It soon became apparent to me that to publish these five novels without readers knowing the events of the missing *Leap Year* would be a confusing mess. Too much happened in these books that continued from what happened in *Leap Year*. Clearly, that missing volume would need to be edited and published too. And while I was at it, why not re-edit the previously published three books – *You Buy Bones*, *The Adventure of the Flying Blue Pidgeon*, and *The Peaceful Night Poisonings* – into an overall cohesive narrative?

MX Publisher Extraordinaire Steve Emecz, THE Sherlockian publisher and the Sherlockian Gutenberg – the man who made Sherlockian publishing accessible to real people instead of guarding a narrow doorway, or deciding that Sherlockian publishing should only be available for a very narrow cadre of self-described elites – was enthusiastic, and ready to proceed immediately. But I needed to actually finish editing the nine books first. It was a joy, and a labor of love to do so.

I had read all of these books serially as published, hopping from story to story as new chapters appeared, back in 2008-2011. But to read the story now, in one place, in order and available in its entirety, made it even more amazing – and exciting for the thought of new readers able to discover this magnificent world: *Sherlock Holmes's London, as seen through the eyes of the Scotland Yarders.*

Even as I dug deeper into Marcy's Scotland Yard adventures, I was remembering the other stories – the previously mentioned *A Secondary Stain.* Her Yarder's Christmas novels, *Gunnysack Goose for Christmas* and *A Mouth of Ivy.* Short-story collections like *Devilry* and *It's All in a Name.* Other novels and novellas like *The Muse of History*, *Ghosts in the Making*, *Courage Rises*, *The Kings and Queens of London*, and the World War I narrative, *The Days of Our Years.* I had amazing fun editing the first nine books that are being published in

2025, and with any luck, I hope to be able to edit the rest of these, along with a collection of Marcy's MX anthology contributions, over the next year or so, in order to fill in Marcy's *Great Scotland Yard Tapestry*.

There are certain authors who "own" other Canonical characters by taking hold of them and defining them. The late Carole Nelson Douglas was Irene Adler's chronicler. Michael Kurland gives us the best portrait of Professor Moriarty. Will Thomas has absolutely defined Barker, Holmes's hated rival on the Surrey Side. The late Gerard Williams claimed Dr. Mortimer (even if only for two books), and Susan Knight is easily becoming the definitive voice of Mrs. Hudson.

But Marcia Wilson tells the True Story of the Scotland Yarders – and presents an amazing viewpoint of Holmes and Watson along the way.

I've said it many times before, and can't say it any better now:

Marcia Wilson has found Scotland Yard's Tin Dispatch Box.

David Marcum
January 2025

Art Notes

Front Page: "The Four Professionals"
Prelude: "Plymouth Pear and Lighthouse"
Prelude II: "Sealing the Paperwork"
Chapter One: "Loose Tile"
Chapter Two: "The Vegetable Lamb"
Chapter Three: "The Kelpie"
Chapter Four: "Tiddy Mun Tavern Sign"
Chapter Five: "Sparrow"
Chapter Six: "Osage Orange"
Chapter Seven: "Bag of Barley Sugar"
Chapter Eight: "Cigar Box and Cigar"
Chapter Nine: "Imperial Stiff Collar"
Chapter Ten: "Phial"
Chapter Eleven: "The Elegant Barley Sign"
Chapter Twelve: "Sandbag"
Chapter Thirteen: "Walking Stick"
Chapter Fourteen: "Goldfish"
Chapter Fifteen: "T'ang Pottery"
End: "Whistle and Club"

Test of the Professionals – Part I:

The Adventure
of the
Flying Blue Pidgeon

Prelude I: Plymouth 1873

Even overlooking the salmon-waters of the Tamar, the air was hot. Hotter than the smoking ashes of the Alexandria Palace back in London. Hotter still than the mid-May rioters trying to free those Ascott women. [1] Tripoli reeled still from the dockworker's uprising, and Khiva – Khiva! – had fallen to Konstantin Von Kaufman. Through it all the old man watched down from his third-storey study, musing upon the world as this small, insignificant portion of it, carried on. These hustling, bustling little people, rendered literally as small as they were metaphorically in the scheme of things, ran back and forth with their ant-like lives. Their river belle was dying against the debutante trains but still they scuttled, caught up in ferrying the newest cargo of stone fruit, mineral and metal. Ferries made way for bridges. Good stone and metal beasts. Water gave way to the gleaming serpents of the rails, slithering on ribs of timber and concrete. Behind them was the rolling green coast speckled with lighthouses and scraps of rock.

Watching these miniscules soothed the old academic the way a bird-watcher toyed with ornitholmancy upon the migrant flocks. Their mindless action, harmless in its smallness, an absently waiting resource to be plucked up and stoked into flame with the proper alchemy.

The small lives of London knew nothing about the greater game of chess in the world. Those who could, fled the thick air of the city for the outer-lying countryside and Plymouth had the advantage of the Channel. Rain freshened the world and sun-browned traders from Roscoff, St. Malo, and Spain plied their hand amongst the ship-men.

19

The visitor high in his host's window frowned, for he had calculated a stronger presence from Santander. Clearly the Carlist War still throbbed amongst Gallica.

His arithmetic was wanting, and this would never do.

In the thick-walled rooms cooled by sea-air, he turned from the window and settled again at his desk. So many students needing his attention. He enjoyed the questions from the young and eager, but if it was to be confessed, the only foolishness he could tolerate was from those who confessed to him outright their ignorance. Those who lied about their skills were a divergence. A faulty equation assembled from flawed components.

It was those who knew they were wrong and sought help that he found useful. And they could be so, so useful . . . .

The gentleman settled against the wall with his horsehair chair and plucked up a few more papers, scanning and prodding and nodding at the occasional flash of brilliance in a thesis or summary or abstract. Oh, the pity of an earnest brain with the most exquisite penmanship and the weakest grasp of calculus!

Above him his generous and obligated host was stamping up and down in the hall, roaring at the latest bearer of bad news but honestly, who would have imagined the States' Modoc War would have ended this way? Make a frivolous bet in haste and accept the outcome like a man. Ivo was a man crafted of thin lava, as far as his personality and social graces were concerned. His son would be different. Ivo had planted bitter grapes and the taste was doomed to sour upon his heirs.

What treasures from the past await the present?

The gentleman smiled at the frivolous thought, knowing the rumination was inspired by the latest news of Priam's Treasure. He gave up the unbearably dull verse of his correspondent. Tea was better.

Surrounded by books and papers and two chalk-boards on either side, he mentally composed the response to Mr. Fisher's interruption of his evening. It had annoyed him. Mathematics was a language of clean joy and music. It oughtn't be defiled by the ignorant. It was true that all information could be useful, but would it?

Fisher was not a terribly useful informant. Once in a great while he would drop off a communiqué and then vanish back to wherever he happened to be at the time. He was a coward and lacked the spine necessary for really useful work but in possession of rare flashes of useful prescience. Now that he had risen to some importance in the lands of cotton it was a surprise to hear from him at all.

His letter was coloured with bitterness. He hated children and there was a sting of satisfaction in reporting this child had a gift for numbers and he was struggling to keep her away from his personal account-books.

A gifted young woman was always worth noting . . . .

The Professor had a tendency to never forget anything he could use later. There was a reason why his brain was whispered to be "as full of memory as forty elephants!"

He did not dispute this. Numbers made him smile. Forty was an even number and an even number was defined by its even split. All even numbers could be broken by two.

Professor Moriarty had two separate meanings in his head for forty elephants.

He thought of this Numerical Child, and smiled.

NOTE

1.   The Ascott Martyrs.

Prelude II: London 1883

The Professor folded over the interesting side of *The Examiner* and tucked it out of sight. Across the room an excitable young clerk exclaimed, which promptly brought over every other man and woman his age to look over the lip of the window to the Thames below.

Inefficient.

One really must pay for the experts.

He briefly considered ignoring the view of the Thames-facing leaded-glass windows and gave up. This was the heart of the Continental Exchange Office. Everyone not on pressing duty was moving to watch the divers at work and he knew the arithmetic of standing apart.

Amateurs!

Below them the great river swirled, filthy from drift and rains at the headwaters.

He shook his head as the brokers murmured and flowed about him. The set of his shoulders and the glimmer in his eyes discouraged coming too close.

The water rippled over a rising black form. The River Police shouted. They swarmed about the pumping-station and the body emerged in sodden sections, like the raising of a boat.

"He that dieth this year is 'scused for the next."

Someone said this in a tone so lordly and imperious, indeed, so present, the elderly scholar had to look. It was that old book-seller, here to ply his trade among the merchants' elite. A barely-read copy of *Cromwell's Economics* hovered in one spidery spotted claw. The other bore up a leatherbound *Sermon at Paul's Cross* – hence the sudden quotation. The books were cleaner than their struggling seller and in distaste the Professor turned away, his normal instinct to calculate and analyse forestalled by a stronger fastidiousness.

"That it is," his beefy customer agreed. "Vamberry was a good sort. The best wine-merchant you'd ever think to see."

A fool, the Professor thought. And he sold you all that wine at a loss because he needed those barrels to hide other things. The world is better without him, and you think he's a good man because he was light upon your purse.

But he remained silent as always. Here was a place of business, and here it was sensible to mingle with the masses even if they hadn't the collective sense within a flock of geese. At least geese knew where and how to fly for the winter.

The other exchangers stepped aside as he passed. The filmy grey eyes of the old bookseller lingered hopefully. He would have to find another victim for his wares.

A Moriarty did not *buy* books. A Moriarty *wrote* them.

The Professor threaded to the higher platform of desks like everyone else on similar transactions, a cool-faced man with measured speech and an even more measuring gaze burning out of his metronomic turns of the head. Outside of his tutoring room he was far from the warm, friendly numerical adviser his students knew. The reason for this was simple: Numbers were his humanity. He loved them with a passion few could fathom, and he learned early on that no one else cared about them the way he did.

No one else could understand him. If he told anyone that numbers had their own personality, that the number nine made a perfect square or that the recitation of the Fibonacci sequence never went far because it made him laugh helplessly. They wouldn't understand and they would at best nod blankly. Between himself and the comforting world of numbers was this sheltering wall.

The wall was imperfect in his youth. The slight fog of apartness and his business dealings had cost him his educational post but he was older now, less prone to mistakes and certainly less innocent.

"Excuse me, sir."

Below them Vamberry's soggy remains were being stretched out on the wet cobbles. A police surgeon awaited.

He turned his from the tiresome scene. "Yes, Mr. Higgens?"

The broker touched a white-gloved hand to his waxed mustache. "The shares have been finalised. Are you certain you wish to trade?"

The professor wished agents looked to the numbers behind the numbers. The stories they would find would be illuminating. And they would at least reduce his need to answer questions. "Yes."

"Then all we need is your signature."

They crossed the carpet together, with the space opening up as more people realised they could see more of Vamberry's corpse dripping muddy slime as the sweating men wrestled the remains into a dead-cart.

A shame it hadn't been Moran's hand. Vamberry wouldn't have been found within a hundred miles of London.

Higgens produced a full quire of paper. His secretary pulled out a chair for the client first and then his superior.

"Not many people are trading in the corn shares," Higgens noted. It was his way of confessing the curiosity was about to expire him. "They're all caught up in the grapes."

Moriarty thought of telling the man the truth: Krakatoa, bursting volcanic ash into the atmosphere, would affect the climate and pinch the crops. Long-season corn would be rendered obsolete save in a few isolated pockets of the world. Only cool-season corn like barley, rye, and spelt would yield stable production.

But then, if the man only knew his history, he would already know from the examples of the world.

From small events come large changes.

He once calculated the necessary drop in temperature to bring about the next Ice Age. Seven degrees. That was all.

Again he said nothing. The man didn't . . . *couldn't* understand. There was no equal among him that would fathom his thoughts. Another stone within the wall.

"Excellent, sir." Higgens was useful in his lack of imagination. He even believed the story that his client had been given the bulk of his shares by a considerate relative. He gestured and the secretary briefly vanished. With a flourish he opened a locked drawer and pulled out his japanned tin of sealing-wax.

The Professor enjoyed this part of business. Higgens was so punctual in his movements, and if they shared something besides the client-broker relationship, it was the satisfaction of a job well done. Higgens folded the papers over in the appropriate dimensions, and held out a neatly trimmed stick of wax. Not a speck of soot marred the bright red. It melted in the heat and he swiftly transferred the drops to a cooling puddle. One press of the seal and all was finished.

"I sincerely wish you well, Professor," Higgens intoned gracefully. "Just as I am certain the Crown is appreciative of your support."

The Professor smiled at the thought of the many governments whom, knowing and unknowing, had contracted his work in the past. And the future. "No doubt."

"Truly, sir. We do not have as many purchased shares in the Company interests like we used to. I suppose the new generation is too caught up in the temptations of striking out solitary into the world." He sighed and grew momentarily regretful. "Now that Mr. Vamberry is gone, you are my last farseeing client."

"Then may you find more."

Higgens nodded mournfully, and they looked up at the return of the secretary, replete with tray and two glasses with a bottle. It was the last part of Higgens' ritual, the ultimate conclusion of it all.

"It would have been more fitting if this had been one of Mr. Vamberry's bottles," Higgens mourned as the wine glittered. "But the 1829 Chenin can hardly be scorned."

Moriarty quashed his relief. "He would appreciate your thoughtfulness." He was determined to never, ever touch his lips to anything with Vamberry's name to it ever again. For the sake of his own sanity and acumen.

Higgens swirled the pale liquid against the thin glass. The wine painted the sides a delicate yellow. Grapes from the south.

The vintage reminded Moriarty of a field of barley-straw under the sun. His calculations were against witnessing this colour for some time.

"The man had a hand with the wine."

"That he did."

"I still cannot believe he is dead." Higgens sipped at the same time as Moriarty. The flavours mingled dry as chalk with a hint of spice. "Who would wish to kill Vamberry?"

"Perhaps a business venture gone wrong," Moriarty offered with a polite and sympathetic *tut-tut* as people expected from a kindly old professor of mathematics. "A wine-merchant's clientele can be a temperamental lot, I've heard." He took a second sip, appreciating the second rush of flavours. "A client might have found disagreement with the quality of one of his barrels. That might be all it took for all we know."

"That is true. Wine-merchants are a flighty lot."

Across the table, Professor Moriarty smiled. "But they do have their uses."

Chapter I

It was no easy thing to be a London policeman at any time, and the 1880's were no exception. Bearing that in mind, there were always some cases that stood apart. One such in the Autumn Equinox of 1883 had inspired Police Constable Crane to sum it all up with a pencil, a cheap brown-paper bag used to hold a few bottles of mind-salvaging pale ale, and the help of participating cohorts:

Scotland Yard's Adventure of the Flying Blue Pigeon [1]

1. *Small-time crook makes career of stealing roofing lead from people's homes.*
2. *Missing lead leads to missing roofing tiles = Property damage and complaints galore.*
3. *Complaints forwarded to angry Chief Miller, who has three ulcers and relatives working in a certain newspaper.*
4. *S.Y. pulls overtime to deal with missing lead on top of current case = Missing waterfront goods and laborers.*
5. *Glocky gonoph [2] adds the roof of some government toff's Pall Mall lodgings to his lead collections.*
   a. *Rainstorm = Damage on some sort of collection of documents that were no doubt as valuable as they were impractical.*
   b. *Toff pitches unholy fit to S.Y. and to SHERLOCK HOLMES!!!! (Underlined repeatedly)*

(Paper bag flipped over at this point. Gregson took pencil.)

6. *Gov. toff for some reason not popular with S.H. Can't imagine why, but H. may be prejudiced against verbally offensive puffer-billies.*

7. *S.H. insists he has more important work to do on the far side of Britian*

(PC Crane took pencil and added afterthought")

W may have something to do with this strange response from H, or it might be another aspect of the general strangeness of H –

(Gregson took back pencil.)

8. *Either way, S.Y. had mixed feelings about H. signing off. If anyone deserved to share the pain of this particular case, surely it was he.*

(Gregson publically proclaimed his willingness to swear Holmes into temporary service, if it meant but a prayer of watching H. tracking a criminal by leaps and bounds o'er the slated tiles of the London roofs.)

a. *W overheard threatening to tie Holmes down "like a Soay sheep" if he even thought about chasing after lead-thieves so soon after a bout of pneumonia and blood-loss from recent stabbing –*

("Stabbing?" [Eruptions from those not present for this conversation, followed by groans of the precious few who actually knew what they were talking about.])

b. *(continued:) Threat was made in front of parade of lackwit Byronian-Wordsworth scholars in honour of Pomona, Goddess of harvest and patron of apples.*

(At this point, several inspectors were shouting their versions of what happened. A constable preferring to remain un-named thus took it upon himself to finish the report with the rest of the drink.)

c. *W's tirade judged better than hairy oldsters in ill-fitting robes contrived of bed-sheets and imitation*

*golden sickles with garlands of apples over their
shoulders.*

9.   *Report of lead-thief north of parade.*
10. *Pursuit of lead-thief leads to thief's natural elements.*
11. *All police not afraid of heights drafted for the aerial
pursuit while the other type pursues below.*
12. *Lead-thief runs back over scene of previous thefts.*
   *a.   Without lead holding burglarized roof in place, the
swifter inspectors suddenly find themselves hanging
off gutters several stories off street.*
   *b.   Certain inspectors rescued by Lestrade, who will
not likely be taunted for his reflexes nor his ability
to lift two-hundredweight Bradstreets in the near
future.*
   *c.   Lestrade insists Bradstreet weighs much more, but
Bradstreet insists just as strongly that Lestrade's
estimation is emotionally coloured and thus,
inadmissible in court.*

End of D----d Report [3]

*   *   *   *   *

Not far away, a tiny woman in sensible workdress and tight cap rested her hands on her hips and stared about her. After the dry heat of early autumn, the sudden rain almost gave new life to the city. Almost. It might be more accurate to say that things had shifted. For her first week of business at The Lancashire Rose, the timing could have been much worse.

Paddington Street was an unplumbed-depths part of London. Despite the silent misgivings of her family, they'd blessed her intentions to open an establishment with her part of the Cotton-Mill inheritance.

Myron Cheatham, occasionally the more talkative of her brothers – not that that was anything to be proud of – had posed his concerns as politely as possible. "It's a clean-enough area, Clea, but is there a reason why you'll have a pie shop by the Paddington Station?"

"It is clean, of course! Think of it. It's a bit up from the surrounding areas. The trains make certain there will always be a flow of traffic in and out, and when there's a flow of people, they'll worry about something hot and ready to eat." She was well aware that the Cheatham-wives were (as usual) staying out of this. "Besides, the shop was already available and has a name for being clean and honest."

"How much lease?" Myron tried again.

"I bought it outright. My share was more than enough, and what I have left from my savings will keep it going the first two years." With a quick jerk, she bisected the platter of smoked fish with her serving-knife. "Who wants to give the first opinion of this?"

In the tiniest silence, her father lifted his big sandstone-hand like a schoolboy applying for his teacher. "I'll try that," he announced, and once the patriarch had spoken, all knew there would be no disapproval.

They would worry, no doubt – they would always worry about the one and only Cheatham Daughter, but disapproval had a way of making things worse. She was a Cheatham after all, and no one dared challenge her for following in the footsteps of her dear late mother, herself a sharp woman of business and kitchen and, be it said, born completely without fear. (And social graces, said those who weren't particularly fond of their teeth in the proximity of the Cheathams.)

Teaching young girls how to cook and manage a kitchen was quite possibly a daft notion compared to the obstacles, but Clea had her reasons. She kept them to herself.

Clea liked this the new life in London, particularly here as it was a comforting distance from the choking affections of their house in Little Venice, and with the Terminus of the Great Western Railway, something was always happening. It seemed to be the favorite grounds for doctors, rail-men, and commissionaires but with the close-access to St. Mary's and the soft waters of Acton, there were daily drifts of women and children seeking laundry or medicinal waters. The variety of everything was a natural stimulation to her senses, and she relished in all the newness in this great dirty city.

Clea also liked the convenience of the post and the fact that one of the only all-night telegraph stations in London were in Paddington. Not that she had ever had to send a wire outside of the usual eight-to-eight times . . . but what if the need arose? The answer was a short jaunt and sixpence-per-mile away.

She was fairly certain a few of the well-dressed gentlemen with strange accents to their clothing were from the Great Western Hotel and dealing with Parliament or the other government offices. Constables and plain-clothed detectives were also a common sight. Children far younger than her young girls were always busy, always moving, always working. She was already used to seeing the little bodies dart forth like sparrows as they delivered messages, baskets, sold oddbits on the fly, or performed as street-sweepers or boot-blacks . . . .

. . . Speaking of boot-blacks, the new customer appeared to be blacked all over.

Clea didn't know he was a detective. At first look, she thought of a train wreck or a fall off the omnibus. Perhaps he had been stuffed up a chimney. How he'd managed to keep his hat on she'd no idea, but he shouldn't have bothered. It looked as bad as his overcoat and what she could see of his trousers at the knees.

Her brothers had come home looking enough like that to make her wonder if the man had a dangerous hobby or had been caught up in something potentially disastrous and illegal. He wore enough soot that she wondered his race.

In the owl-light he probably looked better than he really was, and anyone who looked like that deserved a hot meal. Her sensibilities were relieved when he stepped up and croaked for whatever she was selling that day, keeping well away from touching distance. The slip of a short truncheon shone in the open gap of his coat, and she had an epiphany. Her sensibilities were not relieved at the close-up view of him, which consisted of bright blood-shot brown eyes in a mottled field of sooty black on top of lavender bruises that wouldn't have been claimed by a self-respecting turnip-root.

"Here you are, sir: Hot kedgeree on a cold day."

"Oh, thank God." Lestrade's reaction was purely on impulse. A split second later he realised he had just profaned his language in front of a young girl. In the middle of his flustered apologies he realised she wasn't a child as he'd first thought. She was younger, and tiny.

Lestrade was short. She was diminutive.

And she looked like she knew full well he'd mistook her age. God as witness, it wasn't because of her shape, which was as mature as anyone could hope for, and how could it be missed inside an Emancipation Waist? She dressed with a wise eye in demure dove grey to offset ink-black hair, Prussian eyes, and skin oven-browned to Guernsey cream.

Lestrade stared helplessly. The usual arsenal of polite phrases faltered before a woman who came up to his collarbone, yet gave the impression of being about three yards tall and plated with meteorite iron. ". . . Excuse me." Matters couldn't be any more awkward than they already were.

"You're quite welcome." She was chuckling. "You look as though you could use it." It was a tactful way of saying 'You look like you've been up all night', which was the truth. "Sit down, sir. I'm to pour up the new pots of tea. Dust want brew?"

Lestrade wavered between staggering back to his room with the carry-home breakfast, or sitting down and washing roof-slate out of his mouth.

While he wavered, she pointed a no-nonsense finger to the half-barrel chair by the wall. "We serve all the hard-working men and women off

31

Paddington Street," she announced. "And it looks like a cup won't be enough to keep you awake."

"No . . . ." Better to argue with the Chief than a woman. He sank into the chair and ruefully contemplated his hands. He darkly wondered if a rinse in a canal would make them any less filthy, or would the sheer foulness of the water kill what had to be harboring on his skin?

"Hold, please." Her accent wobbled, as if she hadn't lived long in London. As he watched, she vanished into the shop and emerged with a pitcher of steaming water. "Just hold 'em over the ditch and we'll take care of it."

To do him credit, he didn't complain when the hot, soapy water sluiced off unsightly scrapes under the mawky coating. He just looked relieved to see his hands again.

"You're one of the men from Scotland Yard?" She had switched the pitcher to a tray large enough to carry a large pot and two cups. "This is new tea, mind. Quite strong."

"Inspector Lestrade at your service, Miss – ?" Lestrade realised he could keep from tainting the kedgeree if he kept a layer of the newspaper wrap between his fingers and his food. Luckily it had been baked inside a stiff crust.

"And Clea Cheatham at yours, sir. Welcome to my establishment, but I can't promise the *quality* of my wares will remain in good standing if the smugglers keep *stealing* my wares."

"Eh? Oh." Too late, memory kicked in: *Cheatham*. Diverted goods. Missing goods. Someone "off Paddington Street" had come in person to Desk Sergeant Wraith and "wouldn't go away until her report was taken". Gregson's desk. Not his. Had to tell everyone about it.

Lestrade had heard this complaint in passing, and treated it with the usual smilingly sincere fakery they had for Wraith, who had the demeanor of a watering-pot. This calm, smiling little woman didn't match up with that sot's public report.

He wondered if he ought to tell her that he only knew about her theft because Wraith loved his wroth.

"We're doing all we can, Miss Cheatham." Lestrade normally hated to talk about cases, but now that he'd settled down, getting up was a painful thought indeed. "Part of the problem is we've also got seamen vanishing at the ports. Someone's put up a crimping shop along the waterfront, and until we find it, I'm afraid we won't get much success or be able to pay much attention to missing goods."

"What dust buy at a crimping shop?" Clea frowned automatically at the edges of her breakfast pie, which had been crimped with a fork, and Lestrade was proud of himself for not laughing.

32

"It's an uncouth word for a boarding house that has press-ganging laborers as its real source of income," Lestrade explained. "When the usual workforce of skilled men is missing, employers must hire whoever they can, and that means you have un-skilled labor, and that leads to accidents, mistakes on the job, and a more deliberate consequence with having men who don't know enough to ask questions." He shook his head in regret. "Too many of them are unlettered or unable to speak English. They can't rebel or protest."

"Your job is more complex than I'd imagined, sir. And here I thought having six brothers was enough." Her lips twisted as she lifted her teacup. "I think I have the easier job of it."

Lestrade lifted his tea in a return salute. "I would say you have. At least you don't have to command." Although that statement could have been easily misconstrued, Miss Cheatham's laugh proved she hadn't.

She watched him go as he threaded his way through the crowd. It wasn't like she had much else to do. Business was good but early hours were slow. Despite the fact that he was tired enough to plod like a shod horse, he was doing his best to not touch another person with his filthy clothes. Typically, the "big folk" barely noticed him and kept going their own ways, forcing him to dodge and weave. Strange how thoughtless people were. Clea shook her head. She didn't mind being short, but she did mind that the majority of the world didn't look out for their fellow man unless they were too big to ignore.

Well, a polite customer, and he paid his nine pennies without complaint. She smiled at the fee, which he had wiped clean. Polite and considerate.

NOTES

1.   Slang for stealing roofing lead.
2.   Half-witted, small-time thief.
3.   Except for the hapless Mr. Gregson, the soul in charge of this case.

Chapter II

The stumbling-blocks of the first week had passed. Clea Cheatham was running all over the shop and having a marvellous time – missing corn or no. Sometimes she gave herself a cup of tea or saffron and paused to look. The patrons paused too, on their way between train and wherever, and she was gratified to see them return with friends. Her hand-picked girls were openly proclaimed as students-in-training, for she had learned there was a sharp value in putting the poor to work in a useful occupation. Men were less likely to harass a student. There were those with heavy purses who wouldn't give a ha'penny to the church poor-box, but they would magnanimously pay for a meal and be waited on for a good cause: That good cause of course being themselves.

In this small but significant way, Clea struck an effective revenge against a lifetime of putting up with the worst of her family's clients at the Mill.

She had chosen her girls from the recommendations of local chapels. Jobs in good establishments were the dream. They also enjoyed one good meal, real tea, training with books, and they took home what remnants Clea didn't want to bother with at the end of the day – but Clea of course owned all the left-over tea leaves and fat.

Krakatoa had burst months ago, and she glared at its ghost hovering over London in the form of a cold snap and scattered frozen fogs. Customers hesitated over their food or drink, openly calculating the quickest routes with the fewest slips.

She grew more popular when she posted a map of London. Her Brother Robert was in the Temperance, and he had assured her those establishments knew a good thing when they saw it and preferred to know how to travel swift. Clea wondered if this was his idea of a peace offering.

His milder manner was often silent in the face of the others, and his wife was equally retiring. He was quickly proved right. The abstainers were also loud when they approved.

Her customers behaved. The one time there might have been trouble, Clea managed to make matters plain with a cricket-bat and the show of a knife tied underneath her apron. While she was certain it had lifted her reputation in the public eye, she really had no idea what the average man thought of the average woman. Any lady with tuppence for brains would be looking out for herself first!

"Best be cautious," Robert's wife Elizabeth murmured on one of the rare evenings when they were alone. "This isn't the Mill, Clea. You oughtn't let anyone know you have a knife."

"I can't say I had a choice in the matter," Clea answered impatiently. Elizabeth always made her feel impatient for some reason. "I wanted that pig to put his teeth together, quick. There were childer present!"

"Did they see the knife?"

"Oh, la of course not!" As if she'd be so careless.

Elizabeth hesitated – she often did this around Clea, which made Clea want to speak sharp, even if she did feel sorry for her marrying her friendly-but-addled Robert. But while Clea was forcibly reminding herself to mind her manners, Elizabeth let the matter drop.

There was the chance that word had gotten out about her family. Being the one and only daughter of the great wrestler "Chokehold" Cheatham had done much to create a wall of nerves between Clea and the rest of the world since birth. Blind and elderly though Charles might be, peoples scattered to avoid him when he took a walk down the street.

Clea tried not to think about these things. They made her angry. And when she was angry, she remembered the day when she knew the Mill was doomed.

When she next saw the inspector, only the truncheon inside his open coat told her it was the same man. Cleaned up he was a different species from the weary example that had staggered to her establishment. His eyes were no longer bloodshot – another reason to be grateful. Conjunctivitis had been a part of the Mills, and she needed no reminder of the price humans paid for cloth. There was no knowing how many people finished up blind or half-blind from the motes floating in the flammable air off the looms. She only knew she would never support it again.

Without the thick coat of things she was not about to identify, he was blessedly normal. And just tall enough that she reached his collarbone. That was a relief, actually. Nearly every man she knew was a mountain.

"You must be from the Thames Division." She opened the conversation as she slapped down the daily special: Sole Meuniere with

Capers. His eyes went wide. It wasn't a common meal for London, but Clea was determined to embrace the world through food – specifically seafood because it was as fresh as it ever got in the cool morning hours. The girls needed to show their skills if they were to find good work in the private kitchen.

"I was once. But how did you know?"

She scowled in the fun as she aimed her cutting-knife at him. "For Heaven's sakes, Mr. Lestrade. Everyone else at the Yard has the standard-height rule of five-feet-eight-inches. Thames lets one in on a full five-feet-seven."

He laughed out loud. With perhaps with more boisterousness than her sisters-in-law would have allowed. "More like they continue to let one in at seven inches. I stopped growing early." He touched the faintest shade of evening-beard on his cheek and shrugged. "It helps that it wasn't until 1870 that the standard went to five-eight. I'm not much shorter."

"How much shorter?" Clea frowned lightly, using skills developed by years of eyeing bolts with the mercers. "No more'n half-inch, surely."

"The half-inch it is." He was surprised, but his manners forbade him from asking. She watched him swallow down his curiosity.

"I had another reason for guessing," Clea admitted. "If you were from the Thames, it would explain your knowing what to do with a plate of fish." She managed not to look too smug. "The other Miltonians, they keep their diets to their walks. The vendors talk amongst ourselves, you know. There are always the same coppers that stick around the bake ovens, and the sausage crowd off the market. There are more people to be had for a taste for fish and oysters than the latest joint of meat on the wrong side of the stockyards."

"Very true." Despite the fact he was one-hundred-per-cent cleaner than at their first meeting, including that male wasteland known as the space under the fingernails, he looked as tired as that talk over the kedgeree. "You're quite right."

"So, how goes your search for my missing corn?"

The verbal blast almost severed his mainmast, but he recovered between his first bites of dilled carrot. "I took the liberty of looking at your official complaint," he said cautiously. She nodded, and he looked grateful that she hadn't taken offence. "You are missing a hundredweight [1] of corn plus a hogshead of . . . Indian maize?"

"I am. And I am especially worried about that maize. I try to use up my stores within a certain period of time to ensure its good properties."

Lestrade tilted his head to one side, considering. "Red-Indian maize is not a usual part of British cooking unless we mean the polentas of Saffron Hill."

"If I am to build my reputation on honesty, I must do something, Mr. Lestrade. My teachers were more than cooks. I learned from nutritionists and chemists too. I don't need more than a bit of that maize. A little goes a long way, and if I cook it well enough, they'll cheerfully pay meatless prices for meals that do them as much good. It was cheaper than the horse-feed off the Continent and the ships were swift."

"I believe I understand." His eyes were the darkest she'd ever seen, like a Welshman's. "The Yard was amiss in not speaking to you in greater depth. May I come and ask you a few questions when you are not so pressed?"

"I stop at a quarter-to-three," Clea nodded. "My girl will take over for me then." She turned to trade nods with the tall young woman in the corner with a large water-jug.

"If I may presume upon you that time . . . ?"

Clea laughed in spite of herself. "Mr. Lestrade, if you were imposing on me, you would indeed know about it."

He gave his compliments and left. By then, Clea was figuring him out as a Jemmy, but he had the look of a man who had to have his facts facing his eyes before he'd believe in them. He didn't have the kind of belligerent "let's pick a fight" way most people had who were far short of two yards in altitude. That suited her just fine, as that kind of cocky annoyance caused more fights than it solved problems.

Clea had waited patiently for eight years to catch up with her massive brothers. Her childhood had been spent alternatively as a delicate doll in their huge hands, or as something to condescend – a far worse a fate.

Even now, she held strange feelings about her kin. She might be twelve inches shy of two yards, but she had proven capable of pulling the same amount of work in the day as those big boys before her. Yes, it took her longer, but she could still do it. Being smaller, she prided herself for not squandering her energy in the sillier pursuits. The worst part was Nature had compensated her size by giving her talents her brothers lacked: Mathematical acumen. Thoughts. Consideration. Patience. She suspected her moral code was stronger. Yet what good were such gifts to the last-born and only female in the family?

It wasn't as though her brothers were grateful for a sister who could sum columns of numbers in her head and algebra off her fingers. At first it was fun, giving her a sense of importance as she assisted their father and Brother Myron with the accounts.

Misfortune comes in threes. Myron's financial partner had died, leaving him without assistance. Their father's eyes filmed over past the point of all sight. And Clea was forced to take over the accounting for the Mill Doctor Myron desperately sought ways to save his own small business. Clea had found the third blow in the overly optimistic reports of the foremen. The Mill could not last. Money it made, especially for Foreman Fisher, but it could not compete. The equipment was only getting older. Selling was the only option, and London had been chosen for a new start.

Months passed as her brothers sought their own methods of making their way, and her one set of superior brains was not a match for their combined intent to "keep her safe." Weeks were spent inside their "new" house as, fuming over the rapidly melting assets, she pondered what to do for herself. Eventually she realised she would never get their permission, so she did what she wanted because it must be done by someone. Her mother had done much the same thing, taking soup to the elderly and the infirm among the tenants of the mill. She had gone by herself without an escort and they never questioned that.

It never occurred to her that her mother might have struggled for recognition too.

NOTE

1.   One-hundred pounds.

Chapter III

"**W**atch out for that little rat. He's no good."

The deep voice could only come from Clea's brother Bartram. All her life he had been coming up behind her and lowering Jovian pronouncements into the back of her left ear. She had almost forgotten how to jump by now.

"Bartram, are you warning me away from a Scotland Yard Inspector?" Clea twisted her head up to peer at him – reminding him of how small she was usually placated him. He wasn't quite her biggest brother. He wasn't her smartest – that was Myron – but he had the status because he made by-far the most money.

Which he made through the voluntary career choice of *wrestling*.

Bartram frowned underneath coal-black bacca-pipes [1] despite the pain of a newly-broken nose that was trying to set crooked. A few more years, and he wouldn't have much of a nose left – it would go with his complete lack of a neck and economical one eyebrow. "Clea, he's got no feeling for kinfolk. He's a cold one. Turned in his brothers for some robberies. *He swung his own brother, Clea!* You don't need to be talking to a man like that."

Clea felt ice slip down her throat at Bartram's sermon. That, and the look in his deep blue eyes, made her momentarily faint. No wilting flower, she had always been disgusted at the type of women who fell into vapours, but the concept of betraying a kinsman was something beyond her ken. But to be fair, she didn't think she had many criminals in the family, either.

(Father didn't count.)

"I'll be careful, Bartram." She reached up to pat him on the arm – she couldn't really reach his shoulder. "Don't you worry. I'll just speak to him about my missing lots and then that'll be that."

Bartram looked reluctantly satisfied – his usual expression – and shambled off to wherever the latest match was being held. She watched him go with a rather hopeless feeling. He could bring more in one night than she could in a week or a month – that was a fact. He was also coming home with more than his usual share of injuries. Injuries he hadn't sustained since he was a young pup learning his first tricks.

People paid more for a harder match, but she didn't want to lose the big fool. And he was a fool – a right impressive one at times, which was why she would hold judgment on what he said about Mr. Lestrade.

Mr. Lestrade came promptly as promised, wearing a dark pea-jacket and narrow scarf that him look like someone else entirely – three different demeanors in as many sightings? Clea wondered if he was tapped for undercover work. [2]

"Every time I see you, you're on another suit," she blurted without thinking, and then considered blushing. That was unremarkable for the speech of Lancashire, but not perfect manners here in the ton.

"Ah, I tend to wind up wearing most of London at the end of a day." He looked only slightly embarrassed – point for him. "I was doing some last-minute work along the river." He lifted his hands to his cheeks, which were showing the sting of sudden winds off the water.

"I thought you looked like a waterman," Clea confessed. "What you say makes sense, but I pity who dust thy collars and cuffs." She snorted slightly and poured out another jug. "Dust want brew? It shan't keep."

"Thank you." He pulled out his notebook and pencil first, setting it on the table before taking the cup. It burned, but his gloveless hands welcomed the heat. "To begin with, is there a chance you have any enemies here that would take advantage of your missing goods?"

"I wouldn't know who they'd be," Clea said honestly. "I moved here with my father and brothers a few months ago. We're from Lancashire – former owners of the Vegetable Lamb Mill."

"That explains your speech," Lestrade smiled. "No angry people from the Mill? It isn't such a far trip anymore, not with the train lines."

"None that I would know of. We were against the newer and larger mills. Truth to tell, a mill can be obsolete in only a few years, and it was hard to look at the people who were making the cloth for us." Clea drank her tea quickly. "It's a hard life. When the books showed we would be at a loss in a few years, we sold it for what we could, divvied up, and I put my share into buying the place."

"I hadn't realised Mrs. Corrin had sold at all until I saw you behind the table," Lestrade admitted. "Did you buy the property because it was called The Lancashire Rose?"

40

"Not at all," Clea grinned. "Everyone thinks so – my brothers think I'm keeping my roots and all, but I chose it because it was clean. I like myself a *clean* place. I can tell you, following the dust after six brothers, their wives, plus a blind father is a greater job than stuffing twenty pies!"

"I can just imagine," Lestrade winced with a smile. "My *mamm* was always at us to do something with our hands and the nearest broom."

"Well, a woman appreciates a man who notices dirt." Clea wondered why he suddenly blushed at that. That was not the kind of man who blushed. "At any rate, I'll be churching it by this time, next year."

Lestrade had been writing down the time of day in the top of a clean page. His brows knit together in puzzlement. "I beg your pardon?"

"It's a business term. I'm changing the name of the place in a year. It'll cost me a handful, I know, but it'll be worth it!"

"If you're intending to change the name, why didn't you do it when you bought it?"

"Well, the clients of course." She saw he didn't understand. "Dust have a favourite place you like to go, a place you'd give your business to first when given a choice?"

"I do." In his case it was a small tavern that sold a wide variety of bitter off Montague Street. An ideal place to wash the taste of an appointment with Sherlock Holmes out of his mouth in peace and quiet. There were days when he needed a lot of washing after an experience with the amateur. (He's be off to the Continent next week on one of his queer cases – for who knew how long?)

"Well, there you are," Miss Cheatham was saying. He wrenched his thoughts to the subject at hand. "If I was to change the name of the shop, they would have known instantly that my business was the new one. They would have been against me from the first, sir. Better to continue on for a bit before I slowly turn my own name to the place. If I do change it. I may just keep it."

He stared as if she had said something rare and precious. She tried to explain again.

"Well, if the customers who are used to eating here come up and see a different sign as well as a different woman, they're going to walk away at first instinct. I have to build up their trust first, let them know that things are as good as they ever were?" Clea's voice trailed off. Mr. Lestrade was gaping at her across the table as his pencil drilled wells into his notebook.

"Are you feeling at all well, sir?"

His mouth opened slightly, but words lodged in his throat. "Ah," he began, "Miss Cheatham . . . ." He stumbled to his feet, eyes glazed as his fingers scrabbled for pencil, notebook, and general composure. "Would it be all right if I came back tomorrow? You just gave me a thought about

41

our case that I really must pursue . . . ." He collected himself in shock. "What I mean to say is, Miss Chatham," he stammered, "Do you mind if I take leave of you now? I truly think your insights should be shared with the office."

"Not at all," Clea said grandly, charmed that he thought to ask her permission first. "Be careful, sir!"

She watched him go, her curiosity getting the better of her. He was gone into the masses of London as if he'd never existed. As fast as he was running, she hoped he had the sense of mind not to run across a charging hansom.

"A good thing I've got enough men in my life to look after." She shook her head in wonder. "His women-folk can't possibly sleep the night through with worry."

Inspector Gregson listened to Lestrade's notion with a bald-faced look – the kind of unblinking gaze that suggested the zoo's large, hungry serpents before the weekly feeding. As his rival watched, the big man's pupils contracted, dilated, and then assumed more normal proportions.

"The Kelpie," he said flatly. "That's the only place that would make sense."

Lestrade was taken aback. "That's just an old boardinghouse run by the Holesapples – they're so harmless they're a joke. The old man probably fought for Lord Nelson – Assuming he's that young . . . ."

"It's the only one that makes sense." Gregson stroked his jaw with a growing frown – No one, not even the Home Secretary, could imitate the frightening look of Tobias Gregson when under a cloud of thought – his clouds were more like drumheads. "It's so respectable it squeaks. Always has been. Who's to question an old Navy man decorated for bravery in three wars with a Quaker wife? The worst they've ever done was kidnap abused cats for the R.S..P.C.A., and that was back when they were in their hale-and-hearty seventh decade." Gregson drummed his fingertips on the desktop, vibrating loose papers. "They were in financial difficulties a year ago, weren't they?"

"Yes, a year ago," Lestrade agreed, beginning to get a glimmer. "They split some of their rooms and charged less to get more rates in. Something to do with the fact that the ground level was a small warehouse and the assessor changed their tax status." The Yard had been called in, frequently, because of nosy neighbors thinking the couple had been trying to be sly with their property assessments. Oh, to be so idle . . . .

"See? How many boarding houses on the water-front are also doubling for storage rent? It's perfect."

42

Lestrade conceded it made sense when lined up against the double crimes of missing sailors and ship-goods. "But can it be proven?"

Gregson grinned, slowly. "Give me Youghal. The man can track an ant across foolscap."

"It may take some time . . . ."

"Some time" proved to be three days, during which PC Walsh swore he saw Dr. Watson march Mr. Holmes to the train for the Channel in a heated cab with "dire imprecautions" smoking the air on what he would do if the consulting detective overtaxed his heath in Spain. Desk Sergeant Sharkey said Walsh was lying, but their great-grandfathers hailed from the same village in County Tyrone, so it was natural the Yard would get some free entertainment from their quarrel. At least Lestrade was entertained. He had little to do but be amused as he dug his way down another three inches of paperwork with crimes, notices, and three public health violations that had led to the sort of crimes that can only result from frayed tempers and arm's-length supplies of gin.

He had faith in Youghal. The man looked half his age and acted the same, but his mind was attuned to the jungle of records the way a scent-hound could run a trail under a red herring. Bradstreet held the unflattering opinion that Youghal was determined to be a perfect man here, because his family wanted him to move back to Ireland at the first sign of failure, but whatever made the man a good Yarder worked for the Yard.

On the close of his shift on the third day, Lestrade felt the floorboards under his feet shift in that particular way they did when Gregson grew close – the man was huge and powerful but utterly silent and he took pride in it. It drove Gregson mad that he couldn't sneak up on his rival and drop papers on his desk without his knowing it.

"Good evening, Gregson." Lestrade looked over his sea of blotting-paper to hand over his manners with a perfectly straight face.

"It is for some." Gregson delivered the good news by dropping the one incriminating slip of paper down in the desk before his eyes. "Remember all those property-assessment papers we had to examine?"

"Hmm. That doesn't resemble the signature of our Mr. Holesapple." Lestrade lifted an eyebrow. "Unless he's had a recent stroke?"

"Man's perfectly literate," Gregson nodded. "Whoever pretended to be him on the paperwork wasn't. And he was writing with three fingers."

"Pull the other one." Lestrade scoffed on reflex, and instantly regretted it when Gregson's small eyes narrowed to bright little chips of ice.

"Obvious if you know what to look for, Ratty," Gregson announced with a voice as cold as his eyes.

43

Lestrade hastily averted his eyes to the cramped-up signature, and nodded to pretend he knew what in the world Gregson was talking about.

"We're going to have to do this careful. The Holesapples are probably not even owners of The Kelpie anymore, but they're being kept on as figureheads. For all we know, they're being held prisoner."

"And the sailors think it's still the same friendly, safe place they've always gone to, come in, get their usual rooms . . . and vanish in a press gang." Lestrade scowled. "This is rotten, Gregson. When are we going in?"

"I've got some of the younger C.I.D. posing as idle hands inside," Gregson lowered the boom. "Get some rest. You're coming with us to the raid tonight."

"Me?" Lestrade blinked.

"Yes, you." Gregson's smile broadened, the way a crocodile's mouth expanded its view of long, strong teeth as it opened. "Wouldn't you like to see if I'm wrong?"

"More like you want to see if one of your own men will try to arrest me in the nanty narking." [3]

"Now, it was just that one time." Gregson's smugness fairly dripped, treacle-thick, upon Lestrade's blotting-paper. "And you were in disguise as a street-thug."

"I bloody was *not*!" Lestrade hissed through his own sudden display of teeth – and very sharp-looking they were too, though no one said it to his face, ever. Watson's written comparison to him as a rat was often hailed for its accuracy.

"Oh, you weren't?" Gregson pretended to be surprised and innocent. It was a horrible combination on his face. "My mistake. Well, it isn't my fault you mix in with the criminal element so well, Lestrade. Part of what makes you such a good man for the Yard, I'm sure."

With that, Gregson was gone, and Lestrade was left wondering (again) if anyone would post his bail if he wrapped his hands around a certain officious thick neck in broad daylight.

A few hours later, his rage with Gregson had melted to its usual low level of manageable simmer. He could grumble about the verbal abuse, or he could take it as a chance to join another raid. They were dangerous and tricky, and everything from knives, rocks, ropes and bits of iron could be a weapon, but there was always a chance for a reward at the end, and the satisfaction of jumping into a fight. Lestrade was mortal enough to admit he was frustrated and needing to do something a bit more productive than going to the mat and practicing a few rounds. Hitting his trainer at the club wasn't the same as kicking a greasy, bellowing brute with a club.

There was no denying the day had gone well. Lestrade closed the door to the Main Office in a pleasant mood, though the weather was picking up a wind off the estuary. Hiding a crimping den in plain sight along the waterfront. Who would have thought a criminal would think of such an old trick in this day and age?

Yet it made perfect sense. Sailors weren't stupid. Reckless – yes. To a fault, but not stupid, and canny captains never gave them all their pay at once, knowing the first night a-shore was all about the drinking and bragging and women. If they wanted the rest of their pay, they'd come back on the morrow with aching heads and tend to post-party details such as squaring debts buying up the supplies they couldn't get on-ship.

It was possible, he mused (ignoring the half-hearted screaming of cabdrivers as they fought over a funeral fare), that whoever was in charge of the den merely thought no one would think of such an old chestnut. It wasn't normally a tactic employed by the small crooks of the underworld.

Well, fifty years ago it was. The 1830's had seen quite the run on such activities, orchestrated by clever and low-profile merchants using the mask of respectability to hide some of the worst escapades London had ever seen. Before their times, yes – Lestrade had been born almost fifteen years after the apex of that particular mischief, but the cases had been infamous. The sort of thing discussed at night over low fires and even lower voices, dark with intrigue and tone.

He wondered what Gregson would do after this. Probably send Youghal back on the paper-trail to see what else they could find, if they could find the invisible face behind ownership of The Kelpie. What else would they find?

If it wasn't for the fact that entire strip was on a disputed boundary line, this would all be a matter for the Water Police. As it is, we'll have to share . . . .

A gust blew around the corner and past him, scattering old theatre tickets, train billets, battered paper bags, and playbills that were surely ignoring the authors' rights. Just as quickly a knot of hard-ups [4] raced by, following the wind and stuffing the papers into their bags. Most were children. The old ones didn't have the energy or ability to chase papers for a few ha'pence.

Whatever they made for the day's labours would be turned over to the street-buyers, and that would feed the stew-pot their elders nursed in the mews and alleyways the police ignored. They lived day-to-day and accepted nothing better for themselves. A quarter of London was worse off and they brooked no pity. Wouldn't understand it if it was put to them.

Lestrade paused at the lip of the corner and went from holding his bowler firmly about his head to pulling it off in automatic respect as a hearse clopped by, lacquered and varnished to the last quarter-inch. Even the matched black horses looked as though they'd been inked and then covered in shellac. Black ostrich plumes jauntily bobbed against the sober look.

It was then, as he re-donned his hat and prepared to step across the cobblestones, Lestrade encountered an all-too familiar and far under-small urchin, ragged coat six sizes too large, moth-eaten muffler swallowing his throat, and chalksmears of every tint from his battered shoes to his massive red ears.

"Toby Irish, I thought you'd be in school today."

Toby faced this observation from authority without a blink of his topaz eyes. He merely lifted up the reason for his being out: A brace of roosters that must have passed to the days of their forgetfulness some years ago. The sprout was nearly dwarfed by them.

"I . . . see." Lestrade permitted an eyebrow to aspire to loftier realms. "By any chance, would you be selling 'Little Chickens' inside that big coat of yours?"

Toby shook his head, sending a cloud of chalk and hen-house dust flying from his fine blond carpet of badly-cropped hair. Probably a flea and some bird-lice went flying as well. He was affronted that a longstanding acquaintance such as the good inspector would be implying he'd be selling partridges. Everyone knew a license was required!

Which had never stopped Toby's father from interesting and inventive forays into the fowlmonger business – game-hawkers were quick on their feet as well as their minds, and there was a good chance the slight threat of danger added spice to their trade. Still, they never seemed to make ends meet until the holidays, and during Christmas they could clear up three months' worth of expenses in a week so long as the entire family kept moving and selling and delaying their own holiday until well a fortnight past Boxing Day. It wasn't a perfect life, but it wasn't as poor as most.

The Yard rather missed Old Irish. He'd kept them on their toes and had a tendency to anticipate the future as far as smuggling techniques went – always a step ahead of the latest criminal inspiration, and never violent. To study him was to study the future of guile. But sadly, he dropped dead of a fatty heart. His brother Winnie had given up a profitable income carving tatts [5] and dutifully resumed the slightly-less illegal reins of the family's livelihood – but it wasn't quite the same. Winnie lacked Johnson's imagination and sense of play.

Still, Toby bid fair to step into his old father's shoes – and quickly. Everyone this side of London knew Toby. When he wasn't "working" the family trade, he was getting quite a bit more income as one of London's most accomplished cocksparrows. [6] Lestrade had lost count of the times Toby had been rounded off the street and sent off to the school his grandmother was paying for at seven pennies a week. It was no more than a balm on her iron conscience. As far as he knew, she never inquired to see if Toby was getting the lessons she was paying for. (It all went to paying rent in a squalid sort of human chicken-coop off Convent Garden Market.) Deep in his heart, he dreaded the boy's future.

If the Iron Gran was like any of the old matriarchs he'd met in his line of work, Toby wouldn't meet her until the day before she was ready to marry him off to someone she deemed respectable. Then the quality of his education would be revealed. Jehovah's wrath would descend, with tactics inspired from hours of poring over the Old Testament.

"How much for those worn out old birds, Toby?" Lestrade didn't bat an eye when the boy lifted one finger. "Fair enough. Your usual rate for delivery?" An eager nod was his answer. Lestrade shook his head and, since he was officially off-duty, he could afford to linger on the street. Chances were Toby wouldn't pick his pocket. Lestrade faced him at all times to be sure. There was a definite status among the little boys who managed the High Standard among thieves.

"Hold a moment there, and you can deliver them to my landlady." Lestrade put one foot up on the kerb-line to use his thigh as a desk, and penciled in a short missive. "And you'd best mind your manners with Mrs. Collins, you imp. She's wanted a good dish of *coq au vin* for several days now. Play your cards right and perhaps she won't wash your face for you." Long experience kept Lestrade's expression as stern as the boy's face collapsed in horror. He tore off the paper from his note-book and folded the shilling and a tip inside them.

"You may set yourself up in a bit of business with Mrs. Collins, you know," he advised in a warning tone as the boy appeared to leap into the street. "Once a month for old birds, but they'd best not be tenderised in someone's fighting ring the night before!"

Toby flipped an "I-don't-know-what-you're-meaning-sir" grin at the policeman and took off, his normally swift gait awkward and uneven from the weight of the roosters.

"Mr. Lestrade?"

Just that quickly, the crushing weight of London fell upon the small man's shoulders. No, there was no denying that particular voice. He sternly stifled the warning thump in his heart and turned around.

The speaker was the taller by a full head without his top hat, and three stone heavier – not all of that in the right places. Further signs of good living were displayed on cuffs starched hard enough to shine. (Mr. Holmes wouldn't be able to write on those cuffs. Not without a glass-etcher.) [7] His watch gleamed brightly as the polished head of his walking stick (carved like a Chinese dog), and – as usual – full-spectrum formal dress. From his old-fashioned spats that went up to his knees under his fitted trousers and black coat, to the watch-chain holding a tiny pen and the world's smallest note-book, Powell Madison was back from his vacation on the Continent.

"Mr. Madison." Lestrade inclined his head with formal respect. "I see you've returned safely."

The reporter peered at him with a slight confusion through his glasses. Between them and the large sweep of curling moustache, the impression was the man wore a mask at all times. It made him difficult to read. "You're out a bit late this evening, aren't you, sir?"

"Just finishing up some loose threads." Lestrade answered with the tone of voice that suggested he would die before revealing his business to anyone short of the Queen or the Home Secretary. "Are you in need of police assistance?" A direct question was best with Madison – it saved hours. Lestrade was barely able to tolerate the man as it was, but *The Littoral* was not a newspaper to be lightly treated, nor its reporters treated lightly.

Madison genteelly cleaned his glasses with a bright handkerchief. (Lestrade's cynical eye could tell the difference between silk and Irish silk.) "I thought for a moment I recognised that young boy," he began. With his face exposed, he blinked like a cat in a dust-storm. "A draughtsman's assistant with the side-walk chalks at the last traveling circus."

That's what the coloured chalk stains were all about, you fool. Lestrade merely shrugged. "It's quite possible. The lads are always looking for spare work."

"Well." Madison resumed his air of business with a sniff. Case closed. "How are things at the Yard, Inspector?"

"As good as ever, I suppose." Caution and experience sent a knot of nerves slowly coiling inside his spine.

"Oh? What is the Yard doing about the missing seamen, Mr. Lestrade? Or the rash of thieving of the honest businessman's hard-earned stocks? It isn't right to keep this case unsolved, you do realise."

"No, Mr. Madison, I do realise." Just the effort of keeping a clamp on his thoughts (and inclinations) was enough to bring a sweat to Lestrade's brow. "But I'm sure you realise that just as a decent reporter can't reveal his work too soon, neither can a policeman talk too much about the leads they are following. Criminals can read as well as the honest man, and gossip flows even faster."

Madison met that with a lift of the nose, but he was always polite. Painfully so. Many a time Lestrade had wished the man prove he was human and start yelling.

"I have often thought," Madison went back to the old quarrel that had brought them together in the first place, "that the right of the public to know comes first. Who knows how many criminals would be stymied if their actions were known?"

Lestrade swallowed hard. "I am full aware of your paper's stance, Mr. Madison." And thank God, the other papers think even *The Littoral* is too inflammatory to work within good taste. "And I respectfully say to you that I have no inclination to go outside the bounds of my duty. I hope you understand."

Madison poised. A long moment expanding between them. "I've often felt you made a better constable than you make an inspector." There was no anger at this statement. Merely an opinion posed as a fact.

"My promotion was not my decision." Lestrade swallowed down more bitterness. Other papers tended to waver between being sickly sweet in their praise when happy and vicious when angry. *The Littoral* was as steady as ship's ballast in their opinions of all the inspectors that had sadly caught its eye. Gregson was *The Littoral*'s usual favourite. His slender but excellent connections were often held up as a tribute to the earnest man.

Lestrade was quite a different story. No one knew why Madison disliked him so much. But unique to all the papers in London – and probably the English speaking world – *The Littoral* refused to retract statements or opinions. Their much-loved motto to themselves was "consistency".

Madison was the proud creator of his most infamous nickname: "*Inspector Plod*"> In a world where the nickname "Constable Plod" implied long hours and a brain beaten into pudding by grueling physical activity, "Inspector Plod" was even worse. That attitude had not changed one hair.

They were indeed consistent. Gregson called them "a *littoral* pain in the neck". He might be the adored child for the paper, but he loathed them as much as anyone else. Possibly more. He had to work with them.

Madison was musing over his lenses. "You still harbour some irrational feelings over my work, sir?"

Lestrade was a moment collecting his voice. "I understood your desire to pursue your story," he said in a voice at odds with the rage boiling inside. "But I felt you went outside the bounds of decency when you went to interview my aging parents." Long experience kept him from using more truthful words. Madison was a vulture for an expensive rag that let the high-ups feel smug and superior.

49

"I do what I feel is correct." Madison neither admitted nor denied any wrong.

It was all very twisted, and if one had that sort of humour, almost amusing. During the Aton Bank Murder Trial, Madison had discovered a small discrepancy in his research into one particular Lestrade's history.

Not that he'd lacked for fodder – *The Littoral* was the worst sort of paper as it was, making *The Gazette* appear the height of sobriety, and no paper could resist a delicious scandal: *Two brothers responsible for the murder of a policeman in a bank robbery. Apprehension on part of a third brother who was a fellow policeman of the murdered man. How could it ever be overlooked?*

Lestrade had perhaps declared unofficial warfare between himself and *The Littoral* by completely ignoring the tall, expensively dressed representative for a paper that was so costly the only way the common man would read it is if they picked it up from the gutter the day after. Facing the fact that his testimony and his testimony alone would help the jury decide if his brothers were guilty of murder had taken all his fibre. He hadn't even noticed the stuffy swell. And when the English jury decreed one brother to hang, the other to Dartmoor, his parents had chosen that moment to disown him. Lestrade had been too exhausted to even care at the time.

For months the horror had inked up untold reams and rolls of newsprint. Madison had been a rising reporter, and keen on certain instincts. He knew once the serial petered out there would be lower sales and lower commissions, so he decided one day to go examining the Lestrade family history.

He found the strange discrepancy.

In the plentiful court documents, the doomed Armoricus Lestrade and the institutionalised Paul Lestrade had birth-records to prove their identities. But the youngest son, the policeman, did not.

Further digging revealed to a fascinated Madison that G. Lestrade had applied for a policeman's post in the winter of '62, passing the physician's physical with a written statement to the effect that in lieu of a proven birth-record, Dr. Armstrong had determined the applicant was clearly old and hale enough to request employment of the London Metro. On that word, the Metro passed him into the ranks, where he soon proved a willingness to work.

Lestrade was so used to being examined (French surname. Channel family. An education best described as scraped from the bottom of a barrel. Police-survivor of the Confederate smuggling trials off the coast. Witness to the ethics scandal of '77 – he hadn't paid attention to that either. He'd found out the hard way that Madison had hopped the nearest train to

50

Plymouth and tracked his parents down to the country estate where they worked as servants.

City-born and cosmopolitan, Madison had not been prepared to face a lifestyle he'd long thought was a myth. Here in the provincial lands, servants were peasants. The landowners were saluted with tugged forelocks. Adding to his frustration, the elderly Lestrades hadn't understood a single word of English and only spoke a "rudimentary form of French". (Madison wouldn't have recognised the venerable Bretagne tongue had it struck him, stolen his watch, and pushed him into a canal.)

Looking back, Lestrade wished he would have been that fly on the wall just that once when Madison finally found a willing priest to translate their "illiterate gibberish" in his attempts to discern the reason why only two of their three sons had a viable birth record. He could see it now, in his blessedly puny imagination: Thomas Lestrade staring at the stranger in utter befuddlement. Jeanne Potier Lestrade bending over backwards to be polite to the poor young madman. And for what? A family Bible with the names of *all* the children carefully written in smooth Luxeuil calligraphy . . . .

How bitterly frustrated had Madison been, to see the page for one particular son's name blotted out? Had he not understood a disownment was *forever*? Did he not know that it was disrespectful to speak the names of the *dead*?

On the other side of memory, Madison was speaking. Lestrade gladly pulled his mind out of the past, even if it meant listening to him.

". . . It wasn't as though I learned anything from your parents, Mr. Lestrade." Madison still managed to eke out a bit of annoyance.

Lestrade had reached inside his coat and found his tin case of cigarettes. He did not offer one to Madison. He cupped his hands around the stalk and struck a match on his fingernail in one stroke. For a moment there was silence and flame as the little detective drew the spark inside the tobacco.

"You know, your own innocence led you to that mistake. You see – " Lestrade blew a thin stream of smoke, no more than a grey thread into the air. " – at the time, my parents were Anglicans. And the Anglicans are still the only church in England that insists on birth-records. They had a falling-out with the priest before I was born. Went back to being Romish. That's really the reason why there's no paper to back up my existence." He shrugged wildly, not quite rubbing it in to the self-assured prig. Still, the man actually believed his parents couldn't speak English.

"No man is without something to hide."

Madison's furious words clabbered in the air between them, just as the reporter realised the full irony of the meaning.

Lestrade's dark eyes never reacted. "I quite agree. You seek your information your way," the little detective answered in a low, quiet voice, "and I will seek mine."

There was really nothing more to say.

Madison walked away from the tradesman without another word. He was almost home before words even came to him.

Lestrade finished his smoke, watching the tall man melt into the crowd. His thoughts were suddenly troubling and murky – a foresight perhaps of things to come. A shame there was no such thing as a compass for human behavior.

He pinched the end of his smoke off before it could burn his lips, and a small girl ran up. Her face and ragged yellow hair was clean, but the five dresses she wore – her life's possessions – spoke of the filthy streets. A month ago he'd witnessed the claim of her brother's body to lockjaw. A common death in streets with horse-dung. He handed her the cooling nib, and she pocketed it with a grin. It would join the other stubs to be dried over stingy soft-coal fires that night, and remade into fags to sell to people even poorer than she: The bone-grubbers. The dredgermen who made their livelihood pulling up the corpses of the dead from the waters . . . and the dog-dung-sweepers.

Alone, he lit another smoke.

Had Madison declared war? He never lacked inspiration for his poison pen, and he was willing to wait years for the right moment. Polite poison was still poison. Lestrade was hardly the biggest fish in his net . . . or even the most interesting. Still . . . the reporter had a personal disliking and that should not be overlooked.

No man is without something to hide . . . .

Too true.

The irony of it was, Madison proclaimed to tell the story of the London poor, but he didn't know a single thing about them. Henry Mayhew he was not.

A disownment was a life sentence. He was dead to his family, their extended kin, and those that were loyal to his family. It was a large region, and just as well they were all in Plymouth while he stayed in London. Any sentence in the diaries with his name in it had been blacked out years ago – if it hadn't been sliced, burnt, or just tossed. Lestrade had not been the first man to lack possession of proof of his own life. More than three-fourths of the London poor had no idea there was an attempt to record the simple fact of their existence. They wouldn't understand such nonsense. Why bother? Most of the babes wouldn't see the first ten years of life. They shrugged at it all, and shrugged again when reminded that such proofs were usually the only way one could track the vicious Hell-holes of baby farms, child-rings, or kidnappings. It was what it was. Life was short. They depended on the few charity groups and overworked, un-thanked Anglican clerks to prove they were alive.

Faced with need to make his own way in life, Lestrade found a sympathetic doctor who was willing to write the obvious for the young cab-man – his first London job: *Mature enough for police work. In-turned left foot, too minimal to pose difficulties*. One signature and it was done. A willing sponsor within the ranks helped.

As far as proving he was younger or older than he claimed . . . Well, Lestrade wished Madison luck, in a sardonic way. As long as he was barking up empty trees, he wouldn't be noticing other things the Yard was up to.

Such as tonight's raid at The Kelpie.

Owning an entire building had its own collection of blessings and curses. Hers was older than a few of the neighbors' and wanted a different sort of upkeep two to three times a week.

Mr. Hudson grabbed up a quilted cotton pad and yanked open the cast-iron door to the bake oven her predecessors had so thoughtfully set inside the bowels of the basement. A cloud of steam and the scent of bread, hot stone, and treacle made her hold her breath and blink rapidly. With a swift twist and turn and yank with the flat wooden bread paddle she caught one, two, and finally fourteen loaves of wheaten bread and pulled them out to the waiting cool-shelves.

As a newly-wedded bride, Mrs. Hudson had not been pleased to find this brute of architecture built within the foundation-stones on her first tour of the house. It had been something else to fret over, along with upkeep of the vegetable-plot and the price of bacon on the other side of Marylebone. Twice a week she had to build a low fire and keep the coals simmering for the never-ending war against the damp. In summer it was desperate and only the Doctor, bless him, ignored the discomfort, claiming his training in the military. She still wasn't certain if he was just being a gentleman about it.

But they hadn't much summer this year, and firing up the cantankerous old oven was pleasant against the ever-creeping chill. Even in the midst of baking, the cool never quite left and if she bought milk fresh from the cart it could sit to rise to cream in the far corner. Before his passing, Mr. Hudson had put an iron liner in which saved the earth on fuel. Keeping a house in Baker Street was expensive, and she had enough to do to make all the ends meet and put the rest aside for the future.

The last loaf was done and the new maid took the brook down off the wall and swept vigorously against any dust, being careful to check if the bread was covered proper first. Mrs. Hudson was in the act of saying something to her about the night's cooking when the doorbell caught their ears.

"I'll get it," she told the child. "Finish the sweeping and make sure you cover the lid for the dust-man."

The girl's puzzlement followed her up the stairs, for answering the door was often the task of the younger and swifter, but she was young and new to the post.

She opened the door to a familiar young lad grinning from ear to ear with a fistful of messages and his safety bicycle perched neatly on the kerb.

"Mail for 221b Baker Street!"

"Mind your impertinence, Master Harold," the landlady scolded. "This is not the only address in your route I'm sure."

"Well, sure, Mrs. Hudson. Sure." Harold surrendered quickly. "But not like this one."

His statement was met with a freezing look over a still baking-reddened face. "I'm sure I don't know what you mean by that, Harold."

Harold was satisfied she had all the folding correspondence. He turned and fished a trim package out of a satchel off the bicycle. It had so many latches and tiny locks even the most bored of pick-pockets and thieves would pass it by. "I'm to give this to you in person."

"I don't see how else you could," the woman protested, but accepted the box with only a faint sputter.

"Will that be all, Mrs. Hudson?"

"That will be all until another day. Thank you, Harold."

She watched him go more out of Christian duty than motherly concern – those "safety" bicycles still made her nervous, but he managed to mount his metal beast without falling off and soon he was back in the crowds, going far too fast and yelling for everyone to get out of his way.

Satisfied that if he had his inevitable accident it would be too far away for her to help, Mrs. Hudson set the mail upon the coat-tree in the foyer and sorted what was hers and what was Mr. Holmes's – and the box was both, for it was addressed from Mr. Holmes in Spain, and to her?

Whatever would the man think she needed from Spain?

She admired the stamps for a moment, for they were green and striking, a sharp-angled castle of some sort beneath a sky high with white cloud. She liked the string, which was bound up with what her fingers told her was pure Merino wool, and she gently undid the knot and tucked it away for safe-keeping. A good bit of wool had a hundred uses.

Through several layers of keepable paper she finally found the box, which was real wood instead of paste-board. Imagine that. She marveled at its strength and lightness, just the thing to put up on the wall to keep her own correspondence away from those new kittens. Her thumb slid the door aside and there, packed in a snug nest of crumpled-up linen and embroidery threads, she found a letter addressed to the Doctor, and a small jar of saffron threads tied to a small note.

My Dear Mrs. Hudson,

I have been told by my most gracious hosts that everyone who comes to Spain must know of their prized cloths and threads as well as their cooking. You may notice the cloth is a pale green. This is from a very hard to find plant from the Andes. It is unsuitable for the machine looms but the stubborn craftsman perseveres. I am assured it is much stronger than the usual white cotton fibers. Do enjoy and I shall be out of Spain as soon as this little matter has finished with my attention.

Your devoted lodger,

Sherlock Holmes

Well, bless the man. A bit of saffron would do well to color up that yellow rice the Doctor liked so well, and she wouldn't have to use carrot juice to do it.

But for now the bread had sat and was ready for wrapping. Half for home, half to trade and the customers would be coming soon. Come to think of it, the Doctor would be in soon too. Best to have things ready before then . . . .

NOTES

1. Whiskers curled in small ringlets. Terrible to keep clean.
2. Pea jackets: Originally from *pij-jekker*, *pij* referring to "pilot". The River Police were fond of this dark coat. The lapels were wide, with double-breasted fronts and soft on one side. In Lestrade's time, it would have been made of thirty-ounce wool, but now the weight is as light as twenty-two ounces. Watson noted Lestrade wore a pea-jacket when his work took him to the river in "The Noble Bachelor".
3. "Great fun" as applied to taverns. Lestrade is being sarcastic.
4. Slang for "street-finders" – people that scrounge a living (literally) out of picking up the things no one else wants or can afford to ignore. They are usually the poorest of the poor.
5. Loaded Dice
6. The newest pickpocket in the gang; prized because they hadn't been identified as such. Toby is good at what he does because he can move without being noticed, and picks the beats of the inexperienced policemen.
7. Holmes writes notes on the cuff of his wrist in "The Naval Treaty"

Chapter IV

It was strange the things that could go through Lestrade's mind at times.

On the other hand, it wasn't as though he had much of a blooming choice. Thinking was the only blooming thing he could do right now. It was just his blooming bad luck to be on the wrong side of the blooming thug with the thick muscles, a thicker head, and one eyebrow uniting small, pig-like blue orbs in a greasy face that took second place in its importance against the most amazing clot of wiry black hair the inspector had ever seen.

It would not take any detective (plainclothes, uniformed or private), to realise the raid on The Kelpie had not gone as Gregson had planned.

No one had expected them to go after Lestrade first – he'd been helping bring up the left of the swarm, and there had been several bluebottles on each side. It was all standard procedure: Police invade the structure that has already been infiltrated by C.I.D.'s in disguise. C.I.D.'s jumps to the back of the building and create a chokehold on all the unsavory secret exits lurking by the Thames. A judicious flow of stampeding bodies. A few shrills on the whistle. And the order to halt before the officers of the law usually wrapped up the business. It would be a fitting end to one of Gregson's most aggravating cases for '83 (with part-credit to Lestrade, who owed Gregson and perhaps this mess would square the deal).

Gregson expected the usual blustering, feeble resistance common to depraved individuals who made a living out of press-ganging weary seamen. The Water Police [1] had been called in on this one, and they were now boating their way up and down the section of river, rescue equipment and revival instruments at the ready in case someone forgot how to swim during an escape run.

57

Unfortunately for all of Gregson's brilliant plans, things simply did not work out nicely. For some reason the big bruiser [2] on Lestrade's side of the warehouse had lit eyes on him, and the next thing anyone knew, a human juggernaut had spun grown men like ninepins, and Lestrade's world was clogged with a face a wild boar would have gasped at. Small blue eyes buried in a thick black hedge of untamed hair, beard, eyebrows and double moustaches clamped into him, and then an unlit lamp was blocking his full strike against a load-bearing wall. The pain slapped him senseless on his way to the filthy floor.

At least PC Briggs had the foresight to stuff him between a fallen table and a crate of Kentish apples before jumping back into the fray with Phillips. Lestrade couldn't see much. He was beyond the ability to help himself, so all he could do was watch through a forest of table and chair legs and frantically shuffling human legs. On occasion, a body slammed full-length into the floorboards. Lestrade was rather grateful for those moments, even though the vibration of impact sent waves of fresh agony through his spine. Those tosses were a fair indication of who was winning.

So far, the police force had taken a fall (besides him), twelve times. The same could not be said of the patrons. Lestrade had given up their count sometime after twenty, but they really were tough examples of London's low-life.

Not so long ago, he had found himself explaining what a crimping shop was to the very pretty woman who ran the new eatery off Paddington Station. Lestrade found he preferred to think of her instead of his increasingly slim chances of getting out of this trap without boot-marks on his coat.

"Get that rotten, mucking – "*A chair smashed against a packing-crate.* "Dollymopping – " *crunchcrunch.* "I'll do down, you southern – " *Sound of a fist into a well-padded gut.* " – son of a Surreyside Snakesman!" [3] *Something burst into a million glass pieces.* "Flummut – " [4]

No one could swear like Bradstreet.

Twenty minutes later:

"Lestrade?"

Lestrade winced. "Yes?"

"Are you all right, sir?"

"You'll have to ask an expert, Phillips." Just trying to lift his head made Lestrade break into an icy sweat. "How are the Holesapples?"

Phillips winced in his own sympathy. "Seemed scared, but well enough and grateful. We sent them off in the ambulance just in case they aren't well . . . We sent for a doctor, sir. Have you tried to move?"

"Not since that one time . . . I take it you're all mopping up now that you've had your fun?"

"Ahem." Phillips tried not to look too delighted about his torn uniform, bruised face, and missing helmet. "A few of the rats got away, sir. I'm sorry to say, the big'un that tossed you was one of 'em."

"Too bad." Lestrade closed his eyes. "I was looking forward to signing a statement on him."

"I'm sure we'll see him again." Phillips spoke with the assurance of someone who had all kinds of faith in London, despite all evidence to the contrary. "After all, he who fights and runs away, lives to fight another day." He sank against the wall and un-stoppered his hip flask. "Let's see if we can't get this down ye, sir. A bit of medication until the doctor comes."

Twenty more minutes later:
"Good Lord!"

Lestrade painfully opened his eyes to regard an upside-down Dr. Watson, who looked only slightly less bad than the inspector felt.

"Small world, Doctor."

"Small and crowded." Watson shook his head in wonder. "I was finishing my shift at Barts when a contingent of constables invaded the halls." He knelt, placing his fingers on the floor first to ease his knee down without shaking the floor. "Exactly how did you manage to dislocate your shoulder and wrench your back at the same time?"

"I didn't. T'was done for me." Lestrade realised if he combined talking with exhaling, the pain level was much more tolerable.

"Have you ever had a dislocation?"

"Yes."

"Then I'm afraid you know what's about to happen . . . ." Watson suddenly shifted until he was pressing his foot against Lestrade's shoulder. The inspector had a very narrow brush with unconsciousness as the shoulder snapped back in place. Watson did something else and Lestrade gasped as something made a cracking sound in his back. Watson looked as though he completely sympathised with shoulder ailments.

"He'll live, Doctor?" Gregson's gravelly voice sounded behind the doctor. Lestrade was shocked at the guilt tinting the big man's face.

"I hope he has some reading to catch up on," Watson smiled. "He won't be on duty for a few days, Inspector."

"All the less competition for me," Gregson smirked.

"*Hmmph.*" Lestrade thought about saying something witty, but he couldn't be witty on demand. Watson adjusted his position, put his good arm about him, and cautiously the two got him upright. Lestrade nodded at Watson's silent question, and they slowly rose to their feet. "Get me out of this flash house," he rasped. [5]

Three days later, Lestrade was ready to find the scum who had thrown him into the wall – if only he could crawl out of bed long enough to do it! It helped only slightly that the newspapers were full of the colourful fight and the rescue of the elderly Holesapples. Well, that and the fact that no one had yet been appointed to replace Marwood, Executioner of England.

One had to wonder if said lack of a filled post had something to do with the sudden brazen turn of the criminal mind.

The landlady had been considerate enough to send up the morning and evening editions, minus *The Littoral*'s. Mrs. Collins was a protective old she-bear. She read the papers first. Whatever Madison had to say about him, it must be ripe.

At the very least, the unknown bruiser was out of his regular employers. Lestrade took comfort in the image of the big man trolling taverns, selling his fists and winding up on the wrong side of a rival gang's contract to outfit a ship to Calcutta, Morocco, Shanghai, New York, or worse, some port along the Irish Sea.

Fantasies have no comparison to reality. Lestrade was ready to gnaw hobnails by the end of the third day – he had never been sedentary. His approach to solving cases had been based on his approach to life: Get out and get the answers yourself. He couldn't travel in his mind the way Gregson or – God forbid – Sherlock Holmes could. He actually had to be there in person. His caseload was sitting stagnate on his desk, gathering cobwebs and losing odds with every passing minute.

In a misguided effort to amuse him, Bradstreet sent daily missives on the cases flowing in which distracted Lestrade from his boredom – but sent his heart rate half through the ceiling. Bless his oversized heart, Bradstreet's journalism was not on par with his fine detecting, and sentences like "*Jones found the Holywater Sprinkler of Hyde Park*" [6] without details was enough to make a grown man eat his own cufflinks.

Lestrade's thoughts were going down a very dark road when someone knocked at the door. He glared up from his newspaper. "Enter!"

Dr. Watson opened the door with a quizzical expression. "Good afternoon, Inspector. I thought I'd see how you were recuperating." His bright brown eyes flitted about the poor but hard-scrubbed possessions of the rooms as guileless as a child.

"Oh, excellent. I have a medical question for you." Lestrade slapped the paper down. "Is boredom a leading cause of death?"

"Absolutely," Watson responded with a suspicious twinkle in his eye. "As a Police Inspector, you should know that better than most."

"I don't follow you."

Watson lifted his bag, got a nod of permission, and put it on the table. "If there's a fundamental common ground to our professions, Inspector, it

60

is that we do quite a bit of cleaning up after other people." He clicked open the bag and began rummaging around. "Have you used up that muscle balm yet?"

"No," Lestrade grunted reluctantly.

Watson frowned. "Having trouble applying it? You could have just said something, you know." He pulled out small objects to line them neatly by the bag. "But back to the question: How much of our cleaning up do you think began as some poor chap with more boredom on his mind than common sense?"

"I hate to say you have a point," Lestrade admitted. "My first case as a policeman was helping collect the pieces of a man who drank far too much gin and decided to see how many times he could hop across the train tracks until it caught up with him. What was your first experience?"

Watson actually paused in the middle of his organising. He shuddered all over.

"I don't know if mine can compare to yours. I found a drowning victim." He suddenly dropped his gaze to his busy hands. "A young woman . . . She had floated into the canal of the local mill and was wedged in the dry kex [7] of the bank when the floodwaters were down." Despite the obvious passage of time, the memory was still powerful. "I was just a boy, so I suppose that made it all the stronger."

"That is bad," Lestrade agreed. "Moreso for a lad."

Watson shook his head in disagreement. "We were all looking for her, and the waters were rising. I had to pull her out . . . move her to higher ground before she was washed away completely." He shut the door on the past with a clap. "How is your shoulder?"

"Much better compared to the back itself. How long am I going to keep staring at the inside of this cube?"

"Hmm." Watson looked about him. "It is a cube," he noted in wonder. "Managing short trips out, walking a bit?"

"Not for long." Lestrade exhaled through his nose. "Either tell me I can return to work or find me something to do. Inactivity is not good for body or soul."

"No quarrel," Watson promised. "I'm going to probe those lower muscles to gauge the swelling. Then, to apologise for being forced to tolerate my presence, we'll pick the establishment of your choice." With a grin he handed over a salve-tin.

Lestrade tucked it in his garret. [8] "How about The Lancashire Rose?"

"Excellent choice," Watson approved. "I could smell them working a wonder with John Dory on my way up here, and I suggest we hurry. That kind of treat won't be available for long."

A large man with skin like a boiled prawn was accepting a piled-up platter of steaming food as they made it down to the tables. Mrs. Collins' cooking was decent, yet Lestrade found himself exposed to a culinary lust from the odors rolling off that plate as the big man limped past them, his right leg stiff from an injury.

Watson paused to watch him shamble by, his face creased thoughtfully. "Lestrade, was that Bartram of Lancashire?"

"The wrestler?" Lestrade would have peered, but his back really wasn't up to much. "I have no idea. I've only seen him on playbills." He made a moue of thought. "Well, he's from Lancashire. Why wouldn't he eat at the Lancashire Rose?"

"There you are," Watson chuckled. "I'd just read an article about the man and his remarkable family." The doctor pondered slightly. "Lestrade, it must be he. His sister and older brother are supposed to be savants in arithmetic. Extraordinarily gifted."

"Yes, I know what the word means, Doctor," Lestrade said patiently. He rolled sadly brief memories over in his head. "She did seem a bit confident," he added under his breath. "Quite confident for such a young woman on her first business venture." He paused. "Just how gifted?" he asked as if he didn't care either way.

Watson was too pleasantly caught up in the fascinating memory to notice. "Very rare. She and her brother have a faculty for the higher levels and can recall numbers with ease. If she's keeping books, I would say it is for good manners and proper attention to business – she doesn't need to write anything down."

Lestrade thought about it. "Not anything?"

"No. Not numbers."

Lestrade thought about this some more. "And she's . . . here . . . ." He re-straightened his spine and looked about the establishment with new eyes, trying to find some clue for this mystery.

"It was a bit of a scandal," Watson glanced both ways so quickly the little detective barely saw it at all. The doctor's voice dropped and took on a tone as if he were admiring the quality of the hot tea nested within his large hands. "You see, the family's manager for their mill was clever enough to hide his malfeasance of funds, and her brother was too busy with his own business as an accountant to mind the books. Miss Cheatham found out all by herself, and managed to prove in court the fellow's thievery. She had taught herself advanced French so she knew what the accounts meant – "

Watson shared a conspiratorial look with his companion. French was not an easy language for the English-bred brain to absorb, but the language was essential for anyone who wanted to compete in the mathematical

62

world. "The story ended with a note of his sentencing! It was impossible to recover the stolen money, so the Cheathams sold everything, collected their funds, and moved here."

"Which possibly saved her life." Lestrade was trying not to stare, but this beat any tale he'd heard in a tavern. "That man's friends wouldn't have liked being bested by a woman." He'd seen enough murdered women to prove it. Intelligent women survived if they could hide their intelligence . . . or found powerful protectors. And here she was, out in plain sight?

"Mystery solved. There you are." Watson was satisfied. "I've been living in Baker Street too long if I'm seeing ulterior matters in everything!"

"I should think that would be a natural consequence of living with Mr. Holmes." Lestrade settled into his chair with a heart-felt sigh.

For the second time that day, Watson shuddered, but he was also smiling. "You have no idea. You really have not."

"I've got enough inkling to know you're a better man than I am. For that matter, you're a better man than anyone in Scotland Yard if you can live with the man." Lestrade lifted his hand at the passing tweeny, signalling for service. "We deal with firearms on a daily basis. No need to come home to find it decorating the walls! I don't see how you can do it."

Watson merely lifted his shoulders. He was ever chary to tell tales out of shop, but the general reputation Holmes had of being more (or less) than human needed to be corrected. "As difficult as it is to be to live with a genius," an unusually sober note had struck the doctor, "I'm fairly certain it's even harder to be one." He lifted his cup and a sudden grin flashed across his face. Lestrade had seen Watson in a variance of moods since their first meeting, but he was still surprised at the gentleness displayed in such a hard-looking man who appeared far more at home with cannon and cadence than ordinary life.

"I have to admit it was less of an adjustment to move from Maiwand to Baker Street. Both of them are war zones, but here I have three meals a day," the doctor said wryly, much to Lestrade's shocked delight. "Heavens. He's already coming back for another dish?"

"What in the name of God happened to you?" Clea had no qualms about scolding someone who deserved it. Bartram deserved it.

Had Bartram the sense of a hedgehog, he would have winced and come up with some ridiculous story involving a battle with a stampeding ox or a runaway train and then finished with his victory over the opponent. There was enough fog on the street that even smart brother Myron would confuse a train for an ox. It would have nearly worked. But Bartram didn't try a semi-plausible lie. He told the truth instead.

"Fight went bad t'other night, Clea," he grunted. "Had some of my face yanked out by the roots so I shaved the rest of it off." He reached up to touch his skin. By all appearances, the razor had been used to open tins in its spare time. "What're you so upset for? It's not like I'm sugaring violets for a living!"

"Sugaring violets might be less dangerous." Clea closed her eyes for a moment, feeling the grain of flour on her face. "Bartram, what is going on? Are you working the pits again?" Bullish silence told all. "Oh, Bartram."

"Don't need your criticism, little miss," he snapped, throwing himself down into the table by the chestnut barrel. "What's t'eat?"

Clea held her tongue as she dished up a mound of clapshot, but when she thrust it on the table in front of him, she had all her words rehearsed. "The money you're bringing home won't do a bit of good on tha' death!" she pointed out. "And a fine thing that'll do to *feyther*!"

"He was a wrestler too."

"He quit when he began making mistakes."

His broad face flushed. "You sayin' I'm making mistakes?" He half-rose out of his chair, just as someone cleared his throat.

Clea knew how it looked. Tempers flared under the muck of a London fog with people trapped indoors for hours on end. She was one-quarter Bartram's size, and just because she wasn't afraid of him didn't mean all could be well. Bartram was the strongest in a family of giants – Nature's apology for making him one of the stupidest, she reasoned.

"Beg your pardon, Miss Clea." Inspector Lestrade touched the brim of his hat gently with a forefinger. "I thought I'd apologise for not sending you word about your missing purchase."

Neatly done. Clea felt a moment's respect for a man who could intrude upon a situation and look as though it had been preordained. She deliberately ignored Bartram, who was shifting side to side on his bulk, opening and shutting his hands.

"We'd heard you were injured, Mr. Lestrade." She took in the fact that behind him was a second man, sitting casually with a newspaper blocking view of his lap – or the side pocket where a sap or gun would be kept. Despite the bland expression on his solid face, he looked about as harmless as a cannonball. Doctor fellow, she recalled. Always polite, never tolerant of nonsense. "If so, we're glad to see you back on your feet."

"Not at all." He smiled ruefully. "It will be a day or two before I'm back at the Yard if my physician has any say so."

"He does say so," the other man interjected.

"We'll be glad to hear of it, Mr. – " Clea stifled her reaction to the sound of her brother's rude snort from behind. "Forgive my manners, sir. This is my brother Bartram." She did not introduce him by his title.

"Mr. Cheatham." Lestrade repeated his slow touch of his hat brim – Clea caught on that he was moving gently from injuries. His doctor was scowling enough to frighten a garrotter. "Pleased to meet you."

"Humph." Bartram managed to mortally embarrass his sister by limping off with his tray.

Clea gritted her teeth. "If he doesn't return that washed, I'll charge him double." She swore under her breath. Lestrade's lips twisted. He was trying not to smile. "My brother has the manners of a fatted plough horse," she said by way of apology. "He's part of the reason why all Cheathams have been barred from The Drunken Duck at Hawkshead . . . for life."

"Really, it's not a problem," the inspector assured her. "Any time a person manages not to spit in my face for being a detective is quite a pleasant greeting."

Clea had to laugh. "I think I said before, you've the more interesting job of the two of us. Get back to your palaver with your doctor. I'll have Mr. John Dory up in a few moments."

"Very well done," Watson applauded when they were alone. "Identity confirmed and no blood shed."

"One has to be careful with defusing tempers in a public place," Lestrade winced slightly. "Sometimes the situation calls for simply flashing one's warrant card and acting like the Prime Minister." He lowered his hand to his pocket. "And as long as I have a pocket, I carry my persuasions in it."

"You did well. When I'm with Holmes, I never know if he's going to test his boxing skills on someone, or take them home as a new-found friend."

"Ha! Do you think he boxes just because no one expects someone of his weight to do so? Surprise being the great advantage and all that?"

"I wouldn't even begin to guess with Holmes. I'll die prematurely aged for certain . . . ." Watson discreetly shut his mouth as Miss Cheatham strode up with John Dory and chips.

"Here you are, sirs. The girls are quite proud of this offering." In the four weeks since meeting her, Lestrade had seen considerably less of Miss Cheatham than he'd liked. The cool weather had pinked her cheeks against blue-black hair escaping her cap. "It is good to see you again. Mr. Briggs let us know how you were doing after that waterfront mess." Her wide mouth stretched into a pleasant grin. Ladies smiled. Their finer constitutions would stand for nothing more. Miss Cheatham had more starch. It was a good thing to see.

"Thank you, Miss Cheatham, it looks perfect."

Watson re-cleared his throat with a twinkle in his eyes. "Charming lady."

Lestrade reached for a fork. "Oh?"

Watson's eyebrows slid upward. It was neither as swift nor rapier-like as a look from Holmes, but Lestrade felt the same kind of thought behind those dark eyes. "Oh? You didn't notice?"

"I suppose," Lestrade muttered as he managed to sprinkle vinegar over the chips without hurting himself too much. "I promised to look into her missing goods."

"Here's hoping her establishment remains here a good long time."

"That's two of us," Lestrade unglued just a bit to agree.

Meals were plentiful at the Cheatham House – so long as no one complained at the choice on the table. After spending the entire day cooking, Clea was not about to create any extra wonders with the ovens in the overly-large brick house. Besides, the damp coming off the canals made baking more torment than delight. When their regular cook was out, she merely carried home the platters and "set up shop" straight from The Lancashire Rose to her father.

"Smells delightful, whatever it is," Charles Cheatham opined. Thanks to the maids, who knew to not move the furniture around while cleaning, he was quite good at getting around in the twilight of his world. Clea was glad to see her father up and about.

"John Dory and chips, of course. What else would be suitable for this time of year?" Clunk, the trays were stretched out. "Just the two of us then?"

"Well, let's see . . . ." Charles Cheatham stroked his snow-white beard in a show of thinking. Of all his sons, he was a peculiar combination of both Myron and Bartram, as if each son was a split facet – Myron's patient intelligence and Bartram's raw power. "Myron is off with his little'uns. They be wanting to pick out the good fabrics for winter clothes, and if they take tha' owd man, he's more likely to let them get what they fancy." Father and daughter shared a laugh that was more like a snicker. Myron was smart by anyone's standard (Clea was his equal in numbers), but his three girls had him around their little fingers. There was always the chance – and the hope – that Myron's widower's eye would be caught by a corresponding widow or some appropriate lady with a bit of starch.

Unless, of course, it was one particular widow in question, and that being the bereaved of the late George Masters, Myron's old business partner. Clea thought of the praying mantis whenever she entered the room.

"Cutler and Wallace left this morning to see about setting up some shares with a fishing-business that deals off the Faeroes." Charles shrugged at that. "They won't be back for at least a few days, and you know those two: Good news – we'll hear about it. Bad news – they'll stay gone until they find some good news to bring home." The old man's long fingers, blunted from years of sports-fighting, were still agile enough to dowse the way to his usual chair at the table.

"In other words, they could start out in a fishing business, and wind up with some interests in a Welsh gold mine." Clea had to laugh at the thought. Those two were close as twins, and there was no sense worrying about them – they would look out for each other first and the rest of the world go hang.

"Welsh gold? God forbid." Cheatham grieved. "I don't think they'd know gold from iron pyrite."

"Well, three down – who is left?" Clea prized lightly fried fillets out of the basket. The fish went to a sealed pan perched atop the small iron stove in the corner, and, warm as it was, the meal would be hot before they finished talking.

"Andrew is out on something common, for once. He's visiting some friends he met on the Serpentine. It seems the fact that he once built a boat makes him Grand High Nibs to his peers. They want his advice on a skull."

"That's four." Clea was laughing. She got up to find malt vinegar and ale for the dinner. "Since you seem to be going down the line in birth-order, where is Robert?"

"Scouting an office-suite for him and that wife of his."

"*Feyther,* you don't have to use that tone of voice. The way you said 'that wife of his' is hardly flattering."

"What kind of flattery would I give to a woman mad enough to marry Robert?" Charles asked – quite logically, Clea had to admit. "Dear, I put it to you: What kind of woman chooses to spend the rest of their life with a man who wants to make a career out of *ink*?" Charles had made his point, but he was rarely finished on the subject of his fifth son. "It's not as if we could get the boy to learn his letters when he was a tot – now he's wanting to make the means for the letters?"

Clea did not roll her eyes at the familiar tirade. Her father was mostly blind, but he could "hear" amused derision from across a busy street.

"Bartram I don't know about." Charles finished flatly. "He rises late and returns late. He's been getting hurt in his fights too. I don't like it. He never took such falls back home."

"Now I agree with you on that." Clea set the silverware down and Charles picked them up easily, tucking into the tender fish with

67

enthusiasm. "I tried to talk to him today on that, but as usual, he didn't care to hear a sermon from his baby sister."

"Go easy on the fool," Charles said bluntly. "I was much like him, only I learned from my mistakes sooner. Bartram's problem is he's too good in a fight. Even when he loses, he draws a crowd. Your mother's eyes and four cracked ribs made me stop long enough to think."

Dinner passed in relative silence for a few minutes as the sea-coal crackled.

"So how is my youngest?" Charles asked. "I hear from your brothers that you've caught the eye of a Yarder."

"Give me their names so I can cut it on their headstones," Clea snarled.

Charles roared with laughter. He loved to tease his daughter – possibly because she never took offense like her brothers did. "Bartram's still your big brother, and he's worried about you. He told Myron, so of course they all know. I just thought you should be prepared for the roasting you'll get at the Sunday table."

"Ha. I'll show them a roasting. I'll roast them. The oven's big enough if I joint them careful like and use the largest pans." Clea scrubbed her lips with a napkin. "What should I tell you so you can crow to the boys about how much more you know?"

Charles rubbed his hands together in unholy glee. "Well, tell me everything!"

"There's not much to tell . . . ." Clea was starting to invoke untapped depths of annoyance. "And you are very enthusiastic."

"I would see my daughter provided for." Charles pointed his fork at her with unnerving accuracy. "My sons can take care of themselves – more or less, my dear. But this is a man's world. I would prefer to see you settled before I die."

"You should have thought of that ten years ago when my brothers were picking fights with anyone who dreamed to be my suitor!"

"That was back when you were a Cotton Mill Heiress," Charles countered with the paternal logic that never failed to baffle his daughter. "No one was to be trusted."

Clea momentarily rested her forehead in her hands. "And a police inspector who so far has only passed bland pleasantries with me is an improvement?"

"Heavens, no. But he's the first. And where there's one, more will follow. Before the year's end, you'll have a gallery of beaus to choose from!" (Clea waited.)

"Inspectors are just a higher form of policeman," Charles Cheatham continued as he blithely drowned the fish in malt. "They live in tenement

68

houses with a different family in each room and a pig-cote in the back. Someone might ask for your dance just to rescue a lady from that sort of attention."

"*Feyther*, this is why Mam wouldn't let you attend her parties." Clea finally opened her eyes. "He's a policeman, and from what I can tell, he's concerned about his appearance, is clean, and he has decent friends. He doesn't smell like pigs, and he's got his share of pride, but he doesn't squander it on fighting. He'd never fit in with this family, obviously . . . Did Bartram tell you that this inspector was on the case that led to his own brother's hanging?"

Charles shrugged. "Bartram wasn't there, so there's a chance he's picking up the street rumors as Gospel again." His cloudy eyes were bland and unprepossessing. "I'm not the kind of man who just believes something because I'm told it. You know that. I'd like to say it was due to the influence of your sainted mother – she you can thank your brains for – but it's no secret your dear old papa wore the Broad Arrow[9] in his foolish youth." He shrugged. "He's not our people, but as I said, there has to be a first suitor, and he'll do."

"Well, Bartram was talking to me today when the inspector showed up for luncheon, and for a start I thought he would try to throw a detective through my wall!" Clea hadn't realised she was so upset until she finally said so. "He was as rude as an earless cat! I've seen men arrested for less than how he behaved!"

Charles grunted. "Lord, girl, you know your brother. Your inspector could have been a priest on his one-hundredth-birthday and Bartram would have been poking him." Charles poked his fish for emphasis. "Conflict is his bread, his milk, his meat."

"'My Inspector' now is it? Well, I can't have him scaring business. If he can't respect my shop, he'll have to go somewhere else. I may serve small beer, but that doesn't mean I need someone to frighten my customers into behaving!"

"I daresay not, with that knife you carry under your apron." Charles laughed under his beard. "And an inspector showing up for occasional meals. He sounds useful enough."

"*Feyther* . . . " Clea felt pressed to explain a few things to him. "There is no particular inspector . . . I have ten policemen, plainclothes and uniformed, that pay me regular for a good meal on any given day. They like a clean place to eat and they can't wait around for food when someone might need their assistance. I seem to be getting more and more of them, and by next year I might just change 'Lancashire Rose' to 'Copper Rose'!"

Charles laughed so hard he had to clap his napkin over his entire face.

Bartram picked up the large tankard in a hand that was scarce smaller and tipped it backwards, letting the brew wash down his throat. All about him the tavern continued its bustle, yell, and thump as the good-natured dart game in the back grew progressively less so the higher the stakes were wagered. It was always like this when it was too dark to do a bit of proper fishing.

Being paid to control the rowdies at the Tiddy Mun was hardly difficult. This was just on the outskirts of Little Venice and people knew better than to bring the police. This job was more boring than anything else. Simply standing to his feet and looking in the right direction squashed any misbehavior as fast as a snuffer over a candle. After a week of this, Bartram was bored enough that he resolved to let the fracas go a bit deeper before he did anything.

The fracas died down without his help. He sighed until his ale rippled. Paid to sit, that was all. If the money wasn't so simple, he'd be feeling guilty.

"You look low in the mouth, my friend."

Bartram lifted his gaze. A man tall and slender as an iron bar stood before him, coachman-hat held carelessly in hand. His dress was good cloth but tailored so simply he could have blended in almost any social class. Despite his fifth decade, the blond hair was thick and neatly groomed. He rested his hat before Bartram's drink as he sat down without invitation or query. Frost-blue eyes gleamed at him like an icy canal.

"Long day, sir," he grunted. "A bit of rest and I'll be ready to go all night long."

"Glad to hear that, Bartram. The games are promising tonight." Long, tough fingers knotted together as his "guest" leaned forward. "Now that the fuss over The Kelpie has died down . . . I thought I'd see for myself what happened."

Bartram flushed red – his usual reaction to questions involving himself. "Didn't want to risk getting recognised by that copper, that's all." He sounded sulky, even to himself. "I'd seen him before at The Rose, and there was a chance he'd have seen me."

"Well that's thoroughly understandable," the other man admitted. "You reacted quickly enough that I'm sure they didn't expect a thing . . . but you do realise who it was you threw so gracefully into the wall, don't you?" He didn't wait to be told. "Inspector Lestrade."

"Don't really know him much," Bartram admitted with a growl.

His employer paused for a moment, closing his eyes slowly and taking a calm breath. "Dear Bartram," he said patiently, "Inspector Lestrade is all of Scotland Yard, rolled up into one package." He let that sink in. "He's not their smartest man, and he's not their strongest, swiftest, or with the best social connecyions, or even the best-educated. But he is without a doubt their most *determined* man. Of all the Yarders who get the most attention from the newspapers, I'd put him in the top five. And he possesses a singular quality that makes him rather more dangerous than most."

Bartram grunted. "What would that quality be, sir?"

"Lestrade has little illusions about his abilities, and is extremely vain of his competency. That makes him a very difficult man to control. He compensates for his flaws by being a most professional man – the law, not his pride, is his master and thus he seeks help when his work is too much, or transfers a case to someone else. His informers are loyal, the public's trust strong. He will not fall victim to the usual traps of coercion, flattery, or blackmail. I've tried for too many years to snare him on a charge that would impugn his reputation. Nothing has ever come of it. One can't ruin a man's reputation for honest mistakes, and that seems to be his specialty." There was a sour note to that, as if honest mistakes were a failing.

"He swung his own brother. I know that, Mr. Quimper." Bartram tried to show he wasn't a complete ignoramus.

"Armoricus . . . Yes, that would be a good thing to remember. You see, the inspector could have done the right thing by his family and turned a blind eye to his brothers' misdeeds, but he chose to follow a duty higher than that of his own blood. Vanity talking, no doubt . . . Armoricus hung when dear Geoffrey signed the statement on that unfortunate murder of PC Cooper, and the other brother, Paul, was proven weak-minded." Pale blond eyebrows looked as sharp as knife-blades in the low light. "I try to stay in touch with my lads, you know. Loyalty to one's employees, and all of that. You understand, I'm sure."

Bartram swallowed hard. Fear was not an emotion that suited him. "I understand, Mr. Quimper."

"I hope so." The voice was still quite mild, but Bartram had seen Quimper break another man's arm just to underscore a point. "You are an excellent man, Mr. Cheatham. I would hate to lose another fine employee to Scotland Yard."

"You won't, sir," Bartram promised. "I'll take care of the little rat myself if it comes to it. You know I won't talk."

Quimper smiled for the first time. "I know you won't, Bartram. Disloyalty simply isn't a part of your nature." His smile grew. "I admire admirable qualities." Bartram thought uncomfortably that the lamps in the tavern threw ungodly lights into his employer's pale eyes. It reminded him of the blue sparks a train threw up when braking sudden. "By all means, if you think you can do something about that little man, I'd be most pleased.

And it wouldn't help but improve your sister's business, would it, if the inspector wasn't around so much."

Bartram started, and Quimper chuckled softly.

"Bartram, for shame. I take care of my men, don't I? Anything that concerns my men concerns me." He tapped his strong chin. "A very charming lady, your sister. I saw the article in the newspaper about your rising career. Is it true what it said about her intelligence?"

Bartram's first instinct was to hesitate. A smart woman was usually the butt of cruel jokes, and this was his employer talking of his sister. He struggled for a mild answer. "She's got a head for numbers just like Myron. Only different. Myron's smart about numbers in the books. Clea doesn't need books to keep her business straight."

"You must be proud of having someone like that in your family, Bartram. That is a rare faculty." Quimper's answer nearly made Bartram melt with relief. "She deserves a strong protector, does she not? That's why you spend so much time there?"

"Of course, sir." Bartram felt sweat slip down his neck. He didn't completely understand what was happening, and that made him even more afraid. "She's a nice girl. Nobody ought to take advantage of her. She's number-smart, but she hasn't been outside too much." The family had made certain of that.

Quimper smiled, as if hearing Bartram's thoughts and approving. "Is there a particular reason why our Inspector Plod is paying company to your sister?"

Bartram thought frantically. "She says she put it to him to track down her missing maize."

"Ah, that." Quimper grimaced. "I wondered when that little Waterloo would circle back to bite us . . . ." His fingers rapped gently on the table planks. "Well, he's welcome to try to find the answers on that. Perhaps it will keep him busy?" The man laughed again, very softly. "It might even be amusing."

Bartram was not the kind of man who mixed business with pleasure, much less the "amusing", but he was smart enough to keep his mouth shut when his agreements would sound false. He nodded instead, a safe response, and wished for more ale.

NOTES

1. Thames Division.
2. Boxer.
3. Bradstreet was calling someone a muck-eating, unskilled prostituting yet dangerous effete kind of boy/young man used for common burglary and promising them to do grievous harm. Surreyside was a euphemism for going somewhere for illegal pursuits.
4. Dangerous.
5. A public house used by criminals.
6. Holywater sprinkler: Slang for a cudgel spiked with long nails.
7. Reeds.
8. Fob pocket inside a waistcoat.
9. Charles had once been in prison.

Chapter V

Lestrade returned to his flat with a new course of action – any action being preferable to doing one more jot of nothing. He ignored the aching back, the bed he was so heartily sick of, and went to his desk.

Clea Cheatham's missing goods were a problem in itself. What would anyone but another baker or cook do with a hundredweight of semolina and a hogshead of Indian maize? If he looked at just the contents, there were (too many) illegal applications to the semolina. A dishonest merchant could have removed and cut it with additives – say, a small amount of pipeclay – and sell it on the market cheaply enough that the unfortunate buyer would think there was nothing more than a good price.

The flour they would take home would interfere with digestion, and in large amounts lead to illness. People died from inedible flour. Literally starved to death. The trick would be to sell it in small enough quantities that no one would keep much of the evidence around, and just amended enough that the poor people never caught on. It would be swiftly baked up and there would be nothing left in the way of proof for the Yard's chemists.

Indian maize was a stickier problem. He couldn't think of many uses for maize, overt or otherwise! His father had sworn it was never fit for the horses. It would be difficult to hide. The tint and grain made it stand apart. He did remember PC Berkley saying hot water and maize made a poultice to draw poison out of a wound. But no one would steal maize for such a purpose!

Krakatoa had affected more than the sunshine. The cool airs had plagued entire crop-regions. The maize had been of a type known for its hardiness, a species called the Mandan. (Lestrade was not educated enough to think maize with a taproot odd.) Both grains had been purchased from the same company off the Mississippi ports. A waterfront distributor by the name of . . . Dulse and Chapman . . . been in business for generations, and it was hard to think of their being caught up in something dishonest. They were no more dishonest than the next struggling merchant, and the fact that many of their employees were local no doubt inspired a higher degree of ethics.

The order had been part of a larger order of flour, sugar, salt, and leavening bicarbonates from the Norwegian-Sumatra Line (what a combination that was), a large-weight cargo ship by the name *Iron Autumn*.

Somewhere along the voyage up the coastline, a portion of the ship's drinking water had leaked and partially contaminated the barrels. They had been hastily transferred to some of the empties that were part of another order – robbing Peter to pay Paul, if there ever was a case. Miss Cheatham had signed over her purchase with a contract stating she was aware of the salvage, and had accepted the lowered price and damaged goods. The shipping line's insurance compensated the buyer of the empty barrels, a trader by the name of Mayo who had been under contract to assign a purchase of so much capital per year, and who had simply added enough empty barrels to fill that quota.

Lestrade wondered if things had really been that straightforward. The corn had vanished en route to The Lancashire Rose. No one claimed to know anything about the missing barrels, nor did anyone recognise the driver paid for the freighting job.

Oh, the inexpressible joy of policing crime in a city of millions.

Several sheets of paper and penciling later and Lestrade began to wonder if he was starting to see phantoms. He rapped an absent tune on the top of his desk and went over the facts in his mind, but precious little came to his mind. "You can't make barrels just up and vanish," he said aloud. "Not big barrels like that!" Not without breaking them up and turning them into furniture or firewood, and no one would be daft enough for that . . . hopefully.

Possibilities: Competition? Not likely. Ulterior use of corn? What? Something in the corn?

If only there wasn't the added problem of the missing workers, and the stolen roof lead distracting Scotland Yard . . . .

Corn. Lead. Missing workers . . . Lestrade's head hurt to match his back. "Mr. Holmes would be the person to ask on this one," he grumbled. "He likes the bizarre. Too bad he's so very unavailable right now." What was a joyous stimulation for Mr. Holmes was at this moment a throbbing pain in Lestrade's already-aching neck.

The walk had tired him. He sighed defeat and stood, feeling the strain on his muscles. How he hated this. He was a concrete-and-clay inspector, not some desk bound genius who could figure out things in his head. He had to be there, had to see with his own eyes what was happening. His ignorance penned him in, pounded him with remainders of his stupidity.

"Barrels," he said. "Stick to the facts. It's one or the other. What use would someone make of either one?" He clenched his hands together in thought. The problem was there weren't many possibilities. It all came down to the barrels! The unknown driver – he had been the direct thief, or in the pay of the master. The theft was not random. And if it was not random, it was deliberate. But why deliberately steal corn?

"Maize, barrels," He murmured softly. A prickling sensation was gathering up in the back of his mind. "It is either one or the other . . . ." It hurt, but he had to pace. It helped him think. He did a lot of thinking when he was running back and forth in his cases . . . Maize. Barrels. Maize.

Barrels.

Maize.

Barrels.

"The barrels?" He stopped in his tracks. "What about the barrels themselves?"

Clea was not prepared for the sight of her brother before the hours of dawn at The Rose. "Bartram?" She hurriedly dusted flour off her fingers as she stepped away from the large oven. "Are you all right?"

Her brother deserved that question, and then some. He had a black eye that hadn't perched there yesterday, but he grinned from ear to ear.

"Couldn't be better." He lifted his big hands up. Pouches clinked in each. "I won all my fights last night! D'you know how much money that means?"

"Enough that you'll have a nice deposit on your savings, I hope." Clea sniffed. Bad enough that she sounded like a spinster as it was, but she sounded like an elderly spinster – much worse!

He looked at her as if she lived merely to dash cold water on his spirits. "You sound like Ma," he accused. "You're too young to sound like Ma." Her eyes remained stony. Bartram tried again. "I'm sorry about yesterday," he grumbled. "I know you mean well."

Clea's mouth clicked open. "What did you just say?"

"I said I'm sorry I was rude to you. I know you like your manners."

"That's not the point, Bartram! I expect people to conduct themselves peacefully here! People come here for food, not fighting!" Clea rubbed at the start of a headache. Bartram's apologies were always far worse than his actual offenses. "Dust know what you're even apologizing for?"

Bartram steadied himself. He took a deep breath. "I don't like that inspector hanging around you," he began. "But I'll be civil to him. You want me to be civil to your customers. That makes sense. Wouldn't look right if I singled him out." He caught on that his sister was gaping at him.

"What?" he demanded. "I'm still going to kill him with my bare hands if he upsets you in any way!"

Clea prayed for strength, but settled for pouring a cup of tea. "Thank you, Bartram." Her voice sounded remarkably un-strangled to her own ears.

"And if he makes you upset, I'll wait till he's away from The Rose before I let him have it," Bartram clarified his good intentions. "But I'll do the same to anyone who makes you upset, Clea."

"You're not going to kill anyone," Clea groaned. "Can you not trust me to take care of my own problems?"

"So he is a problem?" Bartram pounced.

"Shut it!" Clea snapped. "That's not what I meant! And I'll believe you, Bartram, when you stop preaching to me and start doing some things that worry me a bit less! Because if we're on the subject of upsetting me, your being out all hours and coming back all colours is much more pressing to me than the prospect of a lounging policeman!" Clea hissed the last part out.

Bartram stopped, hesitating. "I'm . . . sorry, Clea," he mumbled. "Look, what would you have me do? Fighting's all I'm good at! It's all I know!"

"Rather the only thing you *want* to do." Clea sealed her lips against the same pointless tirade. "Look, why don't you try doing something for others once? Not just yourself? You spend too much time in your fights. Get out and do things besides fighting! You could open up a school if you wanted to! Just your reputation alone . . . ."

Bartram's face darkened. "Reputation?" he sneered. "I've had about my fill of reputations." He spun on his heel and, before she could say anything, he was back into the night. She groaned to herself. She hoped he was going home.

Mrs. Collins had sent up a tureen of vegetable stew and bread. He soaked the bread absently as the other tenants romped through the building, paying more attention to the way dawn tried to lighten the world outside the window than the ruckus. The sun never set on the British Empire, but it had enough to do to even show itself in London.

And he wanted to be out there in it, floating soot and all. The sparrows were up and scolding in the eaves, the eternal feathered pest to the housewife who wanted sills unadorned of nests and droppings. Wrens appealed to the British soul, not the common sparrow, but Lestrade felt a relationship to the stubborn little bird. They lived in this filthy city as defiantly as the humans they stole from, overcoming much the same odds as the people on the street.

Lestrade's restless gaze fell on the jar Watson had left behind. He almost smiled at what it represented. The man was growing on him. Mr. Holmes was another matter, but he could respect him from a distance and accept the reserved, backhanded assistance in return.

Lord knew, he hated to think what was going on at Baker Street right now. Mr. Holmes would be smoking a horrid pipe scraped up of everything he hadn't finished on the yestreen, ignoring breakfast, and mostly likely sticking the newest post to the fire-board.

Watson would be pressing him to stop molesting the furniture, at the same time tucking into his own plate – sensibly collecting his strength for the random moments when Holmes suddenly needed him to grab up his revolver and follow. Watson must think his *locum* work was nothing more than an idle vacation. Lestrade chuckled to himself to recall the night of The Kelpie's raid . . . He could too easily picture the scene at Barts: Watson wearily on his way home, his path abruptly blocked by invading policemen. Bradstreet (as usual, taking initiative) grabbing the startled doctor by the forearm and hustling him out the door and into the police-wagon before he could think to protest.

Bradstreet had performed that form of medical press-ganging so often it was a wonder the staff hadn't posted a lookout for anyone in a frogged coat.

Baker Street was a massive difference from Lestrade's own room in Paddington. *Paddingken*, the wags joked, making a pun on the slang term for a tramp's lodgings. There were too many days when Lestrade resembled a tramp at the end of it. His work-style was movement and personal observation as opposed to standing still and thinking. Mrs. Collins' rooms weren't the finest – The innards wanted plaster, and the Forest Glass windows made London look darker than it really was – which, considering London, was almost a laudable achievement. The entire building was clean and warm, but also claustrophobic and bare. He kept his rooms to the pattern and saw them as a means for short periods of sleep, a meal, and some quiet before he headed out to work again. It didn't help that he had permission to do whatever he liked to the upkeep. It was a matter of time he did not possess.

Being trapped only reminded him that he had spent more of his life at work than not since joining the Metro. Without the rumble and shuffle of Scotland Yard about him, the muffled silence threatened a long-buried loneliness in his chest.

Still, it was all he had. It was enough. There was no sense in aiming beyond one's means.

78

Clea was still annoyed.

That annoyance made for a perfect loaf of bread, granted – "troubles melt as dough turns to silk" as the saying went – but there were only so many different ways in which one could pound ire out on a hapless lump of dough. It must have accepted its rise in the warm oven with relief when she was finally finished. She muttered under her breath, and went to the counter for gulp of tea.

Bartram was an idiot. Why must he be her brother?

She had asked God that same question of all her brothers at one time or another: Myron's complacent superiority. Cutler and Wallace's infuriating clannishness that shut out the rest of the family like it was only a game. Robert for his wretched jokes. Andrew for pursuing one worthless hobby after another before his own expenses were paid for.

Much of their flaws also selfishly extended to the women they had married, or were not marrying, as the case may be. But Bartram, closer to her age than anyone else, was the one she saw the most and thus had the most exposure to his maddening qualities.

All my life, I have been up to my neck in this nonsense. The irony was laughable. She prided herself on not having any nonsense to her at all – but look at the family she was committed to!

And here I am, spinster-age, the last of my school to go un-married except for . . . .

She paused a moment, trying to recall the names of the three girls who had known from the cradle they must never marry. Their duty was to see to the comfort of their parents in their last years. Her face burnt up in the heat of her self-castigation. She had not bothered to notice those girls much. "The Three Blind Mice", the unkinder ones had called them. Meek and blind to their terrible fate.

Well, this is no better than I deserve, is it?

Clea was about to sit at her usual table with a teacup. She blinked as a draught skittered chill air over the floor. A grain of flour caught in her eyelashes and she stopped to wipe her face with her apron. When she cleared her eyes, a new customer had joined the ranks.

Now that's a tall one. No, he isn't that tall, he just gives that appearance. Thin as a rail and probably as hard!

He had the look of a man who had just dismounted from the morning train. One dressed in the subfusc colours that would blend in with train-soot and ash. It wasn't until they were safe from the rails that they showed more individuality.

"Good morning, Madam." The man smiled, sending the lightest blue eyes he had ever seen upwards, and he lifted his hat off his head. "May I trouble you for a cup of hot tea against the weather?"

"Of course, sir." Clea nodded to Linda, who was already pouring with a smitten eye. Oh, dear. "Would you want anything else?"

He paused and took a deep breath of the air into his lungs. "I may at that." His smile never left his face, but at least it was understated, not the kind that drove her off the rails. "Everything smells delightful."

"Thank you, sir. We do our best."

"In truth, I was looking for a patron of yours, perhaps you know him. He is a Lancashire wrestler?"

Clea felt her heart plummet into her shoes. "What's he done now?" she asked thoughtlessly.

He threw back his head with a laugh. "My good woman! There is no need to worry! I am speaking of Bartram Cheatham – Bartram of Lancashire. I trust you know him?"

"I ought to know my own brother, sir." Clea put her hands on her hips.

"Good Heavens." He looked startled. "Why, now that I see the eyes, I wonder why I didn't notice it before." He lifted his hat again. "Do forgive my obtuseness."

Clea shook her head with a wry smile. She'd heard much worse by the narrowboaters. "Forgiven, sir. How may I help you?"

"I am your brother's agent, Mr. Jethro Quimper," the man announced, and for an underscore, produced a small card made of the stiffest paper Clea had ever closed fingers around. Jethro Quimper, Agent was stamped over the paper in copperplate with the barest of leafy borders. "I wish to speak with him regarding an upcoming charity."

"A charity event?" Clea repeated. If that didn't sound too good to be true. Clea squashed a rise of hope – she wasn't stupid. "What charity?"

"Ah, he initiated the topic himself." Mr. Quimper continued to astound Clea. "He said he was getting tired of constantly fighting for the gate-pay, pleasant though the recognition may be. He wanted to 'branch out', as it were, and expand his career in other areas. We had some discussions, and he confessed he would enjoy performing his skills at a few charities." Mr. Quimper sipped his tea with an appreciable sigh. "It will be Christmas before one knows it, after all, and that is a hard time for the poor."

"Yes, sir, I'll agree with you." Clea felt depressed just to think about it.

"But forgive me, the point of my conversation was, we found an interesting opening with the Policeman's Benefit. Have you ever attended a Scotland Yard event?"

"No, Mr. Quimper, I can't say that I have." Clea knew she sounded irritated, but why did it seem as though everyone was noting that she served to policemen? At least he isn't going to make a comment about the inspector. She took her good fortune where she could.

"By all means, you should consider attending!" Mr. Quimper cried. "It is a fine display of our men. They work so hard to keep London for us. Why, when my father was my age, this part of London wasn't even safe in broad daylight!" He leaned back, curling his fingers around his cup with a sensual delight in the warmth against the cool air. "As hard as these men work, I daresay London will be completely safe in another generation." And he saluted her with his tea.

"You have my interest, sir." The most attractive part about it was the notion of her brother behaving himself and also doing good without pay. It was better than any fairy tale.

"If I may," Mr. Quimper bowed politely, "if you see your brother sometime this day, please could you inform him that I will be in my rooms off Pall Mall?"

"Pall Mall?" Clea repeated, and collected herself with a nod. "Certainly, Mr. Quimper."

It was not until later that Clea realised what had felt strange. Mr. Quimper would, as a man of business discussing business, given her a card with his place of address on the side. But the card that stated his name and occupation was the sort suited to social visits.

"Ah, he's back," Gregson announced as soberly as a butler sent to speak Tennyson to zoo monkeys. "Now we can relax and stop taking up his cases."

Lestrade half-groaned. "I trust you enjoyed your week. How goes The Kelpie mess?"

"Messy." The big man folded his arms across his chest, putting his wide back against the wall. "One would think that the case would be wrapped up by now," he began, but the little man's snarl cut him off.

"Tobias Gregson, this is where you are about to tell me something I am not going to enjoy."

"Excellent, Ratty." Gregson's flippancy was ruined by the lack of sleep burning in his pale eyes. "But not complete. I'm going to tell you several things you won't enjoy, not by half."

Lestrade felt the skull-throb return. He lifted his fingers to his temples. "Well, don't bedizen it to death. I'm ready."

81

"First of all, none of the men we arrested are talking."

"Wh – How many men were arrested?"

"All but the four who got away – that means we have twenty big bruisers behind bars who aren't saying a single word."

"*T – Gre* – are you telling me we have a waterfront full of men who aren't talking?" Lestrade felt the pain spread to the space underneath his ribs. "Has that ever happened before?"

"Not in my memory." Gregson was driven to honesty by his worry. "Let me tell you, whoever is in charge of these boys, they are terrified." He produced a German stein full of black tea out of the atmosphere and sipped it loudly. "But some progress on the press-ganging."

"If that's a carrot, I'll take it."

"The Norwegian-Sumatra Line has been lax of late. New captains, new first mates, some new lines of traffic." Gregson swallowed tea. "In fact, their complete ignorance of the English language has stifled some of our attempts to question them. They aren't asking too many questions on where their crew comes from."

Lestrade could only stare. He wasn't a citizen of the world, but even he could make a passable "*Hallo-how-do-you-do?*" with Norwegians. Living in one of the largest mixed cities in the world meant one learned talking with foreigners.

"I wonder what their insurance company will say when the barristers get their teeth in that?"

"Better them than the likes of us," Gregson said fervently. "We're still tracking a few clues down that way. Also, Youghal was interested enough in your missive to hit the trod in pursuit of answers."

"I doubt even Youghal could re-discover two barrels of missing corn."

"Nor did he, but he did come across an interesting account of some buskers [1] by the canals off Little Venice. According to their supererogatory witness, a large man with his head half-buried in a scarf 'red as new beef' pulled up a wagon and cracked two barrels of runny pale stuff out into the canal." Gregson grinned smugly at Lestrade's suddenly slackened jaw. "He had all the luck in the world with the big-un, though he had some terrible trouble with wrestling the top off. The second, though, he had much less luck with. It slipped right out of his hands and went into the canal." Gregson took another drink. "The buskers were quite united in describing the language that followed," he finished up. "Lake man. Big man, thick grey hair." The taller inspector pulled a folder out of the same abditory aether that had secreted the tea and handed it over to Lestrade. "Sent the web-foots over to see if the barrel could be recovered." He sighed as the last of the tea finished in his gut.

"Thick grey hair." Lestrade felt a nascent hope die in his chest. Otherwise it could have easily meant that bruiser of a wrestler. He opened up the folder, gratified at the sight of Gregson's meticulous script. For all his bluff, the man was neat as a clerk. "So you're letting me have this part of the case?" He wanted to make certain.

Gregson poured a second cup of tea, even blacker and stronger smelling than the first. Oil floated on top. "Well, the canals are disgusting this time of year, are they not?"

"On par with a flooding slaughterhouse."

"And the weather is going to get worse by tonight, correct?"

"The last I heard."

"Yes, you can have it," Gregson beamed. "I'll stick to the press-gangs. I can do most of my work underneath the roof of a nice, dry tavern – but I'll be thinking of you the whole time, Lestrade."

Sunday dinners were more a Cheatham ritual than church. Clea wondered if chapel would be any less of a bother. Myron's three daughters were behaved well-enough, true, but they had a rivalry going with Robert's two sons – the girls infuriating in their smug assurance of their superiority, and Robert's sons just as infuriating in their refusal to use their heads. Andrew was squiring his new lady-friend, the sister of one of his rowing-mates, but no one believed it would last. Andrew's true infatuation was with the niece of Myron's deceased business partner.

Myron had his own guest, "an old friend" who was the widow of a classmate. Clea was just grateful that the cooking had not fallen to her. They paid the staff for that.

And then Bartram had emerged with Mr. Quimper.

Quimper was dressed on equal par with the Cheathams, but his jewellry was far finer. His white-gold watch swung on its short chain like a star against his fine-cut waistcoat. Clea noted the quality of weaving and the lining of his coat without thinking. Much as she wished she could bury that part of the family's past, it still haunted.

"Miss Cheatham, again a pleasure." He bowed over her hand and met her full in the eyes. For a moment she was struck by the force inside them, which made her hesitate. Everyone took that for a sign of flattery. "Are we to enjoy your mastery at the table again?"

"Not on Sundays, I fear." Clea collected herself slowly. She was glad to have her hand back where it belonged. This man acted too much like the fawning back-stabbers who cozened the family into buying obsolete equipment.

"Ah, what a shame." He passed on several pleasantries, and she answered them with bland politeness that covered just how uncomfortable she felt. For a moment, she hated her brothers for keeping her from practicing in this very dangerous field of socializing.

She was a spinster and she was skilled. She had money of her own and a good family. Clea had seen too many people look at her with naked envy to underestimate her worth to others.

Mr. Quimper did not look like a man who needed to woo her money. He looked like a man who expected to impress her because she was over-looked and under-loved. Clea had seen that look for most of her life but she hardly ever saw it used upon her person. This left her usual confidence confounded.

His statement made, Quimper went on to Charles where the two talked at length over the sport of wrestling, the fickle audience, insurance, the troubles of stolen gate-fees and other winnings mixed with medical costs. By dinner, Quimper was firmly in the camp of men Charles Cheatham adored.

"What did I tell you?" Charles murmured to his daughter over the soup. "When there's one, others will follow."

"I'm not certain marriage is what he's all about." Clea hated the way she sounded. That elderly spinster in her head was back. "Bartram's made it clear I'm the world the sun revolves around!"

"As well as he should." Charles leaned forward and gave his daughter a kiss on her forehead, even though he had to stoop to do so. It made it very difficult to be angry.

Lestrade held the bull's-eye [2] steady as the heavy object thudded wetly to the brick-work of Little Venice's canal ways. Only its shape proved it a barrel. The canal had not been forgiving but here the bridge cut most of the winds on their ears. PC Barks thumped it on the side with his fist and a curse. Water spilled out, along with small, wriggling things in the pale light. The dredgers stepped back hastily.

"Happy Early Christmas, Lestrade!" Youghal beamed. His breath smoked thick as shag. "A pretty sight, eh?"

"Dear me," Lestrade said faintly. The smell could be much worse, he knew. The chill of the year had much to do with that slim mercy. "Hold it still a moment . . . ." He lowered himself to one knee, mindful of the unknown things still flopping on the bricks. The hogshead lid was crushed inward by a single, powerful blow, but there were no sharp imprints to give a clue as to what weapon had done it. He was grateful for the gloves shielding his hands as he lifted the muck-slimed disc and carefully set it aside. Something had tried to colonise on the wood and metal rings, already rusting. He hunched forward, shining the lantern inside the confines.

"Any corn in there would have flowed out by now, wouldn't it?" Youghal asked. He had the job of standing with his lantern, showing light over the bowed surface of the cask. "I guess it's odd luck. We'd have found this sooner if someone had gone missing at the canal . . . ."

"Youghal, may I trouble you for your knife?" Lestrade's voice sounded strange.

"Never leave home without it." Youghal pulled it out in a flash. "See anything interesting?"

"Well, I don't know yet. I see something I never thought I'd see . . . ." A soft scraping sound grated against Youghal's ears. "Here – What d'you make of this?" Lestrade gritted his teeth from the effort of moving against ghost-injuries, and handed the knife back, point backwards.

Youghal frowned at the wet splinters balanced on the tip of his iron knife. "I don't know," he confessed. "The lantern makes it look all yellowish."

"'s not the lantern." Lestrade leaned back. "Take a look at this." He stepped away for Youghal to peer in.

Youghal was silent for nearly a half-minute, thinking. "Lestrade, I'm no expert on wood, but what kind of wood is mustard yellow?"

"Offhand, I'd say no wood meant to carry a shipment of Indian maize," Lestrade said slowly.

"It's yellow." Youghal repeated, flabbergasted. "It's yellow. Is it dye?"

"Why would anyone dye barrel wood?" Lestrade asked.

"What if it's a stain?"

"I like where your head's going, but that's why I scraped it. There's a coating of – I suppose paraffin – but no stain. No stain would perforate the wood fibres all the way through."

Lestrade's baffled voice began to show true frustration. He was out of his depth and he knew it.

"You don't stain barrels on the inside if you're carrying flour," Youghal pointed out with a puzzled frown. "Lookit this – all sealed up tight as a drum. That's not safe!"

"Whatever these were meant for, it wasn't for dry goods," Lestrade agreed. He tugged at a dark metal band wrapped tight about the mouth. "Tight cooperage, Youghal. If you're going to travel with flour, you need slack cooperage." He knocked the barrel at its broadest and it gonged like a wooden bell with a clogged up nose. "This should have been in the report," he whispered out of ear-shot. "Why wasn't this in the report?"

Youghal scraped more splinters and examined them closely. "Blimey, I've never seen anything like this," he said in wonder. "It's . . . *yellow*."

85

"Yes, I believe we've established that, Youghal." Lestrade nodded to the canal-men that they could stand down for a break and reached in his pocket for his cigarettes. The canal-men celebrated in the form of liquid refreshment. It kept them warm in their thin clothes against the chill heading down from the headwaters.

"Yellow as a buttercup. Or a cowslip. A sunflower." Youghal shook his head, still staring at the splinters under his blade. "My father wouldn't approve, Lestrade. He always said that yellow was an unwholesome colour, symbolizing illness that leads to death."

"Wasn't your father a rector?" Lestrade frowned as he struck a match on his thumbnail.

"Yes, and as superstitious as an old Gipsy." Youghal snorted. "Got a fag?"

"Absolutely." Lestrade passed over his tin case. "But for the record, Youghal, Gipsies aren't superstitious." The two detectives sat together on the low stone wall built for the comfort of pedestrians. "Their paying clients, however, are."

"I learn something new every day." Youghal glanced automatically back to the dripping evidence splayed over the trod. "In this case, two things."

"We can safely say we've learned about it when we identify this wood." Lestrade blew smoke and watched its lazy drift across the quiet waters of the canal. Hoarfrost was forming on the edges. "Who do we have for that? Isn't Culpepper's father a woodwright?"

"He is, but he's an oakwright." Youghal said doubtfully. "Oak and nothing other."

"He's a start," Lestrade sighed. "And if he can't provide an answer, perhaps he can send us to a comrade who can."

"Wish Mr. Holmes wasn't indisposed." Youghal grumbled. Lestrade only shrugged. Holmes's absence was not necessarily a burden. The Yard needed a fair shot at what they were being paid to do. "Not sure he'd be of use, truth to tell. There are times when I think his selective memory is a hindrance more than help." He took another puff, his mind devoted to future orders on the barrel's fate. "The man doesn't know the difference between an aerolite [3] and a comet. Would he be able to know the difference between oak and . . . this?"

NOTES

1. Cruising performers or entertainers.
2. Bull's-eye: a small lantern built to project a strong, clear beam of light via a magnified lens in a single direction. It is possible it was named after Aldebaron, a very bright star called "The Bull's Eye" by Romans. Also called a Dark Lantern. It was vital equipment for the Bobby. It was a portable stove (an essential for the miseries of walking without relief in London regardless of the weather. It heated his tea. It was a self-defensive weapon and a signaling device. So firmly entrenched was it within the identity of the coppers that it even showed up in *The Mother's Picture Alphabet* for the letter *P*: "*Also, Policeman, with bull's-eye so bright, / Who goes round to see all is safe in the night.*"
3. Meteorite.

Chapter VI

Scotland Yard:

"I bet Holmes would know what this is." PC Hopkins announced firmly. So far the yellow bits of soggy wood had been passed around as curiously as a prank letter to the Queen. "On one condition, that is."

Lestrade folded his arms. "What condition would that be, Constable?" he asked patiently. He had a feeling he already knew.

"Provided it's poisonous."

Bradstreet snorted, sending the contents of his tea cup over his shirt-front. "Just in case, let's not taste it or anything," he offered. "I doubt 'tis American sassafras."

"I daresay you're right." Lestrade had to give Hopkins points. The lad would be the Yard's most-fashionable inspector someday, down to his Sunday walking stick, but for all his milk-and-water countenance, he was an iron-cored policeman who had gone against his family's wishes and "lowered" himself to join the Yard. There was a brain inside that fresh face, and he displayed an ability to think in a tight corner.

Out of the water, the wood was slowly drying to a milder, less-alarming shade of Guernsey milk. One thing was certain. It was a very difficult wood to manipulate and incredibly heavy.

"Sassafras would have a sweet odor to it," Hopkins commented. "Sickly-sweet. And it would be reddish-orange."

"Let me guess. Someone in your family believes it's one of the elixirs of life?" Bradstreet wondered.

"My grandfather." Hopkins straightened as the doors opened. "Here's Culpepper now."

Cheatham House:

The women and children departed to leave the men with their cigars and brandy. It was in this definitive moment that Jethro Quimper revised his estimation of Bartram Cheatham.

Despite the fact that all the menfolk were alike in size, build, and appearances that were not typical of being aligned with intelligence, they were to-a-man skilled with the amenities of proper social conversation. They knew how much brandy to pour, how far to cut the cigar tips, and their comments displayed a judicious wit. That, and the décor about the house, fairly screamed of a once-wealthy family that had descended in purse-size, but not a jot in pride.

Through it all, Charles Cheatham remained the patriarch and Bartram carried the status of being the primary source of finance. Myron was openly consulted in matters of mathematics and consideration. Cutler and Wallace were hawks to the latest business news and gossip. Andrew was oriented to the politics of society, commerce, and travel through the waterways. Robert, the quietest, had a gift for analyzing an issue and asking the right question, even though his value in the family was obviously quite low. It was all a very well-organised, unhesitant family unit that would make a sergeant's chest swell with pride. What an army the family must be.

Quimper thought of the Chinese blessing that asked for many ugly sons and few but beautiful daughters, and had trouble keeping his amusement to himself.

Bartram was not brilliant, but he was intelligent to a certain degree, and he did have an instinct when he was in deep waters. He had picked up on the pale thread of discontent at the loss of family fortune, and was determined to rescue his kin from their loss even if it killed him. This had placed him in an unexpected higher status among the brothers, and explained why Robert's work with paper and ink was being scorned. Unfortunate business decisions had dictated the necessity of loans, and his family did not approve of his actions. There was strife and complacency in equal numbers within the Cheatham tribe.

This entire situation appealed to Quimper's instincts to garner profit and cause as much trouble among Scotland Yard as possible. He was already enjoying himself.

"So, Bartram." He smiled around a cloud of smoke drifting through the spaces between his teeth. "You were saying there is some . . . *difficulty* with an inspector paying eye to your fair sister?"

"*Maclura pomifera.*"

Mr. Culpepper proclaimed this un-illuminating information as though he were a learned don permitting the surrounding policemen the benefit of his infinite wisdom. Spidery brown fingers, gnarled as applewood, turned the sample stave over in his lap. He looked at the blank faces before him and deigned to lower his language to a smaller plane of comprehension. "A member of the mulberry tree, with wood just as resilient and stubborn to the grain. Indigenous to North America, commonly known as 'Osage Orange'."

"And it is normally this . . . *yellow*?" Youghal wondered.

"Goodness, no! This is fairly fresh wood. Barely aged." Culpepper chuckled, a dry rattling echo. "The more seasoned this wood gets, the darker it gets. The French call it 'blood-wood' for the aged tints. A thing of beauty, I assure you. This garish yellow becomes a satinlike, polished ruddy colour that is most attractive." His wrinkled face turned grave. "This is not a wood for barrels," he told them with disapproval making a stiff paste of his voice. "Not at all. Why would someone commit such a travesty?"

"That is what we would like to find out, sir." Lestrade felt the first stirrings of hope. "Can you tell us why the wood would not be made into barrels?"

Culpepper grunted. "I know oak, sir! No one alive knows as much about the *quercus* as I – "

(Lestrade mentally thumbed the button on the stopwatch of *Time* within his brain at this statement in order to remember it later)

" – and I pay very close attention to alternate woods when oak is unavailable or impossible, or regions where Oak cannot thrive. Osage is a very strong, sturdy wood. It was used to make wooden wheels in the Colonies when Oak would not be had, and it made fine bows by the Red Indians before that. I was asked to repair such a bow for the Museum once." The old man stroked the wood lovingly – before turning solemn and Judge-like. "But it is quite rare, compared to the dispersion of the native oaks. It came originally from a place called the Red River. The American government encourages its propagation whenever possible for its usefulness in fence-control, somewhat as we create hedgerows."

"That's interesting." Lestrade knew he had to say something to prove they were all listening. And it was interesting . . . almost.

"Another hurdle is the dreadfully long amount of time required to flush out the poisonous sap." Culpepper did not notice the looks of shock from his words. "If one air-dries the wood, it will take years of storage, but if one sinks the logs under running fresh water, it cures in a matter of months. Then it is a matter of drying the sap-depleted wood out of the elements.

"Even if one does this, there are people who will contract ugly skin rashes from the wood, and it naturally cannot be used for eating utensils

90

or food storage. Why would anyone make a barrel out of this?" He even sounded hurt.

"We still don't know, sir," Lestrade confessed. "The barrels themselves were empty and on their way to another buyer, but two other barrels leaked and the contents had to be transferred to these."

"Then I am glad that they were thoroughly ruined," Culpepper said shortly.

"So am I." Lestrade wondered what Miss Cheatham's reaction to this would be. "It shouldn't have been put into the barrels anyway – I thought everyone knew it was dangerous to put flour into barrels with those thick iron bands."

"I'm afraid I don't know." Culpepper admitted.

"Flour burns and iron can strike sparks when it hits the wrong thing. Mix that up and you could have a fire."

Youghal's explanation did not voice what Lestrade was thinking: That a fire would have been even worse with the wax lining feeding the heat and fuel.

Culpepper's face twisted. "If that is so, London has dodged a bullet. Osage wood produces the hottest possible fire – almost as hot as coal. Imagine what would have happened if the flour had ignited in that kind of container? It would not have extinguished easily. Indeed, with the metal hoops, it would have been nothing more than a bomb."

Lestrade watched the old man go. "I do not have a good feeling about this," he said out loud.

"Exploding flour barrels?" Youghal rubbed his forearms briskly. "Brrr!"

"So, Mr. Holmes would have known." Hopkins observed. "Poisonous sap . . . ."

Everything was going according to plan – all the more genius because the plan had not germinated until a few days ago. For all his deliberations and careful organization, Quimper was a man who had good instincts when it came to discomfiting his enemies. Bartram proved the value of his attack by the speed in which he fell for Quimper's bait.

"It's that Lestrade fellow. I see him nearly every day at her shop." He began playing with his hands, realised what he was doing, and went for the cigars instead.

Myron lifted thick eyebrows. "I've yet to meet anyone, man or woman, who can resist Clea's cooking." His observation was met with light chuckles that were borderline brotherly-nasty and proud.

"I don't think he's interested in her cooking!" Bartram blurted. He promptly purpled and stared down as a hush collapsed the room.

Charles Cheatham lifted a cigar to his lips, but a cloud had darkened his face. It gave a chilling accent to his cataract-whitened eyes. "Bartram," he began slowly, "you had heard rumors about his sending his own brother to the noose?"

"Oh, they are not rumors, I assure you." Quimper hastened to apologise. "I know that question was not addressed to me. I've known Lestrade for . . . quite some years now. Our families originated in the same plot of land in France." He lifted his shoulders in a suddenly Gallic shrug as all attention came his way. "He's a hard-nosed man, and that's a fact. He loves the law and the letter of the law more than he does his own flesh and blood. Now, I admit his brother did wrong. He did shoot a policeman – but I for one felt it had been a case of hot-blooded panic and not cold-blooded intention. After all, what kind of person would shoot a policeman?"

He lifted his fingers to match his shoulders. "There was another brother, Paul, who is still serving for his part in the killing. He may see freedom someday. Lestrade's witness for him seemed . . . almost preferential in comparison." He made a *tsk* of regret with his tongue.

"Really a shame. Armoricus – that would be the dead brother – always liked to taunt our Mr. Lestrade as a child. Perhaps he let his emotions colour his judgment that one time."

Quimper's regretfully phrased observation was met with polite murmurs of gentle and civil agreement, but the seeds had been sown. Now it was just a matter of time to see if they had settled on rock or soil.

Jethro Quimper turned his head politely to the sound of Bartram clearing his throat. His finest wrestler, source of semi-legal income, and current manikin was leaning forward on his knees, and all five brothers were leaning in with him. A united front, Quimper thought. Perfect.

"Mr. Quimper, it seems as though you have some experience with this Lestrade," Andrew started. He was different from the other Cheathams, mostly from his choice of dress, including an exuberant red hothouse flower on his lapel. Quimper had him pegged as a man with refinery in his tastes, but too few ways to express himself in society.

"Well, I hate to talk ill of a person," Quimper said modestly. "He must be going on forty years old by now . . . if he'd had more to him than being a policeman, he would have promoted up years ago." He overlooked the prejudice of the Chief Inspector. The Cheathams were not the sort to sympathise with anti-French sentiment.

They absorbed the implications in silence. Lestrade was at the age where he should be rising, not staying put. That was a social and career issue they all understood.

"Just so . . . ." Andrew cleared his throat, already disliking Lestrade for not being a step in the society's ladder. "We were wondering: Does your experience offer any suggestions on how to . . . *discourage* him from coming around our sister? She doesn't really need that kind of aggravation." *Better suitors* was unspoken but heard.

Better suitors such as himself. He was almost ten years on Lestrade, but there was no doubt he was very high indeed. Higher than the Cheathams had been in their glory days.

Quimper pretended to think it over, sipping his cognac as he did so. "He respects a show of strength," he said at last. "Not that there's much opportunity for that. He's not the most sociable chap in London." That revelation hardly shocked them. "And he is not a devotee of spectator sports, theatres, race-horses . . . most of the ways in which one would arrange to speak with a man politely and in the screen of the public eye."

"Sounds Calvinist," Charles opined suspiciously.

"No. He simply lacks a social view." Quimper allowed a flicker to pass over his face. "Excuse me, I just remembered. Bartram, you're going to work at the Policemen's Benefit in a few days, aren't you?" He beamed. "That would be a perfect way to have a chance to . . . have a few words."

Bartram snorted. "He'll be there?"

"Oh, yes. The Chief Inspector insists on everyone to attend at least part of the event." Quimper watched, satisfied, as the brothers traded grins.

Night could not come soon enough for the men of the Yard. October 30th would go down in history as one of the most exhaustive of days in a city that was growing familiar with the concept of Irish Terrorism.

"Anyone you know today?" Bradstreet finally asked.

Lestrade lifted bloodshot eyes to his best friend. "Just the landlady's niece. She was scratched by the edge of the bomb, but more frightened than hurt."

"I can't believe no one was killed," Bradstreet said for the twentieth time that day. "What the Bloody Hell was the Clan na Gael doing over here?"

"Who knows?" Lestrade shrugged wearily. "I thought they were sticking to the American side." He rubbed at his freshly cleaned face and pulled the steaming pot to the centre of the table. "Drink up before it gets cold."

Bradstreet complied and the gurgle of warm salep filled the air. Lestrade had finished his first saucer and was stirring cinnamon into a second. Even a dynamiting against the Metro couldn't stop the flow of London. The day had been long enough before the two o'clock blast off

93

Praed Street. Over sixty at last count were injured. No fatalities . . . *Astonishing*. Two third-class carriages had been destroyed.

Everyone knew Ireland wouldn't stop. Most immigrants looked forward to absorbing into the country of their choice . . . but the Irish masses held anywhere they lived was just a temporary thing, a brief exile until the English were out of Ireland and then they could go back and pick up their lives as if they'd never been interrupted. Forget the impossibility of such an idealism. Too many people believed it because they *wanted* to believe it, and England should have listened to Disraeli and done something against the poverty of the people if they really wanted to stop the sickening attacks by terrorists who had lost their moral compass.

Tomorrow morning the Home Secretary [1] would draft three-hundred policemen – a quarter of the number walking the beat – to patrol the Underground and submit a preventative Bill to Parliament. [2] They wished him well. They didn't know what the outcome would be. Nor did they want to think about the near future. At the kindest, each policeman was responsible for about four-hundred civilians, but if you counted the number of policemen who were actually on duty . . . the totals were closer to four-thousand. (No one was foolish enough to question Gregson's slate on the disheartening subject.)

No matter what else happened, the old question on whether or not "Mischief Night" fell on the 30th or the 31st was settled for this year.

"You sure you're up to a bottle?"

Lestrade glared with as much strength as his exhaustion permitted. "That's a wretched question to ask, you know."

Bradstreet muttered something.

"Roger, you really need to stop that." Lestrade fumbled for the clamp holding the bottle of Grozet at bay. It fell off with a satisfying pop. "You do know I grew up hearing all sorts of warped Celtic languages – from bad to wretched. I may not know what it is you're saying from the start, but give me some time and I'll figure it out."

Bradstreet reluctantly laughed, and lifted his own bottle in a toast. "That must come in handy as a police inspector!"

"It didn't when I was working with the Thames. They were determined to put me on the only section manned by the Italians – pardon, I mean, the *Tuscans* . . . ."

"Why did they do that?"

"Because they felt a short man would get along with a short race," Lestrade said sourly. "I felt tall compared to some of them. I wonder if there's a stunting agent in all those cheeses they insist on eating." He watched with satisfaction as Bradstreet spluttered in his drink. "That goes well with the tea stains, Roger."

94

"You're a cruel man, Geoffrey." Bradstreet's laugh was still crinkling his eyes. "Well, you survived."

"Not for lack of trying. They had to transfer me when a smuggling ring crept in. My first work undercover." He looked to the ceiling in memory. "Half-crazed sots. I was so happy to find them on the wrong end of a horse-trading business the year after."

Bradstreet leaned back, which took up a great deal of Lestrade's deskroom. He didn't seem to mind being cramped, but then, he was probably used to it. There was little more than the single shelf of books and the eternal invoice for shoe-repair. Lestrade walked more than nearly any other man alive. It was hard to say how much of his pay went to footwear, but it was thanks to him the local cobblers were feeding their children.

The two passed the silence companionably. On rare nights such as these, Mrs. Collins was willing to devote a spare cot to a weary man of the law and Bradstreet wasn't about to pass up the opportunity. The alternative was to wobble wearily home and risk death by falling asleep in front of a hansom.

"Heard anything from your family?" he asked. Lestrade and Bradstreet had both been disowned from their kin for different reasons. Bradstreet had only just been welcomed back to the family fold – thanks in part to Lestrade and a certain doctor in Baker Street. Bradstreet knew he could ask that personal question of Lestrade, but no one else could. [3]

The small man did no more than continue with his drink and shrug with one eyebrow, a fatalistic movement Quimper would have recognised. He put the bottle down and reached for Mrs. Collins' cold sandwiches.

"Paul's case will be up for review soon," he said at last. "I don't think I'll attend unless the court requires it."

"I don't blame you," Bradstreet answered. Of all the detectives, only he and Gregson knew the full story behind the Aton Robbery. It was a measure of Gregson's humanity that he still treated his worst rival with the same level of sneering jealousy as ever. Lestrade wouldn't have been able to endure pity. He would have sooner transferred to some mournful outpost on the North Sea.

Still, Bradstreet felt that his comrade might as well be manning a lighthouse in the middle of the ocean. Every copper dreaded the choice between someone they loved and the profession they were sworn to serve. Bradstreet had been there when Armoricus put the bullet into poor young Cooper's eye, and he had seen the look on Lestrade's face when he viewed his brother after the handcuffs and legalities were dispensed. Not until the wagon had hauled them away did he speak.

"*He enjoyed it.*" Bradstreet could see and hear that moment as if it had just happened. Gregson was coming up behind him, bloody from the fracas, but he stalled at Lestrade's glazed eyes. "*Roger . . . he enjoyed it.*"

The news had not surprised Bradstreet. Armoricus had been the type to enjoy whatever hold he could employ on someone, and he had been the perfect son. Lestrade had grown up (survived might be a better word) on the wrong end of his brother's humours, and perhaps he had believed the anger that fueled him would stay within the confines of the family.

The truth had been a shock. Once absorbed, Lestrade wrote out his report honestly when it would have been only a small effort to write "*fired in panic*" instead of "*fired in deliberation*".

In family eyes, Armoricus may have died for his younger brother's sin of fratricide, but Geoffrey died every day for Armoricus'. Lestrade's demeanor had not improved from the horror. Cast out from a large and extended family, he had found refuge in the anonymity of London's masses and an even deeper shelter in the law. The law was not the least affectionate to him, and it would react upon her servant just as quickly if he strayed, but she was a predictive matron and one he could live with.

Speaking of matrons . . . .

"Johns and Brewer are still collecting references for their fiancés." Lestrade was clearly trying to change the subject.

Bradstreet grunted. "They just need three each. How hard can it be?"

4

"Says the man who married The Basilisk's daughter and didn't have to worry about anything like that." Lestrade even grinned as he wagged the cap at his friend. "The ladies are both transplanted little seedlings from the Cotswolds. They're concerned that their references won't be good enough for the Home Office to permit marriage."

Bradstreet sighed long and low, drawing his breath out as long as possible. He sounded like an inflated pig's bladder, improperly tied at the neck.

"Because the Cotswolds are always causing trouble in the newspapers," the Runner grumbled with a moustache full of sarcasm. "Well, I'll have a chat with Brewer. One letter from her church, one letter from a charity club . . . and there's always the family lawyer or doctor!"

"Thought you might help." Lestrade blandly returned to his drink.

"And why didn't you offer to help?"

"I'm not married. You are."

"S'trooth, you're right." Bradstreet lifted his drink up but stopped as a though passed through his alarms. "And you just changed the subject on us."

"Not really. I just moved it over – " Lestrade waved unsteadily. " – to something we could actually solve."

"Oh. Right."

The next three weeks passed through London at oxen pace. November grew worse by the day, and the rains came mixed with ice and bits of dirty snow. The police who had broken or sprained negligible limbs had to take it careful, least their injuries be reported by their "negligence" and Lestrade was not the only inspector who turned his eye away from a weary limp or a pained grimace. They were all busy, and anyone with sense preferred a half-broken fellow who was proven to work than a newcomer who might pay attention to policy more than the fear of losing wages. More than a few had the perfume of "painkillers" upon their breath, but as long as they could work through the day, no one called them on it. The Brotherhood took care of its own.

It was times like this that the Home Office did the most of its quiet gritting of teeth. The fraternal closeness between the police was infamous and often useful in their behalf, but it was also the beginnings of winter and this was when they lost a lot of their good men with the strongest work-ethic, who, struggling through old injuries, managed to get themselves under hospital care good and proper with a simple fall or blow. Gregson, who was so often the voice of cold-hearted gloom for them all, pointed out that it was the end of the year, and with one-in-four policemen hospitalized or "retired" by injuries every year, now was about time they were due for whatever it was that was bound to happen to the remainder of the one-in-four.

Gregson's temper was the first thing to jump ship when he was having a hard time of it, and he was having a very hard time now. The silent seamen had turned from chore into millstone with the outbreak of scarlet fever. The big man's language on the turn of fortune was heard quite clearly by the others. His worry over his subjects turning out on a technicality was replaced with the chilling possibility that they could all die before court.

Two did die during the quarantine, and four more other prisoners as well, thanks to staff who were ignoring the current safety standards. Their dismissal without wages was a pallid victory. The rest showed signs of pulling through after the first week.

From the gaols it came, and away it spread, burning through the slums.

Lestrade found himself inexplicably relieved at the excuse to not be around Miss Clea because of his proximity to the seamen. He sent a note of warning to her about the latest in fevers and reminded her of the ill-effects of being too close to the trains.

Clea took the warning for the apology it was, and ordered her girls to bring their used clothes in for steaming at the end of the work-day. If they were going to be around the public, they could be careful with a two-hundred-twenty-degree bath against the disease.

One girl was quarantined. The doctor later said the good hygiene had been a factor in her recovery, but Sally was out of work for over a fortnight on a diet of rice-water and whey. Her parents were not so fortunate.

Scarlet fever from the gaol and police stations. Measles emerged from the German quarter and then a strange, high fever with sweating and delirium blew from the Eastern Docks. The newspapers were full of their usual platitudes, and Clea read with interest the speculations Mr. Culverton Smith wired to the reporters from his Sumatran plantation. His manners were horrific, but he had the ring of confidence.

Clea saw the dead-cart roll past her shop every day. Sometimes two, three times. The chill of winter had never been so threatening to her before. Most of them, the cold had just finished what starvation and disease had started.

Tenant-houses burned like matchwood from the least carelessness with the gas or the lamp. After the third fire-truck in one day, Clea faced the truth of living in a city: More people meant more buildings, and one mistake had the chance of going further than the countryside or even the small, congested towns such as their old home.

Among the reliable patrons was Dr. Watson. Every other day after the rush of noon, he would pause with his back to the wall and have a strong cup of tea. Always the perfect gentleman, he managed to eat and drink and converse with the utmost manners, and if the girls hadn't been sternly schooled about fantasies, they would have been utterly smitten.

No doubt the girls were completely wrong about their notions on how the handsome man spent his days. After his long hours as *locum* and that cup of tea he indulged in a personal custom that would have had them puzzled, he wandered London, one street at a time, in a slowly-expanding spiral on foot or carriage.

"And he just walks around, aimless as a lost duckling," PC Marion complained.

"He looks like a sight-seerer, someone new to London." PC Proctor was always more patient than his partner.

The two men watched the crowd flow for another minute as the doctor did indeed, drift through the throngs.

"Heard he played at Blackheath," Proctor said at last. "He'd have to know London some, wouldn't he?"

"Maybe they don't let medical students out much."

"Maybe."

"Now look," Marion nodded with his chin-strap jutting outwards. Their oblivious quarry had pulled out a tiny notebook and was jotting something down in a fever. "He's like a newspaper-writer, but what's there to look at around here?" The taller constable flapped his shoulders helplessly in his confusion. "Just a dirty-great square overlooking the mews!"

"S'trooth."

Had the men known Watson's purpose, they would have been more puzzled than ever.

Mrs. Hudson was stirring up a glaze for the evening roast when the draught over the kitchen tiles warned her the front door was opening. The loose window-pane rattled in its casing as the air sucked in, then out. The little woman tutted and set down her bowl and whisk, ordered her new maid of all work to mind the flour, and checked her hands against her stout apron as she climbed the half-step up out of the kitchen and into the little corner just under the stairs.

He was prudently putting the key in his pocket as he placed his hat neatly upon the coat-tree. A few months ago even that movement would have been stiff and wooden, like a marionette under the strings of a student puppeteer. He was also taller and straighter. His stick walked with him instead of for him.

"Ah, good afternoon, Mrs. Hudson." The young man smiled wearily. "Something smells wonderful. One of your good solid meals for tonight?"

"A small roast, nothing more than a bit of beef with plenty of potato and new cabbage. But you'll be more interested in this, I daresay." She pulled a thin, stiff rectangle of paper out of her inside pocket and handed it over.

Once upstairs, Watson built up the fire and changed. Holmes's letter crackled in the pocket of his dressing-gown. He plucked up a small pipe before he settled into his usual spot, slippers up, and split the wax seal along the seam.

Holmes liked to use his clients' stationary whenever he could, claiming the expediency of the location. Watson suspected he just wanted to quietly build up an archive of different papers.

The fact that Holmes never once threw away any of those papers, but kept them helter-skelter into a fast-swelling folder, supported this suspicion. He was also supported in his circumstantial evidence that, after getting a written letter from the stationary, Holmes would thereafter send a wire.

Mrs. Hudson came in with his freshened suit to find her lodger laughing and trying to smoke at the same time. It was not going well.

"Good news, I trust?" she asked drily.

"Good enough, Mrs. Hudson." Her lodger removed himself from tobacco long enough to catch his breath. "It would seem that his hostess's nefarious Uncle and Grasping Hand upon Her Fortune owes his reputation with whist in his 'personally commissioned' cards."

Mrs. Hudson's eyebrows slipped skyward. "Do you say?" she murmured in that special tone of voice that was some remarkable, un-mappable zone between amusement and disapproval.

"Yes, and by some broad stroke of fickle fate," Watson wiped his eyes. "the cards were commissioned through the very same company that made Holmes's 'special playing cards'."

He waited for her to think about it.

"He'll be owning the building before the night is out," she predicted.

"Oh, I doubt he'll keep it," Watson was quick to say. "What would he do with a Spanish mansion?"

"Before that day comes, the scoundrel will be forced by desperation to play a clean game with Mr. Holmes," the lady admonished. "And then he'll know the true meaning of fear." She pulled the cover off the supper tray, which was a bald hint that he ought to start eating before it grew cold. "Mind you, he may just give the said mansion back to the little niece. Mr. Holmes does love his little tricks when he's sticking a pin into a bully."

"Ah, but who of us are immune to that love?"

"You're a bit of a scoundrel yourself, Doctor Watson."

"Remind me again why we must attend charity functions?" Lestrade asked out the side of his mouth. It was doubtful he needed to lower his voice. The Old Rugby Playing Field was crammed with noisy humans.

Youghal shrugged. "Civic duty?"

"We're bloomin' Yarders. Civic duty is our job!"

Youghal shrugged again. "You have to admit: Our presence does make things safer for the civilians." He touched his fingers to his hat-brim as he spoke, beaming at a young woman herding her charges across the grass. "Cheer up, Geoffrey. If the Police Surgeon can volunteer his time for this, so can we."

"Youghal, for God's sakes, make a convincing quarrel. The Police Surgeon is about to retire. Not that that isn't well-deserved. He probably still remembers when he was hunting the woolly mammoth!" Lestrade crammed his hands into his pockets and subsided into a glower. "Well, what's going on?" he snarled at the forest of hats.

"Nothing much right now. They just finished with the Hurley display – I'm a little disappointed, mind. Not a single broken bone."

"Poor you," Lestrade scoffed.

"And what has got you in such a sweet mood, Geoffrey?" Bradstreet had come up with a Kendal Mint Cake in hand. Lestrade thought of the sugar in it, and shuddered. [5]

Lestrade nodded, pointing generally with his hat. "I've been on the look for a large, grey-haired Lancashire man, but so far they're all black as Lancashire coal in the top and beard. And I don't like mandatory volunteering. It goes against my grammatical grain."

"But surely not your alliterative one," Bradstreet grinned.

"We're also moving into the season of the Prince of Peace, but we're celebrating it with blood sports."

"Game, set, and match," Bradstreet managed, without appearing to conduct any effort, to yank out his spare tea-can and hand it to Lestrade. "We have tried everything under the sun to have gentler amusements, but how are we supposed to compete with the entrenched charities? Even the seamen's benefits have been around longer than the police!"

"Don't remind me." Lestrade sipped the hot drink gratefully. It did wonders to ease his mood.

"We even tried that chess tournament, and you won't charge me if I confess I'll be happy if I never again see a charity chess set for the rest of my life." Bradstreet paused and dealt with the problem of mint on his lip. "Then there's – Oh." He stopped.

"Oh? Oh, what?" Lestrade craned his neck but could see very little of use.

"Large Lancashire man, grey beard, did you say?"

"Where?" Lestrade couldn't see anything.

"Look at the edge of the contesting ring."

Lestrade was already pulling his spyglass out.

"Speaking of seamen, why is it you stick to those things and not a proper pair of field glasses like every other normal man under the sun?"

"You can focus sharper with one eye," Lestrade said absently. "They're cheaper, and there are fewer parts in a spyglass to break, for Heaven's sake – Oh, I see who you mean. Damn. In every other aspect, Bradstreet, I would say you had him, but the man's blind as a bat. I can see the cataracts from over here – and he's being guided by a young man who is obviously his own sprout."

"Too bad." Bradstreet pulled out his field glasses and popped the caps off the lenses. "Let's just see . . . Goodness. Look at all those red rose-laden lapels. Can they possibly be any more Lancashire and still be in London?"

"You have me." Lestrade was interested despite himself. "But if they're right here, they're probably not dynamiting Parliament, eh?"

"They travel in packs, don't they?" Bradstreet wondered as if to himself.

"That's human nature, Roger . . . Hold on, who is that coming up to meet the gaffer?" Lestrade abruptly gasped out loud.

"What?" Bradstreet demanded, and then saw for himself. "Bloody – !" He growled. "Is that Jethro Quimper?"

Lestrade lowered his spyglass with shaking hands. Bradstreet watched as the colour drained out of his face.

"Geoffrey?" Bradstreet touched his shoulder in concern. "Geoffrey," he repeated. "You want I get a closer look?"

Lestrade took another drink of tea, trying to work moisture back into his mouth. "I thought he was still on the peninsula," he muttered.

"Stands to reason he'd come back for business once in a while." Bradstreet sucked his cheeks in. "Someone should have told us."

"Devil take that." Lestrade tapped his spyglass in his open palm. "He's moved up in the criminal circles. Too important for humble Yarders." His voice scathed.

Bradstreet wished he couldn't agree. "He's friendly with the big ones clear enough." He looked at the small playbill in his free hand. "Hold on . . . Well, rubbish."

"What?"

"Playbill doesn't say anything except there will be Lancashire-style wrestling."

"I do hope an ambulance is standing by," Lestrade said with feeling. Lancashire's particular style was considered one of the most aggressive in the world.

"They'd have to," Bradstreet said in unconvincing tones. "Here comes Youghal. Let's see what's got a flame under his pot?"

Youghal was beaming as he threaded his way, shoulder-first, through the crowd, pausing to shout something at every Yarder he encountered. His open face was flushed against the cold weather. "Did you hear?" he gasped. "Bartram of Lancashire is going to show us his wrestling moves!"

102

NOTES

1. Vernon Harcourt.
2. The Explosive Substances Act.
3. See *You Buy Bones*.
4. A woman had to provide three references supporting her good character before she was allowed to marry a policeman. The fraternalisation within the force helped this hurdle of paperwork many a time.
5. Quiggin Mint Cakes have existed since 1840 on the Isle of Man, and when a Quiggin moved to Kendal in 1880, the Kendal Mint Cake was born.

Chapter VII

Bartram was at crosshairs. He had waited patiently for the other events to take place. The Hurley demonstration had been the only one able to hold his attention for long, but no one had broken anything and he felt strangely down-let from that fact. Why would a sport be forbidden by half the schools in England if people didn't get hurt in them?

As time passed, his excitement began to build. It was the usual anticipation of entering combat. Not for the sake of the fight itself, but the eternal hope that he would actually face something different. *Challenging.*

Getting injured did not mean he was challenged. Getting half his beard yanked off by a furious opponent wasn't a challenge. Nor broken bones or being called a new name. It was the not knowing what would happen that he enjoyed about wrestling.

But this would be different.

"How is it?" Charles Cheatham asked. Despite his calm voice, the old man's hands trembled on the candle-coal head [1] of his heavy walking stick. He remembered those days and missed them.

"A big crowd," Andrew popped in while Bartram of Lancashire began breathing in and out, warming his blood for the moment when he would step into the ring. Several children were tossing chalk on the battered grass from the previous demonstrations. "There are a lot of women here." He paused and was startled into returning the open smile of a very pretty young woman with a strategically missing button on the front of her coat. "Why? It isn't proper!"

"You're a right idiot, big brother," Clea popped up cheerfully. "They're with their families." She beamed, all snow and roses with pink cheeks against her creamy skin, and tapped Bartram on the shoulder. "Lower that great head down for a good-luck kiss." Bartram complied with a bashful smile.

"Now, no displays, Clea," he grumbled. "How am I supposed to find a wife if everyone thinks I gotta look after you every moment?"

Clea smacked him on the pectoral. "As if you have time to look for a wife! First off, you'd have to actually leave off the mat more than four hours a day, and the next, you'd have to give me a bit of breathing room!"

"Don't you worry any," Charles reached out and patted his daughter's shoulder without missing it. "Your brothers have you well in hand, my dear."

"That's enough to worry about, and true." Clea sighed and went to find the spun-sugar seller. "Try not to break anyone, Brother."

"I'll try." Bartram of Lancashire called back. He was grinning from ear to ear. *I'll try, but maybe not very hard . . . .*

"Let's get to the front." Youghal grabbed a shocked Lestrade and pulled. The two stumbled to the front row – Youghal with enough Irish jubilance for three – and Lestrade with the enthusiasm of an overly watered cactus. "You're not really enjoying yourself, are you?" the other man observed as this thought struck him.

Lestrade pondered several possible ways he could respond to that, but remembered that he often had to work with the overgrown boy-elephant, and opted for some tact. "I've been up all night for two nights, may I remind you? The insignificant matter of exploding barrels."

"Oh. I forgot." Youghal looked slightly abashed. "You just need to drink some more tea, Lestrade. It will do you good."

"I don't know if my nerves can – !" Lestrade shut his mouth as the crowd erupted into blood-hungry cheers. Bartram of Lancashire was standing before the crowd, arms lifted to the sky.

That, he thought, is a very, *very* large man.

Clea was so glad to be away from her business and eating someone else's food for a change that she hadn't realised the danger signals. Bartram at his sweetest was Bartram at his second-most protective. Either Bartram was difficult.

At first she was just glad that he was doing something that wouldn't get himself hurt (for a change), and she settled to the side next to a pile of odd-sorted objects that a little boy explained would be used for the following event of road-bowling. When she asked what the cannonball was for, he responded it was the bowling ball.

"Oh." She blinked, and ignored the covetous greed on his face at her paper bag full to bursting with barley sugar sticks. "Are they going to bowl it on the road?"

"It's called road bowling, Miss," he pointed out, still polite – he wanted her sweet badly. "You know someone who'd like to have a go? T'wd 'a bit safer than wrestling with Bartram of Lancashire!"

Clea roared. "Right you are! I have no intention of such an action – my preferred method of combat is a frying pan!"

He grinned at her, all teeth and gingery freckles. "Number Nine, miss? That's the weight me mum prefers."

"Aren't you the rapscallion?" She teased off a bit of broken barley sugar and handed it up to him. It was gone so quickly she wasn't certain she had done anything. A faint roar went up in the crowd. "They're lively today," she commented.

"E's demonstrating to some o' the policemen," the urchin answered, smug in the fact he had a higher view from her perch atop the equipment pile. Clea didn't envy him, as it looked ready to tumble apart at any second. "Uppos, there goes Constable Burns."

Clea strained to see over the crowd. "Bother, why are people so tall?" she fretted. "What's happening?"

"Not too much, Miss. Cheatham's demonstratin' a different throw per policeman. E's going down the row." The boy was positively gleeful. Cockney Heaven had come early. "Looks like the Chief's told 'em all to hold still and wait their turn! Cor, if I'da known this, I'da brought me da!" He yelped in delight. "There goes Youghal! Now look, if he ain't getting' back up all smiles!"

"I still can't see a thing." Clea wondered if she should risk injury by going through the crowd.

"Orf a mo' it's Lestrade. This oughter be good."

Clea felt her jaw click open. All colour washed out of the world as something terrible flashed through her mind. The numbers tumbled to a particular combination. A moment later she was punching herself through the crowd, and a certain Baker Street Irregular was hopping down to take advantage of the discarded bag of forlorn barley sugar. The dirt and grass didn't bother him. He ate more than that in his regular meals and, anyway, he owed Wiggins for last week's cuppa whey.

Lestrade heard the triple snap of small bones breaking before the flood of pain spread up his arm and into his brain. It was followed by an angry flush of tearing in the area between the bottom of his ribcage and under his arm. The brown grass of the field went grey and flat.

Cheatham took a step backwards, giving his opponent plenty of space. Lestrade thought that was wholly unnecessary. He only thought of finding the truncheon in his coat pocket. It wasn't like he was going to actually use it.

106

Besides, his coat was being held by that gnome of a rat-catcher in the sidelines.

Lestrade tucked in his breath and stood up. He could smile before angry Chief Inspectors. He could smile before arrogant diplomats and gentry before their most frozen contempt. The day he couldn't bestow the same courtesy on a drooling fool like Cheatham was the day he retired and took up mucking stables for his living. Or worse, be a butler.

"Very good, Mr. Cheatham." Lestrade held out his hand. He held his breath again, feeling the sweat chill on his face. Everyone could see his smile. They believed he was all right. "Remind me not to anger you."

Cheatham's thick face dulled with brief confusion, but he knew how the game was played. "Stay away from my sister, Inspector." He returned Lestrade's handshake, his hand huge against the other's.

"I haven't even approached your sister, nor do I intend to." Lestrade kept his smile as his thumb shifted, stabbing deeply into the nerve at the junction of Cheatham's thumb and forefinger. Cheatham's face set as it was his turn to pretend nothing was wrong. "I don't know if you've ever had a single thought in your thick skull, Mr. Cheatham," Lestrade hissed through his teeth, still smiling, "but it would hardly be proper for a policeman to play court to a Cotton Heiress."

Still beaming, Lestrade let go of the other's hand, and stepped away. He even raised his arm to wave a greeting to Bradstreet across the green. The wizened old man handed him his coat back – pockets unpicked. Point to him for that.

"Here ye go, young sir." The graveled voice spat phlegm on the grass past the ropes. Strong shag tobacco hovered about him like a factory cloud. "Hold still then and I'll set ye to rights." Lestrade was grateful to have the man pull his coat over his shoulders.

"Would ye be needing anything, young sir?"

If he calls me young sir one more time, so help me I will arrest him for being intoxicated. "Not at all." He breathed, trying not to grit his teeth. "I'm fine, thank you." Getting through the masses re-defined punishment. He hadn't been crowd-jostled so much in his life. Bradstreet and Youghal called his name, but he couldn't think about that. He needed to get away and find his breath.

He made it to the relative privacy of the memorial garden by the stables. No one felt particularly drawn to the wet spray of the fountain in this chill. He sank to the stone bench and wondered if he should take a look inside his shirt. He decided just as quickly not to. He held his breath, tugged off his glove – *Ohdearthathurt!* – looked down and watched his left hand swell before his eyes. The breaks were already black points under the skin.

Good God. I'm going to get killed. And it won't be in the line of duty. That wasn't fair.

Lestrade wondered briefly if the custom of the bride's dowry was started as a way of funding all the damage and medical bills from the battles of two families joining. It would explain why the groom's family kept the money when the marriage contract was severed. He could easily see it all going to splints and bandages.

"Mr. Lestrade!"

Of all the faces Lestrade did not care to see at that moment, it was Miss Clea's. Things were made worse by the fact she looked as pale as the chalk in the ring, and her hand was over her mouth. The feeling worsened when she knelt to his side.

"My God, Inspector, I am so sorry. My brother had no cause to do such a thing . . . ."

"I'll be all right, Miss Cheatham," Lestrade said slowly, but his face was pale and he held himself quite still.

Clea felt ill. "You can't be all right!" she yapped. "Bartram, I'm so sorry, my brother . . . ."

"It's hardly your fault," he pointed out in that same pained and faint voice.

"The hell it isn't!" she shot back without thinking. "He can't stand the idea of someone looking at his baby sister!" Incredibly, Lestrade's shoulders were trembling from the effort of holding back his laughter. "What the hell is wrong with you?" She shouted. She felt like crying, she'd used strong language, and he thought it amusing? "What in God's name is so blooming rich?"

"Ah, I think I'll plead a crack on the head." He gulped hard and went rigid, clutching at his shoulder with a stricken expression.

"You've said too much all ready," she glared. "What is it?"

"Merely an . . . *ob* . . . ." He held his breath and tried to stand.

"Oh, no, tha!" She tried to push him back down. He cringed.

"Miss Cheatham . . . .this is a charity. No one is going to want to see me like this."

She glared at him with a later-for-you expression that made her angrier when he ignored it. "I'll help you up," she vowed, "and I'll even squire you around to show you aren't hurt . . . but you can at least explain yourself!"

"Done." He lifted his good hand in weary humor. "I promise." He lifted his arm. "Perhaps between the two of us, we can get me on my feet."

"Hold on . . . ." Clea pondered, and then put her arm around him on the good side, his good arm over her shoulder. She reminded herself she'd done the same thing in the past with many a brother. Lestrade was

108

reminding himself it was completely necessary if he wanted to get out of here, and he wasn't trying to be sly about being in contact with her. *What is that perfume, anyway? It smells like a pomander . . . .*

"First, explain why you were laughing at me."

"I wasn't laughing at you," Lestrade said patiently. "It was just . . . what you'd said."

"What about it?"

"Miss Cheatham, no one can avoid looking at Bartram Cheatham's sister. They would be stone-blind and they'd still turn their heads to you. And I'm not saying that on a shallow judge of your appearance. Far from it. I'm saying it as someone who has noticed how others react. You're the flame to moths." Lestrade somehow had the strength to colour at his words, which slightly lessened his awful pallor. "Good Lord. You have no idea what I'm babbling about."

"I most certainly do not," she responded. "We're going to have this conversation when you're put back together."

"First," he promised, "you have to help me pretend I'm sound."

"And then what?"

"Then I speak to . . . that man over there . . . ." He nodded to a thick-built man with a black beard and a Highlander pin on his frogged lapel. "He'll help me claw my way out of here on some pretense."

A few moments was all it took. Clea watched the Yarders bundle up their mate with gentleness at odds with their bluff appearance. A blond man took the reins and they rattled off. Clea felt ill. Yet it wasn't until much later in the privacy of her bedroom that a strange realisation came to her: He didn't smell like pig.

"Just hold on, old fellow." Bradstreet's deep voice was soothing, but his thoughtless pat on Lestrade's back was not. "Oh – sorry – sorry!" He apologised in distress almost as deep as his friend's. "Sorry," he said again. "We're almost to the doctor's." An incoherent mumble was his answer. Bradstreet glared up at the next available target. "Gregson, for God's sake, go easier on those curves! You're not going for the Wessex Cup!"

"The brutes want to run in this weather – May I remind you I'm not the usual driver?" Gregson roared back. He did manage to slow the horses marginally, which made the cobblestones feel larger and sharper than they really were to the passenger. Things worsened as they hit the freezing advection fog off the Thames. Gregson swore under his breath.

"Henceforth, you're getting practice – if we survive!" Bradstreet promised. He turned back to Lestrade. "You're shivering, Geoff. Have another drink."

"Not sure I – !" Lestrade's protests were made moot by Bradstreet in short order. He gasped – Bradstreet's personal vintage was less a respectable label and more like paint thinner scorned by East End gin mills. He coughed, sending fresh agony through his body. "I swear I'll kill you for this," he promised faintly.

"I think he's going to make it!" Bradstreet crowed.

"We'll let the experts be the judge of that," Gregson promised, somewhat alarmingly to Lestrade. It was all he could do to lie motionless on the floor and anticipate every turn of the wheels. The pain of the rigged fight was only spreading outward, like a wildfire.

Parts of his ribs felt like they were disjointing and falling away. Miss Cheatham had every right to be furious at him. He had been a royal idiot – Lestrade wasn't sure how a royal idiot could be worse than a common idiot, but his scattered thoughts chose to let that slide for now – to pretend he hadn't been injured. He had to have aggravated the wrenched shoulder. Clea had mercifully distracted him with her underbreath commentary about brothers and how it wasn't true at all that Nature never made mistakes. Just look at her family.

He was almost – not completely – convinced that while they were struggling through the crowd to Bradstreet, Quimper had seen him. It had been a fleeting glimpse, no more, but it worried him. Holmes could brag about his superiority all he chose. Lestrade wasn't going to take that without the salt until Holmes figured out how to trap Quimper in a net of his own corruption.

It was going to hurt whether or not he talked. Lestrade decided to go ahead with it. "Where are we . . . going?"

"Watson's *locum* for Dr. Thomas in Kensington Street right now," Bradstreet said blithely.

Lestrade closed his eyes. "Is Watson the only physician in London?"

"We could check around," Gregson called back insincerely, "but he's about the only doctor around that doesn't ask stupid questions, and he doesn't charge more than he must."

"Shut . . . up . . . ." Lestrade tried to glare but that required movement. He lapsed into helpless misery as a form of passive protest. What felt like many more minutes passed, but it couldn't have been all that long because Bradstreet's terrible choice of fortifier had not finished taking hold. A dull burning sensation had slipped from Lestrade's gut to his chest by the time Gregson managed to pull to a stop. The cab still felt as though it were moving.

"Lestrade?" Dr. Watson's dark face blocked the dirt-smeared London sun. "Inspector Lestrade, how do you feel?"

How does he manage to keep brown all year around? Lestrade realised he was lushed. Obviously Mr. Holmes was even more a slave-driver than they had thought. Visions of the hapless doctor forced to chase after an oblivious consultant across the countryside, demanding he get his proper meals and sleep, was a difficult one to shake off.

Oh, Splendid. I am corned [2] *as a priest. Am I still on duty? Was the Benefit the same as a personal day? Is it a personal day if the Chief Inspector threatens to send everyone who doesn't attend to the Lambeth Detail?*

Lestrade was a moment collecting his voice. "Like a bloody great ape picked me up and threw me into the ground," he gasped.

"Oddly enough, that's almost what happened," Gregson supplied helpfully.

"Someone threw a Scotland Yard detective into the ground!" Watson was horrified, outraged, and indignant at this attack upon the representatives of good British Law. Even Gregson thawed. As quickly as that, John H. Watson made eternal friends.

"Your shock is most gratifying, Doctor," Bradstreet said warmly. "But it does happen more often than you might think." He clapped the smaller man on the shoulder. "Still, that is what almost happened."

"What did happen?"

"Scotland Yard's Seasonal Charity," Lestrade said through his teeth.

"This happened to you at a *charity*?" Watson's mouth actually dropped open. It couldn't have been easy to shock the man – not where he was living. Lestrade felt a ridiculous sense of satisfaction at his reaction – rather like a boy who finally prodded the Beefeater to react to mud balls.

"There was a demonstration of combat on the grounds," Gregson started, but the doctor threw his hands up in surrender.

"First of all, may we get him inside first – and what did you give him?" Watson bent, sniffing at Lestrade's face and quickly recoiling. "That can't be poteen!"

"Now, Doctor," Bradstreet answered far too calmly, "a man of the law would hardly be carrying that!" [3]

Watson's only response was to level a deadly eyebrow. "Just help me get him on the stretcher." From the icy tone of his voice, he didn't think much of men who gave their wounded compatriots Cockney-rejected drink.

Lestrade somehow endured transport without fainting, screaming, or swearing. Barely. Blessedly, the freezing gritty London air was replaced with a much more welcoming sideways view of a burning fireplace, paneled walls, framed certificates, and a sparse collection of weary-looking books. The medical chart on the wall didn't make sense. Lestrade tried to imagine why Watson would use a graphed image of a human head for a dart game, and gave up.

"Dislocation, wrenched back, and – " Watson picked up Lestrade's hand as lightly as if it were the feather off a bird's breast. Lestrade winced and pulled his breath in deeply. "Three broken metacarpals. I hope this isn't your favoured hand."

"I can manage," Lestrade managed.

"Just a moment, old fellow, I'm going to reset this – the breaks are dislocated and pressing against the large wristbones from the centre to outer edge. As soon as we set those, you'll find your pain level will be much more – " Watson made a quick movement and lightning struck thrice. Before Lestrade could draw breath and accuse Watson of things that would never occur to his own lodger, he found the pain had indeed settled. " – bearable," the doctor finished.

"If I could, I'd sigh with relief," Lestrade mumbled.

Watson quirked an eyebrow. "Would you like morphine for the next step?" he asked politely.

"Would rather the medication follow the treatment, if it's all the same to you."

"Good man." Watson's smile was quick, and Lestrade was struck by how genuine it was. For some reason he felt glad of the man's approval.

"Gregson, Bradstreet, may I trouble you put your hands here, and here . . . ."

Although Lestrade knew what was coming, he dreaded being pinned down. Watson set his hands above and under the dislocation and looked Lestrade dead in the eye.

"Count of three, all right?" He began. "One, two, four." A wrench sent a shudder through Lestrade and for a moment the world went cloudy.

"Thought you – said – *three*?" Lestrade wheezed.

"Yes, well, the surprise takes the edge off the pain." Watson produced a small vial. "Having said that, a small amount of morphine would not be amiss in this matter, but please tell me if you've had any stimulants or depressants in the past week."

"None whatsoever," Lestrade said firmly. "Outside the usual coffee, tea, and cigarettes."

"Good enough." Watson slipped the drug into the needle.

Ten Minutes Later:

"Why don't you ask Lestrade if you don't like the story?" Gregson protested. "He's right there behind you!"

"Kindly don't tempt me."

112

Lestrade watched with glassed-over vision as Watson put his hands on his hips. "I'm not asking Lestrade. I'm asking you. Lestrade has enough morphine in him now that I doubt he'd face an army of rabid foxes with more than a polite interest." The doctor leveled what Youghal called a Gloaming Eyebrow, sparing neither Gregson nor Bradstreet. "For Heaven's sake, give me some credit for finishing Netley. Our incapacitated friend weighs at twelve stone, which is less than Bradstreet. Even less so in the summer, when I'm running full-tilt at one of Holmes's windmills!"

Lestrade snickered. It hurt, but he didn't care. The Don Quixote analogy was perfectly divine. The London theatre must surely weep bitter tears at the loss of Sherlock Holmes every night.

"So I'm merely curious as to what on earth would drive a Lancashire wrestler to pick Lestrade up and use him for an auger."

Bradstreet had accepted Watson's offer of "decent beverage". "Well, it was Bartram Cheatham," he said as if that explained everything. "We believe he plays a bit creatively with the definitions of the law, and we're certain he works the unsolicited fights off on the East End for extra pay. We're certain he's up to something shady . . . but so far we have nothing we can pin on him . . . ."

NOTES

1. Channel coal. Oil shale used to make paraffin. Charles is patriotic to Lancashire industries.
2. Corned.
3. Poteen is the Irish potato version of moonshine, and still as illegal in Ireland as "blockade whisky" is in Appalachia.

Chapter VIII

"Hold – hold – hold." Watson had his hands in the air. "Mr. Cheatham was at the Charity for a demonstration of his Art. He picked Lestrade out of the crowd for said demonstration . . . and then threw him into the earth, pulling his back, breaking three hand-bones, and dislocating his shoulder?" The doctor let his disbelief show. "Cheatham is three of Lestrade put together! How could he make such a mistake?"

Proving he wasn't completely the imbecile that Mr. Holmes thought he was, Lestrade kept his mouth shut.

"Ah, you have us there," Gregson said awkwardly, proving he wasn't the smartest inspector that Mr. Holmes thought he was.

"The last time I read the pink pages, the rules of Lancashire wrestling were against breaking bones," Watson growled.

"It's still the most violent sport outside of Cornwall," Bradstreet pointed out. "Next to Hurley, that is."

"Hurley is not that violent," Gregson complained. "Not if the players know what they're doing!"

And when was the last time you saw a full team of skilled Hurley players?"

"*Ahem!*" Watson cleared his throat with amazing volume. "I may not compare to Sherlock Holmes, but I do know when I see a smokescreen." He threw himself into a chair and pointed to the couch. "Be so kind as to sit. There is a box of cigars left behind by a rather annoying client, and it would please me if you could help smoke them."

"Put it that way . . . ." Gregson led the way to the couch and passed the little wooden box around. Rum-soaked Caribbean may not have been the right bribe for a prideful doctor, but they were good enough for Yarders.

"Lestrade wasn't actually his opponent. He was just demonstrating his wrestling moves. He'd already had about six or seven men before that, and nothing bad had happened to the ones who'd gone before."

"But a few minutes later," Watson filled in grimly, "Lestrade is the one who hears the snap of his own bones." "Is this something to watch out for? Something like Guy Fawkes coming up – people seeking symbols of the establishment in order to cause mischief on them?"

"We're always on the look for that," Gregson grumbled unhappily. "Not that we can return every battle we're given! No, our Cheatham checked out too clean for that nonsense. He'd been asking around to attend events that might bring a bit of money in, and his agent suggested he work as part of the entertainment." He sighed. "But his agent happens to be as clear as a twelve-yard sundial."

"Aren't they all?" Bradstreet murmured.

"Hmm."

There was a strange note to Watson's voice that brought even Lestrade's attention out of his personal drug-soaked euphoria. The doctor was stroking his moustache, buried in thoughts. "Lestrade, may I trouble you to recall something about the time your back was wrenched for you earlier?"

"Hmm?" Lestrade promised.

"The thug who put you out of work . . . could he have been Bartram of Lancashire?"

Lestrade tried to sit up. It was a mistake. Several minutes later, he was still gasping for breath.

"Good Heavens, man! Use the oxygen in your lungs for breathing! The expletives can wait!"

"Holy Mary," a very Protestant Gregson said mildly. "You know what you're saying, Doctor?"

"I don't have much to go on, but – Lestrade, hold still. I need to confirm a suspicion."

"Hold still? I wasn't aware I had a choice," Lestrade growled. Watson had managed to ruin a perfectly pleasant moment with alcohol and opiates. It was beyond unfair.

"I need to see your arms . . . ." Watson removed his shirts as gently as possible, and drew his eyebrows together. "I still have a copy of that medical report. Bradstreet, bottom drawer, L-file. There aren't many of those I warrant. I keep a separate section for Scotland Yard, so he should be the third or fourth file . . . ." Watson ran hands light as goosedown over Lestrade's drug-addled ribs. "If I was a better physician, I would be able to see this in my head . . . " he muttered to himself.

"Here's the file." Bradstreet sounded as bewildered as Gregson looked.

"In the fight at the waterfront, you said the attacker 'ploughed through' the other detectives in his eagerness to get to Lestrade, put his hands on him only long enough to send him flying through the air, and it was the impact of the lamp and the wall what did all the damage . . . ." Watson's private mutters became even less intelligible. "The only way those injuries could match up is if he put his left hand under your right arm, and spun your balance with his right hand corresponding and lower part of the body, at the inside thigh just above the knee. Lestrade, you must have spun like a top!"

"I felt like one."

"In order to throw someone like that, it would have left marks on the skin. I didn't ask. Were you bruised in those areas?"

Lestrade gamely tried to oblige Watson's curiosity. "I was limping like you for a time."

"I'll take that as a yes." Watson had found what he was looking for. "And I can see for myself Cheatham threw you in exactly the same way your assailant at The Kelpie threw you into the ground."

"But he was demonstrating different wrestling moves," Bradstreet egged. "Why would he do something like that?"

"I think we have established a wrestler has a fish-eye for Mr. Lestrade. If it is the same person, then he would naturally re-create his initial successful move against him."

"I guess you'll have a tale to tell Holmes when you get home," Gregson said sarcastically.

Watson looked puzzled. "Hardly."

"Oh? Working on a case?" Gregson was being annoying, which just showed to Lestrade how jealous he was.

"I don't speak to him about my ships unless they sail into dark waters. At any rate, Holmes is in Spain right now. Something about subversives in a palm-frond plantation." Watson shook his head. "Believe me, gentlemen, I sleep better when I don't know everything Holmes is up to."

"That's just as well," Lestrade grinned. "Because he doesn't tell any of us mere mortals what he's up to anyway."

Watson laughed softly. Affection shone in his eyes at one of the most difficult men in London. "You have the right of it." He pulled his bottle out and topped everyone's glass. "In my short term in the military, gentlemen, I faced the sight of Englishmen going mad with tropical fevers and shooting into their own troops. I saw hundreds of different and creative ways in which man can attack another man, was drafted to be the emergency medical support in case the tiger hunts in India went terribly

116

wrong, and then of course, Afghanistan." He swirled his drink smoothly, brown eyes wry. "And during it all, I was only shot, stabbed, and beaten a few times. Now that I share rooms with Sherlock Holmes, I can truthfully say to you my level of danger has increased, and I remain haunted by my old friend Colonel Hayter's words when he shook my hand goodbye."

"Oh? Don't stop now." Bradstreet was grinning fiercely under his nose. "What did the man say?"

"He said, 'It's a quieter life you're returning to, John my boy.'" Watson lifted his glass in a toast as Gregson sputtered brandy across the carpet. There seemed to be a lot of that going around . . . .

Clea did not trust herself to speak with events so fresh in her mind. She shivered and wrapped herself deeper inside her thick coat as the air sharpened with the cold. It was an easy way to shut off her family. She was wordless all the way home. The men were so caught up in the success of the day, Bartram's pay for attending the event, and their "putting one over" that "little Inspector", they never noticed until they were almost home.

Little, she thought. They say it like it's something to be ashamed of. When they use that word on me, it's like I'm something weak and delicate. She was sick of being "little" and there was nothing she could do about it.

Not when her world was populated by giants.

Watson would have known Holmes was back even if the tobacco smoke wasn't piling out of the cracked-open window over Baker Street. Mrs. Hudson was flapping her apron at one of the Irregulars as he ran off, barefoot in the cold. As she turned, she caught sight of her other boarder and they both smiled at each other: Sherlock Holmes was back and all was right in the world.

"Good evening, Doctor," that wonderful landlady proclaimed. "I hope you're in the mood for a bit of chowder."

"It would be perfect for such a day as this," Watson answered with feeling. He hung his coat in the foyer with relief. He would wear his warmer item tomorrow, and send this one off to be cleaned. His fifteen-pound medical bag went with him up the stairs to the sitting room.

Holmes was clad inside his mouse-coloured dressing-gown – a true indication he was glad to be back to his old habits. He lounged full-length as best as his frame would allow on the settee, engrossed in acquiring a collection of smoke-rings in the atmosphere. Watson took the time to wonder just how much his friend had contributed to the miasma of London, but despite living in a perpetual fog-bank, the detective had gained healthy warmth from the Spanish sun. His grey eyes were alight with mental activity and they sparked as Watson pushed open the door.

"Ah, Watson. How is Inspector Lestrade? I wonder if an injury ordained at a charity event qualifies for paid medical leave."

Watson ruffled his moustache as he dropped his bag to the floor and rolled his shoulders. "Are you adding prescience to your list of skills? He'll recover, but I would have given much to have seen that 'demonstration' – it hardly sounded fair!"

"Nor could it be. Cheatham is an elephant among fighters, my good fellow. His ilk is one of the primary reasons why I selected boxing and the singlestick." Holmes pulled smoke in and created another geometric marvel. "Wrestling was not originally for large men. It was created by men of Lestrade's stature for combat against a larger opponent. I shall remain a boxer until this perspective is corrected." His dark brows popped up like a buoy in his pale face.

"Well, it wasn't pretty," Watson said curtly. "Three bones broken in his hand, strained ribs, dislocated shoulder again . . . ." He poured himself a drink. "Bradstreet offered comfort in that hideous distillate he insists on carrying."

"Worse than that Oban whisky you adore?" Holmes drawled, honestly curious.

Watson glared. "Holmes, that vile concoction is possibly the first reason why Ireland was ever conquered." He knocked his own "distillate" back without a qualm. "I think gin would hurt less." Another drink. "Forgive my manners. How was your trip?"

"Bah." Holmes flipped his wrists. "Petty and far from satisfying. Positively acerebral! Two rival plantations and just enough idleness to cause mischief. If it hadn't afforded me a brief vacation and a gratuitous amount of pin money, I would say it was not even worth the air I breathed. I'll grant you," he added, "now that I may contemplate freely in the ataraxia of our rooms . . . there was a delicious irony in dealing with the criminals of a small market that depends upon a religious holiday. Were I not already latitudinarian, I would be ruined on Palm Sunday for life."

Watson chuckled. The brandy had loosened the tightness in his shoulder and he felt more than ready for supper. "Then I needn't trouble your recollections, but I will insist you explain how you knew about Lestrade's damage and my attendance."

"Simplicity itself. I was there." Holmes flipped another wrist at his flatmate's surprise. "Not dressed as myself, mind you. I'd picked up the playbill of the event as soon as I crossed the Channel, and I decided to pay a quick view of Mr. Cheatham's skills at the gate." Holmes managed to

118

snort in a way that would abash a plough-horse. "I was singularly under-impressed."

"The man has lost no more than one out of twenty-five fights!" Watson protested.

"Inevitable," Holmes retorted. "Native gifts of mass and circumference, combined with a creditable knowledge of the art learned no doubt at his father's knee. There simply aren't enough opponents in his size to give his true talents full reign. Stagnation is the only outcome. Well, he knows it. It leads to certain . . . *aggressiveness* in the game that conveys his lack of peace about his livelihood." Holmes ruefully set aside his empty pipe. "That and the quality of the company he keeps."

"I've seen him at his sister's establishment," Watson mused. "I hope you aren't meaning that kind of company. Miss Cheatham is the soul of propriety!"

"Not at all. He has been seen quite often in the company of one Jethro Quimper, a self-avowed agent of sport-fighting, trade-goods, shipping, and a bit of racing and investments thrown in," Holmes murmured. The sardonic humor had melted out of his lean face like ice under the sun.

"That his latest prize-fighter . . . or perhaps simply 'prize' would be more accurate, would be on the outs for our good inspector is cause for concern."

Watson slowly elevated his own eyebrow over the newspaper. "I'd be worried about Lestrade too, after seeing what he did to him in the name of a charity!" The doctor was offended to the depths of his soul. Holmes almost smiled, but Watson's honour could beat a king's. It was serious because Watson was serious. While forgiving to a fault, his biographer would not allow the use of charity for sundry pettiness.

"I have said before that Lestrade is the best of professionals. Be assured that title carries with him no particular sense of joy or false pride. It was long before your time. It was a dearly won reputation, and he will pay for his ethics for the remainder of his life."

Watson lowered his newspaper. "You've explained that much, Holmes. Do go on."

"Lestrade was a lowly constable when Quimper inherited his father's predilection for law-bending," Holmes complied. "Two of his employees were, unfortunately, Lestrade's older brothers. Nothing was ever proven to connect Quimper. He is a cunning rascal and clever as the serpent. But all circumstantial evidence points to the fact that they and several others were sent to thieve a gold depot off Bond Street. Lestrade attended, and it was he who witnessed his oldest brother murder a fellow constable in cold blood. For that he was hanged. The second brother remains in Dartmoor, and I do not have confidence in his freedom." Watson's expression was met with a shrug. "Family is not always what one would like it to be. I believe it made matters all the worse that Quimper, as well as his brothers, planned on our inspector's blind eye," Holmes smiled wryly. "As I have said, the best of professionals."

"Gruesome," Watson summarized. "I can't fathom the workings of a man who would prey upon familial bonds – such an action would render those bonds forfeit." He shook his head sadly.

"Enough of that!" Holmes burst loudly. "I have stagnated in Spain for too long and I am anxious to find something of merit! The stolen lead still has great possibilities."

Watson almost groaned. "I made no complaints when you went to Spain because of its weather," he said in a hard voice. "Do not pretend you have fully recovered from the fluid in your lungs, nor tell me you have faithfully been taking your doses of *Aesclapius tuberosa*."

"My dear Watson, what would lead you to deduce I have not?"

Watson did not quite sigh. "I am a medical man, Holmes, not a detective. But though *A. tuberosa* is unmatched in its ability to battle lung attacks, it does have a most unfortunate side effect in the breath. Without being crude, your breath merely speaks of shag tobacco, not the trademark 'rotting chestnuts' odor of the tincture. Finally, you only crack a window to smoke when a bit of cool, damp air would benefit your bronchial tracts." His expression thus turned to stone at his deeply amused friend. "In other words, you aren't going anywhere without me."

Clea dressed for dinner in a worsening mood. Judging from the noises floating up the stairwell, Mr. Quimper was the celebrity of the night and Clea was again grateful she did not cook on weekends. The temptation to put something vile in the man's food would override her good sense.

How could Bartram be this way? Her father and remaining – and allegedly more-intelligent – brothers were supposed to have more sense! They had let their acumen be replaced by another person's – an outsider's! *How could they?*

Her lips were set tight. They were sealed with enough force that she felt her chin shake. As soon as the maid left she sank down on the side of the bed, holding her work-apron over her knees.

The apron symbolised her struggle to be accepted. A working woman wore garments that buttoned in the front. A lady's buttoned in the back because a maid was essential for the skill. She wore the first when she was at The Rose but she covered it all up with a one-piece apron that kept anyone from knowing how she buttoned her dresses. A peace offering.

It was not her only discretion. After a childhood in pneumonia, the doctors had insisted she live her life with unrestrained, untampered lungs.

120

Thus it was that her family supported her Emancipation Bodice because they didn't want her to die like Mam. For her part, she didn't embarrass them with forward political views and she didn't press her nieces to give up the tightlacing. It was hard, but she did it to keep the peace.

And did they understand her efforts to make everyone happy? No matter what, she was their baby sister. A clever babe trapped in amber. It wasn't just the birth-order, either. It was being the only sister, the tiniest member, and the only "real" female in the family since Mam died. Not that the women seemed to account for much in the whole unit. None of her sisters-in-law even tried to stand up front. Her father had no interest in re-marrying. The only woman of any status . . . was . . . Clea.

She was beginning to realise her bitterness about that status. It wasn't real respect. Not by a long chalk. It was as if she symbolised everything the family tried to cherish. The liberties they allowed her to take in family conversations when they would not tolerate the same from their own wives and daughters . . . was that true tolerance they had for her?

Or . . . *indulgence*?

For years she had hoped to grow up. Then she had hoped to grow tall. Then she had hoped that she would grow in stature. But their regard for her had only improved by small degrees and hardly improved when her academic skills approached Myron's. Indeed, they excused it to the guests and family friends by saying "takes after her mother", as if she was hardly at fault for being able to cipher long sums in her head. They wouldn't admit they were living beyond their means, so she went ahead and found her own way of living before the inevitable times grew bad. They wouldn't say she was correct. They only admired her for opening her own shop, and they knew not to try to tell her she was working below her means. But she knew they talked behind her back.

The whole Cotton Mill Heiress nonsense was a hollow bubble supported by spent money and crippled children. They had never been that high of a status anyway. Mam had walked alone to the poor in the tenant-rows, giving out soup and bread. She helped with births and deaths. No lady here would do such a thing and keep her reputation!

Here in London, their worth was even less than it had been in Lancashire! It allowed them a choice house along one of the most beautiful canals in London, but they were not high enough to afford a house outside the Jews' neighborhood (an aggravation to Myron), and Bartram had to sell his fists to keep them out of debt while Myron toiled equally hard at his desk to maintain their lost standard of living.

Clea had spent her entire life swimming like the frog in the pot of water. The water had grown hot, one degree by one degree, and now she was boiling, with still no hope of escape.

121

"Miss Cheatham, no one can avoid looking. You're the flame to moths."

Clea's sense of being crushed at her own helplessness was tainted with absurdity. No one had ever given her a compliment without bringing her brothers into it. Quimper's subtle praise of her eyes had been a perfect example.

The inspector hadn't done anything improper – he had merely spoken to her in public, and that had been enough to collect her family's hatred. It made things worse that Clea liked to talk to him. She liked being able to hold a conversation with someone without half breaking her neck peering up, and he didn't treat her as though she were little more than a doll to be kept on a shelf.

They wanted her married, but on *their* approval. *It will be someone clever, like that horrible Mr. Quimper who smiles too much.* Clea rose without strength and listlessly returned to her dress. She could have recalled the maid, but at this moment she couldn't even tolerate the company of another woman. *It will be someone who can recoup the money we've lost. They don't mind my shop because they believe it won't last. They think once I get myself into a proper marriage I'll leave the shop, or run it as distantly, as a Duke collects land-tithes from peasants he's never met. For now it keeps the dear girl busy, keeps her mind off our loss, that's a sweet girl.*

"Good Lord." He'd stared at her. *"You have no idea what I'm babbling about."*

"No," she said aloud. "I do not. No one has ever braved my family long enough to tell me anything about myself."

Chapter IX

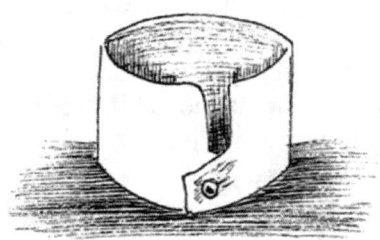

"You're still mad at me."

Clea paused while rolling crust out, and then continued ignoring Bartram.

Bartram was not used to being ignored. It was difficult to ignore Bartram. He shifted his weight to one side, then the other. Ignoring Bartram took a remarkable amount of discipline.

He, however, was not just as large as a boulder. He resembled a boulder also in his ability to wait.

"I saw what you did, Bartram," Clea said lowly so the tweeny couldn't hear over the roar of the oven. "I'm ashamed you treated your sport so badly."

Bartram blinked. He had not been expecting that sort of sally. It did not occur to him that his sister had been thinking about what to say to him for three days – and for most of three sleepless nights in the privacy of her room.

"Not my fault he got hurt," he mumbled.

Clea stopped rolling and merely looked over the counter at him. Since he was sitting down, they were almost at eye-level. "I know what a fighter can do, Bartram. We do have the same father. That toss isn't normally allowed. He was lucky not to have a broken arm or neck! What would that have done to your reputation?"

Bartram felt even more confused. She wasn't acting how he'd expected. No snaps or yaps about his treatment of a paying customer, or how it looked. And he wasn't certain she was wrong.

At first he'd felt like a boy about to play a good trick on another boy. There had been a mischief to the plot that appealed. A marlock.

And it wasn't like a lot of the other tussels back at the mill, where men fought with their clogs, kicking their shins until blood flowed and bones were notched for life. A few finger-bones was just a side-laugh compared to clogging.

The laughing and joking following the ride home had made Bartram feel as though he was finally on standing with his brothers. They were all older. Not a day passed without one of them saying something about how his size was greater than his mind. But there hadn't been any of that following the Charity. Bartram had loved it. Normally he would have felt left out against the rest, and he would have talked with Clea to pass the time and sense of awkwardness.

But this time . . . Clea had sat alone, and he had been one of the ones to ignore her.

Bartram wasn't sure what he should feel first. He floundered. He latched on to the default of his father's example against his actions.

His father had not disapproved. He had come from a rough generation of wrestlers harder than Bartram's. All was legal if the judge wasn't looking. And it wasn't all that different from what he and his brothers had done against all the boys who had looked at Clea. But it was easy to chase off the beaus in Lancashire. Here it was different. They were in a city of millions and they were no longer the figureheads of authority. That went to men like that little rat of an inspector, or to men like Quimper.

Quimper had wanted Lestrade hurt too. Quimper had to be happy. With his new eye on Bartram's life, the wrestler felt a strange mixture of pride to be so important, and worry that he would not be good enough for his employer. Bartram had never been "good enough" for anyone for very long, and Quimper's approval was about the strongest he'd ever garnered.

He had to make Quimper happy. Quimper could restore their family. Maybe their fortunes would improve to where Bartram could step further back from the pits that worried Clea and their father so much. Back home, he could never wrestle enough. Now it was all he did, other than work for Quimper as a bar-guard for one of his taverns, or his odd night-time jobs. He'd never contemplated the possibility that enough was enough.

Make Quimper happy. Part of that happiness depended on getting rid of that detective. It would also do Clea good, even though she wouldn't agree. Mr. Quimper was interested in her. He was rich. He was the better provider. He could restore the family.

Bartram's rusty mind slowly churned its cogs in search of a doable plan that would not upset his sister any more.

Paddington Street – Mrs. Collins' Rooms:

I really must find a hobby, Lestrade thought. It was a wholly new idea, and Holmes would have been pole-axed at his ability to think outside of the box, but there was no sense in denying truth. He needed to do something that would keep his mind from self-destructing.

"How many fingers am I holding up?"

Lestrade growled something that was the inevitable result of being a man who, pushed too far for too long, must finally snap at the first available target.

Dr. Watson never even blinked. "Such animals aren't designed for that kind of treatment," he pointed out. "Not without an independent supply of oxygen and immunity to volcanic fumes, at any rate. It appears you'll live, but we'll get back to your arithmetic later." He held up a glass of cloudy water. "Do you think you can drink some of this?"

"That depends. What is it?"

"Something that will re-join the cleft in your skull in short order."

"Can I have a written statement to that effect?" Lestrade groaned as Watson slipped his arm underneath his back, and by half-degrees, slowly elevated him to a drinking position.

"I can write you anything you want on a prescription receipt," Watson promised, "but I say nothing of you being able to read it." The doctor waited until the bitter drink was down. "No starch in the collar until at least tomorrow morning. You need to keep moving your neck."

Lestrade's vanity quailed. "Tomorrow?"

"Tomorrow. They're wonderful things, stiff collars, but not practical when you've gotten a case of neck-strain."

There were days when Watson's medical declarations were as peculiar as Holmes's deductions in crime. Lestrade chose not to question today. Holmes would just shrug and save his *I-told-you-so*'s for later. Watson was the man who took matters into his own hands.

"Lestrade, I must confess, I once wondered why you were such a hard worker at the Yard. But if this season is any indication, it must be safer for you to be on duty than off." He glanced at the mark on the wall where the detective had, suddenly attacked by a spasm in his healing ribs, doubled over and struck his head.

"Sound deduction." Lestrade closed his eyes. "Mr. Holmes would be proud."

"Hardly," Watson snorted. "He'd be scolding me for not knowing what was going on with you."

"You mean you're not going to bring him here and investigate the mysterious crimes against an inspector?"

"You're not his patient, you're mine," Watson scolded. He folded his arms across his chest, and seeing as how his sleeves were still rolled up, the biceps were an impressive sight mixed with the stern expression on his face. Oath to harm none aside, the doctor was looking much less like a doctor and much more like a major. "Mayn't I inquire as to why you are so determined to be back on your feet so quickly?"

Lestrade glared. "I believe you've been described as a man of action, Doctor. And I seem to recall early on in our first series of meetings, you appeared to be ready to chew carpet-tacks if it would only alleviate your boredom."

"I would have, if it had been scientifically proven to alleviate boredom without damage," Watson retorted.

"Well, you have a half-mad lodger to occupy your mind. I have a family of wastrels on the next flight, a family of sparrows on the sill, and the morning ritual of arguing hansom-drivers and knockers under my window, plus a view of theft-free leaded roofs, and, on occasion, a whiff of the river which lets me know that the weather is about to change." Lestrade's confession only fueled his frustration.

Watson glanced at Lestrade's single shelf of books, noted they all had something to do with reference, except a volume of Shakespeare. He wisely decided not to suggest reading or musical instruments.

"Unlike my 'half-mad lodger', you have been following your regime," the doctor said at last. "You weren't hurt nearly as badly as at The Kelpie, so we aren't talking more than three days, and that's over with tomorrow. Can you hold it together for four-and-twenty more hours?"

Lestrade's expression was an interesting mixture of frustration and hope. "I don't have much choice." He slowly sighed, which felt quite good. "By-the-by, Mrs. Collins demands to know what that salve is you've given me. She borrowed some for a cut on her hand and it sealed up in a heartbeat."

"I hope she cleaned the cut out thoroughly first!" Watson exclaimed. "Comfrey is a quick sealer. You can trap foulness inside a wound if you don't take precautions."

"Mrs. Collins washes her floors with undiluted ammonia. It's a wonder we all haven't died of nosebleeds."

Watson gagged slightly. "It's a beeswax-based ointment with comfrey and yellow-root. I put in Solomon's Seal for the tendons. Are you taking that vile potion I gave your landlady?"

"I'd rather argue with you than with her, Doctor, and she is convinced I need it three times a day. You're going to have to tell me what that wretched brew is." Lestrade lifted his hand ruefully. "I've never knitted together so quickly in my life."

"Don't be dependent on that happening every time," Watson warned. "It's white snakeroot. I have the devil's own time ensuring it's the proper kind. There is a plethora of plants with 'snakeroot' in the name." He sighed. "Treat yourself gently and you'll be back on duty without incident."

"Amen!" Lestrade blasphemed to the ceiling.

"Has there been any word about our friend the wrestler?"

"Nothing good." Lestrade did not let his feelings show. "For a man who takes up half a city street, he's oddly difficult to track."

Watson chuckled. "We could always have a quick luncheon at The Rose."

"That's not very funny."

"I could bring my service revolver."

Lestrade had to laugh. The humor leaked out by degrees to be replaced by a thoughtful expression.

"I should go. Miss Cheatham was convinced her brother had killed me."

"You sound like you're going to attend your own funeral."

"The way things are going?" Lestrade slowly bent to pick up a pencil off the floor. Movement, sweet movement. He didn't care that it hurt. He was ambulatory again and things were good. "I'm feeling a mixture of things right now. The least of which being that an overfed wrestler with blow-addled brains thinks I'm making sheep's eyes at his only sister."

"I disagree." Watson examined his nails. "You've been nothing but courteous to Miss Cheatham."

"Well, he's a jumpy sort," Lestrade said gloomily. "I wish I could arrest him just for the company he keeps. That agent of his . . . we've been trying to get him pinned for . . . *years*."

"Perhaps Cheatham can step out of line, and you can arrest him anyway," Watson offered. "And get information on the agent that way."

"That's not a very warm comfort," Lestrade pointed out. "Cheatham is the type of man who will go down fighting. He makes Gregson look like Tiny Tim!"

"Brrr," Watson shuddered. "My imagination needed no cues such as that!" A quirky smile appeared on his face. "Let's go to The Rose," he grinned. "You want to go anyway." His eagerness made the other man suspect Holmes was not the only lodger at 221b Baker Street with a taste for disaster.

"Yes," Lestrade agreed softly. He owed it to Miss Cheatham to show he was back on his feet again. The look in her eyes at the fountain created a strangling sensation in his chest every time he thought of it. The idea that he was the cause of her being upset was a disturbing one.

Lestrade was used to inspiring disturbing feelings in other people. It was part of being a policeman. But he was completely out of practice with that response outside the bounds of duty.

Clea pressed the door to the oven shut, and quickly flipped the flourdust out of her apron. She coughed slightly. The air was dry today, made worse from baking. Bartram had finally retreated – of a sorts. He was off in the dark corner of the shop, nursing the same cup of tea for a quarter-hour.

That meant he was thinking.

Thinking took Bartram a long time.

Good, she thought. He needs to think. And if he couldn't get his mind to work, she'd be just as happy if he tried contemplation or reflection.

He was the most aggravating in an aggravating family, but he was the closest to her in age, and (hard as it was to admit) he was the one she saw the most. Her older brothers weren't like him at all. Their usual policy to the youngest-born could only be described as "passive ignorance" unless something worried them, and then they were all over her like ants on treacle. Robert was perhaps the least offensive, but he was caught up in his own marriage and his own children, whom he adored and spoiled.

Things were even worse when her father was in on the plot too. Like now.

Clea felt the surprise on her own face light like a storm when the bell rang. The doctor was holding the door open for – *Thank God, he is alive!* She wasn't ashamed of being worried. Bartram had never killed anyone . . . yet . . . but there had been some close calls.

"Good morning, Miss Cheatham!" The doctor pulled his hat off with a smile. Mr. Lestrade did the same, more slowly. It reminded her too much of his return to the shop after the waterfront raid. "May I inquire what is on the menu today?"

"Perfectly ordinary herring and potatoes," Clea responded. She included both men in her smile. "And how are you gentlemen on such a crisp day?"

"I, for one, am glad it is crisp. It is much more preferable to being wet," Watson offered with a smile while tipping his hat.

"I agree." Lestrade had noticed the corner was populated. As Clea watched, he lifted his hand to his brim again, and his lips turned up in a slight smile. "Good morning, Mr. Cheatham. I trust your hand has recovered?"

Bartram lowered the newspaper he'd been holding and stared with that flat, fish-eyed look he gave when he wasn't certain if he was being mocked or not. He settled for one of his non-committal, zoo-grunts. "Your hand, sir?"

"Recovering nicely," Lestrade drawled peacefully. "Doctor, you choose the table. I'm not particular."

Watson, however, was. He had a fine sense of survival and chose a table closest to the door far away from the wrestler.

Clea gestured for the tweeny to dish up plates. For a moment she debated if she should deliver the food herself, or make it the girl's job. Oh, hang it all. Some knot of ire clabbered under her psyche. Mr. Lestrade was determined to act like all was normal in the world. The least she could do would be to stop skulking.

She crossed the room with the tray and set it down herself. "You're looking right better than you did the last I saw you, sir."

It was the first shot across the bow.

Are we to have that conversation now? I'm ready if you are.

Lestrade heard that mental snap as loudly as if she'd shouted it across the room. In the meantime, she was looking at him with her hands perched on her hips as if that was the only thing that kept her from wringing his neck. The direct stare was worse than the psychic message. He could see what she was thinking as she scraped him over with her eyes: *He looks to be normal enough, but there's a patch on his forehead that I'd swear hadn't been there before. His hand is still wrapped up. Is he pretending for my sake? I'll not put up with lying, not in my establishment. Who lets him leave the house with a starchless collar?*

"I feel much better than I did, Miss Cheatham, thank you." *This must be what it feels like to be keelhauled under a barnacle-crusted ship.* He lifted his teacup with the right hand. "How is business?" *No, Miss Cheatham, I am still convalescing, and "having that conversation" is beyond my slim abilities right now. Perhaps forever.* "I am sorry about your stolen goods." *I am very sorry about the collar, but I'll not hide behind my doctor. I do have my pride.*

"*Tsha,*" Clea waved that off. "Thank you for sending me that note in your absence. That was nicely done." *If you think I'm going to let you have your way over this, you'd best take your business elsewhere. We are going to have that conversation, even if I have to track you down. I hear there's a private consulting detective on Baker Street.* "I can't imagine what it all means," Clea said, perhaps to both levels of discussion they were inflicting upon each other. "Dust have a notion who was behind this?"

Watson ever-so-slightly stiffened, prepared for battle, but Lestrade's C.I.D. training had been as bone-deep as Watson's Army procedures. He never reacted to the question that could betray his suspicions to the gorilla lounging in the corner.

"No, I'm afraid we haven't learned who would have the motive for such a strange crime. We're still working on it, but it's difficult to learn anything. There were rumors of contraband being smuggled into food barrels for a while. There is the possibility a rival gang mistook your goods

129

for an easy pick." Lestrade spread his hands. *Can we please, my good woman, hold this topic off until a better time? Your brother . . . .*

Clea began laughing. "My barrels holding illegal cargo? Oh, I like that idea!" Her face warmed at the thought. Watson thought to himself it was a shame she didn't seem to realise the responses she conjured from the people around her. That easy warmth and humanity could charm a serpent. Tragically, she had no more sense of her talent than a child.

That warmth abruptly died a slow death as she turned. Her brother was rising to his feet and lurching slowly to their table. Watson abruptly picked up his fork and stabbed a potato with it. It made a dull ring on the metal plate – probably left a dent.

"Mr. Lestrade."

Lestrade paused with the teacup halfway to its destination. "Yes, Mr. Cheatham?" *Man, do you not see how your sister dims when you stand close to her?* What are you doing to her? Out of the corner of his eye, Watson was looking less like a civilian by the second. The detective realised in slight shock that, if he simply gave the word to attack, Watson would obey without hesitation. *No wonder Mr. Holmes keeps him around. That's a handy attitude.*

"Maybe I shouldn't have thrown you the way I did." The wrestler stopped, suddenly unsure as to what he should be saying. He wouldn't be getting any help. Everyone present save Watson had forgotten they were eating and now waited, breaths suspended, for come what may. "I get carried away sometimes."

"I can well believe that, Mr. Cheatham." Lestrade chose his words carefully. It was easier than one might think. Bartram was merely a physical version of Chief Inspector Miller – a verbal bully who seemed to think Lestrade would infiltrate a French plot as soon as he had one moment of spare time. Either one could hurt him. Only Bartram could leave marks. "Still, we both appear to have survived." *But I make no guarantees for how much longer . . . .*

Cheatham's battered face still struggled with words. "No sense in us bein' enemies." His effort was painful to witness. "I'll buy you dinner summat. When you're back on your feet."

"That . . . that won't be necessary, really." Lestrade's nerves kicked into full Clyde Engineering locomotive horsepower. Clea stepped backwards slightly, no doubt so she could stare at both of them with the same astonished gaze. "You have a difficult job, Mr. Cheatham. I would be surprised indeed if you could remember to hold your strength back every time."

Cheatham turned that over as ponderously as stone wheels grinding a quern. "Meet for dinner sum'tyme," he persisted. "We can talk."

Lestrade had been witness to many offers, but that had to rank among the disturbing. Dr. Watson was paying far too much attention to his meal. Much as he liked his food, Lestrade intuited that whatever might happen, the other man had decided blows would not happen – yet.

"All right." Lestrade astonished himself. "It will have to be at least a week from now, sir. I'm returning to active duty."

The wrestler probed Lestrade with his eyes, but the little detective had no idea what he was plumbing for. "Good," he answered. "I'll leave word."

It was no exaggeration to say that everyone at The Rose watched him lurch out the door. The door shut against the wave of cold air. Clea realised she had been frozen at stance. She began to whirl to give the fool inspector a piece of her mind but – just – stopped herself.

Bad enough you sound like an old spinster, Clea Marie! You don't need to channel for your mother's spirit too! "Why would you want to talk to him?" she demanded.

Mr. Lestrade was taken aback. "He seemed to need it."

"He's my brother. He doesn't need more than ten meals a day, a steady income, the adoration of the crowd, and a keg of cheap drink. Everything else can go to seed."

Lestrade had faced all sorts of conditions in which one's composure was absolutely necessary. He put his tea down and counted to ten. "I am sorry, Miss Cheatham. But I feel it behooves me not to have a wrestler on my list of antagonists."

"You might as well," she snapped bitterly, "because it's clear you're on his."

They watched her go in awkward silence. Watson impaled another potato. It made a final-sounding clink on the plate.

"That was . . . ungainly."

Watson snorted through his nose. "I'm gratified to see you have recovered your powers of speech," he noted wryly.

"I hope that isn't a comment." Lestrade gingerly rubbed his injured hand. "I swear to you, I am completely out of my depth." Of course, he often felt that way in his line of work, but this was outside duty.

"For what it's worth, Mr. Cheatham is out of his depth too. I had no idea thought could be a source of pain." Watson glanced over the street to make sure no one would hear them first.

Lestrade found himself smiling. "He would look right at home at one of those Neolithic museum exhibits, wouldn't he?" The thought was a charming one to savour.

Watson tried not to chuckle, but it leaked out. "All right," he sighed. "If you're insistent on this nonsense . . . ." He muttered something about the rigidity of British spinal columns, reached into his wallet, and pulled out a card. "Keep this on you at all times."

"I already have your business card."

"This lists all my contacts for the rest of the month. Provided Holmes does not shanghai me into some ghastly part of Britain on a dovetailing crime, you should be able to reach me at one of these addresses." Watson's worry showed. "The man means to harm you, Inspector."

"Doctor, I appreciate what you're saying, but . . . The Yard lives with this all the time. There's no point in living in fear."

"You're saying you live in a war zone."

"Too right by half."

Watson accepted it. He didn't like it, but he accepted it. Soldiers operated on the understanding that once in a while, there were treaties and a cessation of hostilities. Civilian life was a drastic reversal. It was supposed to be the land of benign peacetime, and illegal to assault people without permission of the Crown, but people still managed to inflict horrors on their neighbor in the name of civilization on a regular basis, with a casualty list that rivaled anything the ineptest general could achieve in the field.

It was no wonder Watson had been lost at sea since his discharge. Open warfare with spear-laden Afghans and reused bullets had not prepared him for the depths of human selfishness back home.

Lestrade put the card away, and Watson visibly relaxed. "I'll be sure to give you a call, Doctor. Especially if it turns out I need an emergency stitch-job by someone who knows how to hold a gun simultaneously. I'm rather appalled that retired Army surgeons aren't a premium on the job market."

Watson grinned, delighted. "I think it's our difficulty with following orders."

"You, Doctor? You have difficulty following orders?"

"Well, there's no clear-cut sense of rank among you civilians." Watson defensively pointed to Lestrade's unadorned shoulders. "You don't even have epaulets or brass buttons to let us know who we're supposed to listen to!"

"We have Detective-sergeants! That's the rank of *Inspector* for the uniformed ones."

"Marvellous. You have one rank."

"So what is Mr. Holmes's orientation of rank? We're all dying to know down at the Yard."

"Not rank so much as amazement," Watson answered comfortably. "He tolerates my vices. I try to wean him off his."

"Sounds like an equation for a perpetual motion machine . . . ."

Bartram watched them go, laughing at a joke. The knot in his chest uncoiled and left him feeling relieved but empty, as if the anger had been a battery fueling his body.

"My dear boy," Jethro Quimper's voice nearly sent him tumbling into the street, "you are at half-odds. Did you have another encounter with that inspector?" The agent was dressed for near-best in a blue wool frock coat against the cold. A spray of bittersweet glowed at his lapel. A small bouquet of dried flowers rested in the crook of his arm – another gift for Clea. The bronze walking stick resting under the black kid gloves worried Bartram. He'd heard rumors of what Quimper did with that stick.

"He came by to eat," Cheatham grunted. "Can't outlaw him. I think he was here to show me he was all right." Cheatham had done the same thing many a time to his opponents. He straightened and put his hands in his pockets. "I told him we should meet some time. Have a talk, like."

Quimper grinned. "That sounds like a splendid idea, Bartram. Why don't you make it someplace public, so he needn't fear an unpleasant end in a dark alley?

Bartram studied him, his huge face flat with uncertainty. "You don't mind, sir?"

"Why, not at all. It would be good to finally clear the air between you, wouldn't it?" Quimper leaned forward on his stick, his weight pushing the tip into the frozen pack of the kerb. "You can pick any of my taverns. It would ensure nothing would happen against your favor." He was still smiling.

"I don't go to any taverns but yours, sir." Bartram puzzled.

"Of course not." Quimper laughed, genuinely amused. "Why don't you see if you can arrange a family meeting, hmm? Not with your father, of course. It wouldn't be good for his health to be out in this sort of weather."

"He doesn't need to know I work in pubs," Cheatham agreed. "You're right, sir." Bartram rubbed his still-pink face. "I can bring my brothers in. We can have a civil meeting with him." *Civil, right. Civil War.*

"Remember," Quimper wagged a friendly finger. "He respects strength. Bullies always do. There's no sense in wasting too much civility in his kind. You have to hit hard and fast." The tall man's eyes burned like topaz in the overcast light. "A good humiliation is what sticks."

"Halloa! Watson!"

Watson and Lestrade stopped, not entirely surprised to see Sherlock Holmes waving his stick in the air and pummeling his body through the

133

shifting crowd. There was nothing to do but hold still and hope he would not come to an ignominious end against a flying meat-cart or cab.

"I thought you said he was ill?" Lestrade watched as Holmes managed a deft maneuver through the costermonger's side.

"Don't be fooled," Watson said darkly.

Holmes panted to a stop, his lean face flushed with excitement. It was contagious. Lestrade felt his own blood heat in response to the other man's exultation – something of interest involving crime would be his only motive. "Inspector Lestrade, how good to see you on your feet again. I see Watson has released you."

"Temporary hiatus," Watson said sternly. "What has roused your interest?"

"A murder, of course!" Holmes responded. He struck the kerb with his stick. Ice split. "I was on my way to the canals. Would you gentlemen like to come?"

"I might as well," Lestrade retorted. "I was injured on a personal day. I might as well work on one too."

Watson shrugged and lifted his medical bag. "Would I need this?"

"One never knows. People have been declared insufficiently dead before," Holmes answered mysteriously, turned his back to whistle once for a four-wheeler, and thus missed the interesting expression shared between fellow lodger and occasional ally in the legal process.

"You do realise you're the closest thing to a jury of peers the man has," Lestrade muttered.

Watson did not argue, but he appeared caught between disapproval of hearing criticism of Holmes, and resignation to his fate. It was a common blend, and Lestrade normally tried to be considerate of Watson's affection for Mr. Holmes – Lord knew, Holmes needed a friend badly. He resolved to be more discreet in the future.

Holmes barked something and shrilled once to signal a four-wheeler. A cab stopped in front of a coney-cart, causing a near-wreck. Ignoring the shimmering observations, he argued with the driver over the length of the trip, winning by agreeing to pay half in advance. As a former cab-driver, Lestrade was thoroughly embarrassed at the finagling and found great interest in the opposite direction – but before they knew it, all three piled in for the western canals.

Watson exhaled fog. Before the heat of their bodies created some warmth, it was going to be uncomfortable. "Well, don't keep us in suspense, Holmes."

"I received a note from Gregson." Holmes leaned forward, his grey eyes now quicksilver with the hunt before him – and possibly amusement at being able to witness Lestrade and Gregson together again. "I had offered to concentrate on the lead-thieving. Several of the constables working on the vanished laborers discovered a disturbance at the canals this morning.

"As you know, canal water is much quieter than that of the rivers that feed London. It is a directed flow, calm, and regulated. Ice forms with regularity despite its depth, especially about the old stone gates and bridges that shield the water from the sun. One of the sharp-eyed constables – Crane – noted there was a large hole in the thin ice at the Old Stone Gate by Little Venice." He smiled quickly, pleased at the show of initiative. "He engaged a few hookmen who soon fished up a gruesome catch."

Lestrade closed his eyes. "Right after I ate," he groaned. "It's a bloater, isn't it? I hate bloaters." They knew he did not mean the kind of bloater one ate for breakfast.

"Gregson's note was vague on the condition of the body. We shall see soon enough. The medical examiner has already been by, so we must accept the leavings of the scene." Holmes sniffed his opinion of that.

"We really don't have much choice, sir," Lestrade said gently. "The Yard brings you in before our own men when we can, but we can't make a habit of it."

"Then you must teach your examiners my methods."

Lestrade needed precious little time and no imagination to conjure up the nasty consequences of a lowly police inspector telling a properly trained man of medicine how they should do things. If his colouring suddenly washed out, he hoped the others would assume it was from his convalescence.

"How does this have anything to do with what the papers are colloquially calling the '*Flight of the Blue Pidgeons*'?" Watson's journalistic instinct leapt to the fore.

"The lead-thieving has ceased, has it not?" Holmes asked as if that explained everything.

Watson dealt with the situation sensibly. He pulled a small notebook out of his bag and a tiny pencil. While the cab pitched them back and forth, the doctor demonstrated the under-appreciated art of writing while moving.

Lestrade waited until the temptation grew too great. ""I say, Doctor, do you get sea-sick?"

"No, never." Watson looked up, bewildered. "That's a strange question to ask, Lestrade. Any particular reason why?"

"Oh, no particular reason." Lestrade noted that Holmes was sitting with his eyes half-closed, but his lips were smiling. "Just curious."

135

Chapter X

"Good morning, Miss Cheatham."

Clea never before dreaded hearing those particular words. Who they were coming from had a lot to do with it. Bartram's agent, family friend, and current financial advisor to Myron on their fortunes lifted his hat off his head at the same time he bowed forward, producing the spray of flowers. From the viewpoint of someone who liked to dance, she was impressed at his coordination.

"Such a dreary day. It stands a gentleman right to do something about it. Particularly a lady of such a sharp mind and distinction as yourself." Clea was surprised to see some warmth had made it to his eyes this time.

He still looks like those carrion-eaters that tried to rob our Mill . . . .

"Thank you, Mr. Quimper." Clea made a point of cleaning her work off before she accepted the flowers. They whispered in her hands. She looked at them instead of at their benefactor. "I'm . . . Well, I am afraid I don't recognise some of them." They looked like carnations, but were delicately shaded in yellows, pinks, baby-blues and even – astonishingly – mint green. Clea had not thought a green flower possible.

"Nothing more exotic than common carnation," he assured her. "The florists place them in coloured water. When the color reaches into the petals, they then dry them, fixing the colours." He smiled, pleased with himself. "You see, even the ordinary and overlooked can become a rare thing with just a bit of attention."

Clea felt her face burn. Her heart hammered in her chest. She did not know what to do: Throw the flowers in his face, or give him thanks she did not feel?

This is your establishment.
But he is Bartram's agent.
And now Myron's advisor.

He holds our family in half his hand.

Clea had never thought much about snakes until now. She felt very much like a wren scolding at a threat. The snake, of course, would ignore her and continue to rob the nest.

"Most kind, sir." Clea's voice was fainter than she would have liked. Next to her, the tweeny was staring in open-faced admiration. Another disciple of Mr. Quimper. "If you would be so kind," she swallowed dryly, "I should put this up . . . ." She made herself speak the words. "My father hopes you will attend dinner with us again." She would not be petty even if it killed her.

Quimper tilted his head. Another sweep of his hat matched his smile. "I would be most delighted. Your family is a pleasure as always, Miss Cheatham."

Clea watched him go, his duties against her discharged. In a crowd of three-and twenty diners, her students, and the boy who swept the floor, she had never felt so alone.

She put the flowers up in the back. They stared at her. Clea did not think she could look at a blossom ever again without thinking of the message behind the gift.

You could get a better marriage proposal, girl. She heard her mother in her mind.

This is the only marriage proposal, she screamed back. I'm old enough to have my own family, yet I have no more than a wealthy . . . kite for a suitor, and a plainclothes detective who paid me my first honest compliment, and I still don't know what to do. I thought it was bad enough to be trapped by the plans of my own family. This is worse. My family's plans are now Quimper's. He hates Mr. Lestrade, and he's ensuring my family does too.

Lestrade's innards clenched. It was a small crowd around the canal: Three constables including Crane. Lestrade recognised Briggs and Phillips. He was relieved there were solid, reliable men on this section. The worn-looking hookmen. And Gregson. A lumpy canvas tarpaulin drained dirty water into the canal. At least the cold air kept the odours back. Holmes jumped out before the before the cab braked. Watson stifled a barracks oath. The detective threw up the remainder of the pay and the cab took off without as much as a thank-you-gents.

"Up and about, Lestrade?" Gregson waved his mitten. His wife was a splendid knitter, and he smugly displayed the rewards of his marriage in the cold. Show-off. "I have something you'd find interesting . . . Oh, have you eaten?"

137

Lestrade glared. "It's good to know you can work in my absence, Euclid." He pulled his muffler higher. "What have you?"

Holmes had already nipped forward and was pulling the canvas back. "Interesting," he said with a ghoulish enthusiasm.

Interesting was not Lestrade's word. The supine corpse rested its arms stiff against its sides – possibly from the effect of the freezing water. It was a small man, a head shorter and leaner than Lestrade's regulation height. Bristled dark beard sprawled over the leathery face like wire wool, already whitening with the first grains of forming ice. The eyes, lips, and tongue were eaten by fish. The freezing over gave an effect like shroud-linen. A neck too scrawny for its round head was withered and drawn inward, perhaps from cold. The throat was bare of the top buttons of his shirt-front.

Men tore their shirts when drowning.

"Crane knows his walk." Gregson nodded at the constable.

"It looked a little old, sir." Crane touched his brim. "But I'd been off yesterday and Woods doesn't know the cause so well. The light looked funny, not like it does in the morning, and I took a closer look, saw how there was a hole all scratched-over with a new coat of cat's ice." [1]

"He'll still get a talking-to, Crane."

"Well, Doctor? Would you like to give our Police Surgeon a hand?"

Watson tilted his head to one side, curious in a clinical way, and slowly lowered himself on his good leg. He touched the face gently, testing the movement of the joints. "Immersed two days, I would say," he noted. "I must say I'm surprised at its decent condition."

"How could you hide a body in a canal?" Lestrade muttered. "For that matter, why? How deep are they – three or four feet?" They'd plucked the barrels up from a yard of depth at the most.

"Deepest canal's the old Roman cut at Fossdyke." Gregson was delighted to educate Lestrade. "Four feet at its worst. But fall in and you can't see your own hand in front of your face. Whoever killed him was just hoping to hide him until the fish turned him past all recognition."

"Well, that was just stupid." Lestrade took mean relish at throwing in something Gregson didn't know. "Fish don't eat as much in the cold months. If this had been summer he'd be a rack of bones in a day." He saw Holmes look at him sharply, suddenly, as if he'd just said something clever, but Lestrade was damned if he knew what was clever about it.

Lestrade studied the corpse from where he was while Holmes pondered the state of the open eyes. The body was of the ubiquitous London criminal type. A man shaped in the under-nourished, unwashed predatory life of criminal London in charity-shop clothing. A tin watch hung on a paperclip chain. Probably stolen. What hair remained on its head was graying brown.

Lestrade busied himself searching for a smoke, staring at the neatly-set stonework at his feet.

Watson leaned forward, gently ruffling the eyebrows, causing quite a few living eyebrows to go up. "Welsh," he commented.

Holmes's smile spread. "A foregone conclusion if you judge a man by his ornamentation." He pointed to the exposed wrist. A small red dragon snarled back at them, a leek grasped in its paws.

"No. The hairs," Watson answered absently. "The Welsh have a tendency to grey prematurely and to have double hairs. See for yourself."

Holmes took him at his word. He pulled a small lens from his watch-chain and hovered over the dead man's face.

"Interesting. I wouldn't have known the race was differentiated," the detective murmured. Once, the Yard thought Mr. Holmes had been lacking in feelings. That was before they realised his emotions were not separated from his thoughts, and all were combined like a volatile stew behind his grey eyes.

"Most signs are small, when they exist at all. It doesn't occur with all Welsh, but the double tendency is unusual outside the blood." Watson shook his hand dry and pulled out his notebook again. "I'd estimate his age to be about thirty to thirty-five."

"He is a former sailor," Holmes added, "a rope-splicer attached to hashish. You will find he had lodgings somewhere off the Fleet Street Market, and that he was a bit of a seeker of thrills. It no doubt factors to the circumstances of his death." Holmes lifted a recalcitrant arm, displaying the soggy fingertips. Over the dead-white layer of swollen skin they were smeared with what could only be traces of lead and tarry hashish. "I daresay his long exposure to the lead was beginning to affect his behavior, too."

"More than likely, if he was working with lead this long." Watson looked sad at the state of the world. "They know it's dangerous, and yet they'll do it anyway if it means more pay."

"What killed him, sir?" Constable Crane had edged around Gregson and was regarding the morbid find with uneasy fascination.

"Look at his shirt-front," Lestrade nodded. "When a man loses air, he makes that motion." The cloth was rent by fingers.

"I see you've saved the most intriguing for last, Gregson." Holmes had reached inside the coat-pockets of the dead man. He pulled out a handful of dripping metal.

"Lead," Watson exclaimed softly.

"Mind you, I never saw that much of our boy when we were chasing him over the roof-tops," Gregson put a match to his cigarette, and exhaled smoke that looked worse than the greasy yellow fume off the factories. "But he fits the body type I do recall. You, Lestrade?"

Lestrade sighed. "It isn't too big or too small to be the man we chased."

"A fine point," Holmes commented with enough acid to etch fine glass. "If I may finish this examination – ?"

"By all means." Gregson shrugged. "Crane, tell those poor hookmen they can go home. They've been out in that ice half the day as it is."

The hookmen did not wait for Crane's blessing. They were poling their way across the canal with a flask of gin before the words were done. Juniper fumes drifted back across the thick water with the unpleasantness of asafoetida wrapped around their necks.

"Grim job," Watson noted. He seemed immune to the irony. The policemen watched him with the usual interest of men who are viewing an unpleasant task that needs not involve them. "Holmes, would you mind giving me a hand?"

The detective complied, and the body was slowly tilted to one angle.

"Watch what comes out of his mouth. We're looking for brown water. At the very least, we need to find some sort of colouration in the fluid."

Gregson had seen Lestrade's nerves. He offered his horrible fags. "Have you noticed something about this little skit, Ratty?" he asked softly.

Lestrade decided to take it. He would say nothing of enjoying it. "Something in particular, Euclid?" He flinched as unadulterated leaf shot straight into his bloodstream. Small wonder Gregson chose the stuff. Who needed cocaine or coffee?

"Watson never writes about his own participation in these investigations – not unless he's painting himself as an ignoramus." Gregson spoke as the man privileged the sight of Watson's "little writings". Lestrade knew full well the doctor wasn't ready to set it out his work with Mr. Holmes in print yet. Nor had he seen much of the doctor's samples save some un-flattering descriptive terms of himself and most of the Yard. But Gregson had seen Watson's full manuscript and was indirectly rubbing it in.

"Well, I suppose that makes sense." Lestrade caught Gregson's bewilderment. "No one wants to buy a story with the author's marvellous qualities. Besides, if the readers caught on that he knew something, they'd be trying to send their business to him as much as to Holmes. Watson likes excitement, but I don't think he wants that kind of attention." *Come to think of it, who would?*

"Dunno." Gregson frowned doubtfully. Although Lestrade thought of frowning as Gregson's natural expression, it added nothing to his natural lack of charm. "I suppose I can understand that. I mean, I can figure Watson's the type who couldn't say no to anyone who asks for help . . . ." He lowered his voice. "But he strikes me as protective, in a way. He doesn't seem to want to take the thunder from Holmes . . . ."

"I dread the notion that Mr. Holmes needs protecting – but if he did, Watson would be my choice."

"Ha!" Holmes barked. "Inspectors, we have a new wrinkle."

Gregson and Lestrade hurriedly pulled on their tobacco and stepped forward. The constables clustered like doves spotting an old woman with bread.

"This man drowned, but not in the canal." Watson pointed to the rivulet of clean water that was still trickling down the dead man's chin. For good measure, Watson had collected a sample in an empty drachm phial from his bag. [2] "As your own surgeon will tell you, this is clean water. No silt, no signs of residue. Nothing that would indicate he filled his lungs with this water." The doctor nodded with his head to the murky canal. "His lungs were already full of water when he was sunk by his coat-pockets. I cannot tell you more than that." He suddenly squinted at the phial in question. "Odd. Look." He passed over the clear glass tube in his fingertips. The distinction was unmistakable. Holmes held the tube for inspection.

"Fragments of ice." The amateur smiled. "Watson, in your experience, can water freeze in the lungs before the rest of the body?"

"Unlikely! The water had ice chips when it was inhaled at the point of death. At the most it partially dissolved but it froze again when the tract opened to the water outside."

"I dare venture he was bundled up and made to pretend he was an upright but drunken comrade on his way here." Holmes somehow made "venture" a positive fact. "No one watches a drunken man make his way home." His sword-sharp eyes promptly flayed open the flesh of every inspector, constable, and hookman present. The sins of Lauriston Gardens were a dreadful ghost to haunt the men of the law.

Lestrade sat back on his heels. "That would imply a slow murder. The signs are unmistakable. We learn that in the first stages of our training!"

"He could have been asphyxiated to the point of unconsciousness, then the job completed." Watson's eyes were as black as night as he contemplated the death.

"If the water was cold enough to put ice in the lungs, then it was denser than this warmer water of the canal. That kept the canal from adding

141

to the water in his lungs. The body had to have time to cool further before it was dropped here. The coroner's examination will be interesting."

"Watson, would you be so kind as to take notes on the state of the body?" Holmes murmured. "I should like to look about."

Gregson and Lestrade looked at each other. As one they followed Holmes's grasshopper movements to the stone gate-way that spanned the canal.

"What do you think, Mr. Holmes?" Gregson put it forth. "Is he right?"

Holmes was lying flat on his stomach, ignorant of the thick frost, peering at the pedestrian walkway with his watch chain-lens. "Watson is a common man, Gregson," he said without looking up. "He is utterly, fiendishly ordinary and pertinacious except in one particular matter." The detective ripped up a wisp of dry grass and peered at it with feverish interest. "He is never wrong in his medical instincts."

"Never, Mr. Holmes?" Gregson smiled doubtfully.

Holmes merely looked up at him, serious as a stone slab. "Never," he said sternly. "Given the choice between the Royal Surgeons and Watson, you should choose Watson every time." A faint thread of accusation laced through the detective's voice, and Lestrade recalled the Yard had (politely) asked Watson to consider working for them in 1882.

Granted, Watson had met their first three criteria by default: He was not an addict, kept reliable hours, and had a work ethic. It was amazing how many applicants failed in those regards. Yet it had not occurred to Lestrade that Holmes would have been angry at their offer. It wasn't as though they were going to steal him!

Well, Holmes could be a peculiar man. He was known for his odd possessive jealousies, and it was just as well they caught on that he was jealous of Watson's time. It saved trouble later to know where the boundaries were.

Watson lowered himself into a roiling hot bath and exhaled. One had to experience pure misery before knowing pure bliss. For nearly a minute he rested with his back against the rim, eyes closed as steam filled the tiny bath. Water-droplets formed on the salad burnet hanging in its potted basket by the window like a tropical vine after the sunny rainshowers of India, where the weather was daily as swullocking as a day in a greenhouse.

For a long time, Watson simply soaked his bones and watched mercury bright droplets of water swell with the clouds of steam, growing larger and larger until finally one then another fell into the dish of melted soap against the sill. The old window was poorly set and mis-angled, but that error caught every scrap of stingy sun in London.

142

Sun and rain together. "*A wolf is getting married*" the old folks said here, but when he was transferred from India Proper to the North-western provinces against the troubled Afghanistan, it was "*Da gidarh wade*" – the *jackal's wedding*. The bones of his extremities ached on par with his wounds and he took the time to simply stay put, listening to the blood-beat in his ears. He ought to go in for a full steam tomorrow.

Contrasting the peace and calm of his outward appearance, his mind raced. Raced. He considered the word delicately and smiled at the accidental justice. His mind was indeed racing from the events of the day, the same way the impatient young foal champed and strained to join the older horses on the track.

And it wasn't so long ago that you were one of those foals.

While his friend steeped his aches and pains, Holmes bent over his chemistry table by the window. Anyone who had been with them at the canal would have recognized the looks of the tiny phial of misty liquid he was pouring so very carefully, drop by drop, into an assortment of slides and dishes. The mother-phial perched in the lip of the window that was adding so much chilly draught to the sitting room.

"Hmm!" he exclaimed to himself on occasion. His black brows drew together, and then sprang apart with violence. "Now isn't that a bit out of the ordinary."

From upstairs, a muffled voice betrayed Watson's departure of the bath and an attention to their upcoming meal. Holmes was aware on some level that his body was protesting its treatment and food would be pleasant for it, but if he ignored its tiresome chatter, the signals would go away. Tobacco helped.

Watson strolled in wrapped well in a heavy weight dressing-gown by the time Holmes had finished smoking his way through the problem at hand.

"Our landlady has outdone herself." Watson breathed in fragrant steam off the heavy tray in his hands. "Holmes, if you do not join me, I shall declare your palate handicapped."

"Mmm ?" Holmes muttered absently. "Watson, it is quite unlike you to interrupt my train of thought."

"And so I would not, if you had fulfilled your personal obligations." The doctor narrowed his gaze. "I believe I said something about regular meals and rest before I left our rooms this morning."

Holmes regarded the (so far bullet-free) ceiling, but he had to laugh. Watson could be as bad as a broody hen.

"I promise it will not be beyond your abilities." The doctor spooned boiled potatoes and bacon into their dishes. "And I vow to you, if I witness you sitting here, and eating without complaint, I shall not trouble you for the rest of the evening."

"But what if we have a visitor?" Holmes murmured. He knew he sounded like a diva, but teasing Watson was such an enjoyable pastime.

"If we have a visitor, I will bar leave you to your nicotinic contemplation." Watson pressed his hand over his chest. There were days in which it was clear Watson was joking. On other days he was not readable.

Holmes surrendered in good grace.

"I say," the doctor finally rubbed at his forearms after looking twice at the fire-grate. "It feels cold here."

"The window is open."

"Whatever for?"

"I need to keep the sample cool, Watson. Albeit not as drastically as I believed." The detective put away a last bite of bread and rose to bend forward and dip down, not unlike a hunting heron. "Here it is." He plucked up the tiny phial and returned to the table. "Hold it carefully with the pincers. The heat of your hand could be enough to disrupt the matrix."

Watson gingerly complied. His right hand had not suffered from Maiwand, and his grip was delicate and steady as he held the phial of canal water with the tool. "I see nothing unusual."

"Do you remember noting the ice crystals in the water?"

"Of course. They are the same flakes that I see here."

"Are you certain?" Holmes murmured with a quick, fey twist to his sharp lips and a glitter in his grey eye that was hardly to be trusted.

Watson slowly closed his mouth on the verge of a protest. Holmes could be peculiar, but he had a motive for everything. He squinted and looked closer. He held the phial before the low light of the table-lamp.

His gasp made Holmes clap his hands in delight. His words made him laugh.

"Why, some of this is not ice at all! I see scales off a fish!"

"Ah, but not at first, Watson! But as vital a clue as the ice, the confirmed presence of fish is even more so."

Watson stared at him in steady bafflement for a few breaths, trying to figure out the meaning behind those strange words.

"What is the clue?"

Holmes bowed, introducing Watson to his microscope where a mirror was already poised to reflect the ambient light up and into the stage. Now thoroughly intrigued, the doctor settled before the device and peered down the eyepiece.

The blurry, some-like form adjusted into focus, revealing a cycloid scale typical of the soft fin-ray fish fish he preferred to catch for the table or sport: Salmon, trout, loach . . . .

"This looks like a grayling scale more than anything else, but I suspect it is from a more common owner." Watson shook his head. "A grayling would have little business in London waters unless they developed an air bladder."

"Bravo. You see the domesticated *Carassius Auratus*, commonly called the silverfish. One or two scales may have possibly come from their sibling goldfish. They were subtly tinted. One was markedly so with an interesting reddish brush along the spine. I have set that one aside to admire later."

Watson only shook his head. "Holmes, what could be important? Goldfish and silverfish are carp. The canals are packed with carp and other common feeders."

"Goldfish are not as common as one might think." Holmes turned grim. "I do not believe these fish were from any canal."

Watson thought about this for a long minute. Sometimes it still unsettled him, Holmes's unnatural patience with letting him muddle through his own reasoning to an outcome that may or might not be correct.

"The water in the man's lungs was far too clean to be in the canal in the first place. That ought to be proved without much difficulty in a court."

Holmes nodded. "And we may be grateful that the canals are reprehensible conduits of runoff from the dirty streets and roofs at this time of year! But we have extra data in the form of these scales."

"Extra data?"

"Our killer is careless." Holmes grew serious enough that when he took back the sample, it was to peer darkly into the delicate contents of the thin glass phial. "Careless from his over-confidence. Perhaps arrogance."

"Arrogant because he took a life?" Watson felt rather like a fish himself. He just needed to find an awkward cast to catch the hook.

"Arrogance because this man was drowned in a private fish-pond not far from the canals." Holmes's long white fingers tapped impatiently upon the table-cloth. Watson picked out the opening of Handel's grasshopper-quick Water Music in the pattern.

"Holmes, I do not see."

"Oxygen."

I beg your pardon?"

"Carp are favoured pets of the limpid ponds, Watson, for they need little upkeep. I doubt even a mathematician could tell us how many of these little fish are thrown into the canals or even the Thames after they have been won or purchased on impulse at one of the markets. They can take cold temperatures admirably – you have seen the open bowls being sold in the marketplace for holiday table decorations!"

"I once had the pleasure of dining with a Raja who allowed fish to swim in a stone reservoir that chilled his wines," Watson commented with a sudden smile on his face. "He had silverfish for his white wine, and goldfish for his Tokay."

"No red, Watson?"

"Red Gurnards in a salt pool!"

Holmes snickered in that special way he had when someone's creative initiative allowed him some unusual artistic license.

"Most of the tame fish end their lives swiftly in the wild. Not from lack of ability as much as the liability of their colouring. The brighter the fish, the easier the supper for the heron or crane, or the larger fish. Eels are especially talented in hunting." Holmes's distaste at anything snakeish was clear. "The killing-pool of our unfortunate friend was a private pond in which fish were stocked, but it was also kept very clean. Such waters may be found in the small properties of the wealthy, in order to add delight to their innumerable garden parties. They are nearly always within a stone's toss of the house itself. All the better to discourage hungry fishers. I should not be surprised if this was a fountain or reflection pool."

Watson's experience with India had left him a little prejudicially slanted in favour of refection pools. "You may have some trouble determining the pool in question."

"Possibly." Holmes's eyes were clouding over with distraction. He rose and replaced the phial back in the tiny cold draught by the window. "And possibly not. It all depends on the vanity . . . ."

"The vanity of . . . ?" Watson asked, and then stopped himself.

Holmes had already forgotten he was there.

"He what – ?" Lestrade knew he sounded unreasonable, but he didn't care. "How did Bradstreet get the common cold? What . . . what microscopic infidel could get through that paint thinner he carries on his hip?"

Hopkins shrugged under his heavy coat. "Doesn't seem right. He never even noticed the cholera outbreak."

"Which one?" Constable Crane wondered from the side.

"Either of them."

Lestrade stamped to his office with a vague sense of betrayal. Bradstreet got sick only about once every other year. It threw his evening plans awry to say the least. Three days abed! Well, his wife's mothering and that Scottish liquor and heather honey ought to take care of him soon enough.

Good God, but it was good to be back in the office. He gleefully threw himself into the dry legal forms and dull summaries. It couldn't compare to trodding the concrete all day, but something was better than nothing. Nothing was his own version of Hell and he dared anyone prove different.

Updates on court hearings. Appeals. Complaints registered and deemed worthy of an inspector's regard – never in short supply. Only two suicides among the Bobbies? That was good. And looters plucked off a flooding culvert blocked over the Thames' neep tides. Ugh, they'd be fumigating the entire gaol after that!

London was large enough to encourage all sorts of disasters, limited only to the imagination of the persons behind the acts. By the time mid-day shone its harsh, sooty light into his tiny window, a quarter of the papers were dealt with – they were all piffling, humdrum little bits of clear-cut crime and punishment – and he was ready for his second round of strong Pekoe. Lord in Heaven, grant that all of our criminals be this stupid every day. He picked up the next envelope off the pile without thinking, stopped when he saw the return address. A small symbol was stamped in grey ink on the lip. Lestrade would recognise that five-petal rose anywhere.

Sod it.

He slit the letter open and was re-reading the contents when Youghal popped his head inside the door.

"Hullo, Lestrade." The young man smiled. "How's your hand?"

Still reading, Lestrade lifted his bandaged break. "Healing nicely, thank you. I'll just have to remember not to get into a fight or three with it."

"That's what I told Johnson, Todd, and MacAlpin. All three of them got their toes broken in that fight at the waterfront."

"You've just got to love those icy wet blocks for boots. Did you tell them where we keep the wraps and knitbone?"

Younger and elder policeman chatted a bit on the topic of feet for the Bobby. Neither dreamt to suggest their mates go to the doctor for the breaks. Even an honest Crow would tell them there was nothing he could do but wrap it up tight, and the Bobbies already knew how to do that for free. He would then tell them to be careful of walking and put that foot up every chance they got, which they couldn't do if they didn't want to be dismissed for laziness. The Brotherhood took care of its own, but you couldn't squander your chances. One single slip, be it real or mistaken, and you'd be tarred for years.

Youghal made a face as Lestrade described a former break that managed to split the three outer toe-bones on his left foot 'cross the middle, and how the landlady had made him drink a swear-to-Heaven-its-true slimy tea every night that tasted like a marsh-mallow root with the dirt

147

still on the bark. Because of – or despite – all of this mothering, he'd been back to normal in only two months. "Well, glad to hear it. Was wondering if you'd like to join us at The Elegant Barley for a drink tonight?"

Lestrade was a moment in collecting his voice. "Ordinarily I'd say yes, Youghal, but I've been invited to dinner elsewhere."

Youghal parted in good grace. When he was gone, Lestrade rested his chin in his hand and dropped the letter on his desk. It angled butterflylike over the previous correspondence.

Dinner indeed. Lestrade had no real idea on what "dinner" meant to someone like Bartram of Lancashire . . .

. . . but he doubted Clea's cooking was part of it.

The Bronze Farthing, despite the humble name and elderly two-storied architecture, was downright arrogant in its general air of defiance. The night-crowd was a goodly share of the weary men who spent long hours working the Thames' Grand Junction, starting at the quiet waters of the canals and finishing with the sweet water of the upper Thames. Their tiredness mixed with cheap drinks and buskers to a natural gallimaufry of debates, arguments, long-standing grudges, and open declarations of war.

From the first storey one had a fine view of the ruckus going on at the ground floor. Diners here paid a bit more for the honour of not having to deal with those fine debates.

The tall man with an oversized cloth cap and rope-stained fingers watched several promising examples of linguistic fervor from his position at the rail that ringed the balcony diners. He and his companion had met at the tavern nearly an hour ago, "waiting for a comrade", as they explained to the barkeep. His hawk-sharp eyes missed very little, and several times a quicksilver smile flickered over his thin lips as something struck his fancy.

"If the man I suspect is behind this fascinating example of varied crime," he murmured, "we should see him here. Perhaps not tonight, but soon." Not many more minutes had passed when he lifted his eyebrows and tilted his head to his drinking companion. "You're not very verbal tonight, my dear fellow."

Watson allowed a single moment to pass after Holmes's innocuous remark, and then simply turned his head and looked at him. The false scar Holmes had painstakingly fastened on his neck to suggest a vicious fight and an inability to talk gleamed with an unwholesome life of its own.

Holmes was rather proud of that act of artistry. It had taken nearly two hours and a half-cup of bran from Mrs. Hudson's kitchen that he hoped she did not plan to use.

Good old fellow that he was, Watson was not going to leave the confines of the character Holmes had drafted for him, even though their table was perfectly private. To clarify that, the balcony that ringed above the bottom-level of the tavern was vaguely private, but the selfishness abounding at every table ensured no one could hear a blessed thing past a six-foot radius.

If Holmes had known Watson was capable of silence on this level, he would have employed him for this kind of work long ago.

Watson was still glaring at him over his mug of shandy-gaff. [3] He had barely blinked since Holmes's ridiculous remark. Holmes buried his smile in his stein. Watson's fingers twitched on the table before sharply tapping the letter "*K*" in Morse Code.

"Really, it's a fine disguise." Holmes's confession garnered no expression of appreciation on the doctor. "Normally I would ask one of the C.I.D.'s to help me out, but there wasn't any time." He waited another moment. "I put it to you. We must re-work your writings, my dear fellow. You always have yourself cited as a man who is easily impressed at my trivial abilities. I assure you, you are not so easily impressed with me tonight." A new movement in the front of the tavern caught his eyes. For a moment Holmes looked quite amazed before he slumped back into the disguise of a salt-stained laborer. "Well, well! Friend Lestrade is keeping pleasant company in this day and age," Holmes marveled, still too quietly for anyone to hear him. Watson's eyes widened, and he slipped to a shadowy part of the rail to observe unnoticed.

Lestrade looked anything but overjoyed to be in the company he was keeping – half a rugby team full of giants with ink-black hair and sunburned meaty faces.

"Bartram Cheatham," Holmes's eyebrows had gone as far into his browline as Nature could permit. "I wonder what he is doing out of the gate on a night like this? Was he finally disqualified?" The detective could not keep the hope out of his voice.

Lestrade would have rather faced many other fates than agree to dinner with a man who had decided to be his enemy. The invitation, however, had not been phrased in a way that brooked any kind of refusal.

"Glad y'could make it, Inspector," Bartram began.

Lestrade could smell impending disaster. Bartram was not the family's usual figurehead. That honour appeared to go to the oldest of the bunch, a greying man named Myron who had the look of an office jockey. Most men of that stripe had more comfort in numbers than people, and Myron was not looking comfortable now.

149

"You implied this was your only free day," Lestrade reminded him quietly. He noted a pale flicker in Myron's face, and did not know to be worried or encouraged with the oldest brother chose a chair far away from the whole proceedings, tilting his chair back against the thick plaster wall. The youngish one named Robert seemed to want to gravitate to Myron, but lacked the nerve to do so.

Cutler and Wallace, who had been introduced to him as "businessmen" were another story. They were ready to fight, but not look the kind who fought outside their own plans. Surprise them and they would likely flee. Andrew was openly trouble. He had a saucy air and the look of someone willing to fight . . . and win.

He should have warned the other detectives about tonight. He'd known there would be trouble, but he'd foolishly thought this would be just himself and Bartram.

Idiot, idiot, idiot.

Bartram was smiling. It was not his usual face in Lestrade's presence. Over the throng of the crowd he made a beckoning signal and Lestrade barely made out the nod of a waiter, stepping to the back kitchen. "I ordered dinner ahead of time," he grunted. "Hope you don't mind."

"Not at all," Lestrade said slowly. He was seeking a quick exit.

Holmes leaned so far over the rail Watson grabbed his sleeve. The detective glared his annoyance, saw the doctor's icy stare, and switched to a contrite smile, the kind a child uses when trying to charm a humorless guardian. "I fear our good inspector will be in need of assistance," he whispered. "Bartram has just signaled to bar the windows and door."

Watson's eyes narrowed, which made the tattoo Holmes had painted on his cheek to coil inward, like a pit viper readying to strike. No one need to ask for Watson's help in a fight. All they need do is point out the injustice.

"I think it is about to start." Holmes's grey eyes glistened in a feverish anticipation as a waiter strode through the crowd. "That wrestler looks a bit too eager for that tray to be set down. I suspect the contents will be the instigation."

Lestrade stared unblinking at the potato pie before him. In the back of his mind, he noted that several of the Cheathams were wearing stunned expressions. So they weren't all like Bartram – bully for them.

"Well?" Bartram smirked in his face. "Eat up. I tried to find something suitable. Cheer ho."

He barely heard past the roaring in his ears, but . . . Two thrashings, public insults, taunts, and collusion with the devil responsible for a brother's death, another's imprisonment, and his own disownment.

150

And now the insult of a potato pie. A man can only be pushed so far. Bartram was still smirking when Lestrade, displaying his reputation for being quick and energetic, rose to his feet and made Bartram a hat of the steaming vegetables.

"Blast!" Holmes swore and, to Watson's horror, leapt over the balcony and plummeted a full storey to plant his feet in the middle of the plank table. Every object on the surface catapulted into the air. Before anyone could react, he had selected a promising victim in the ranks and was pummeling him with pugilistic eagerness that Watson, as a doctor, could not approve of.

Watson reserved the exasperated sigh for later. Once a British soldier, always a British soldier. Following a mate into battle was never problematic. It was a vital quality for the few hardy souls who tried to protect Holmes from himself. He joined the fray with considerably more dignity than his friend. He used the stairs, but he also took a moment to pick up his large walking stick on his way down.

Lestrade's plans did not include walking out of the tavern in one piece – he doubted walking would even be a factor. But the look on the wrestler's face as he was kick-boxed into the wall was headier than the strongest drink. For the briefest moment, Lestrade's faith in a dry Brythonic God was refreshed.

"Foul!" Andrew Cheatham blurted. "The little rat's fighting French!"

"I *am* French, you idiot!" Lestrade dropped, good hand on the floor to leverage his turn, and used the torque to spin himself into a *coup de pied tournant*. The impact into the breast-bone knocked Robert into the wall-beam, and if the kick didn't put him out, his skull against the age tempered oak surely did. The Bronze Farthing had been a tavern before Henry VIII first contemplated legal infidelity. Someone with a fist of iron and the stench of Thames mixed with French cologne – obviously Andrew – grabbed from behind and yanked him off his feet – an instant disadvantage – he braced himself as his attacker lifted him for a sobering punishment.

"My friend is kind to your lack of education," Lestrade heard his rescuer's voice from literally out of the blue – and he had the time to ponder the irony.

The reinforcement had dropped into the centre of the plank table, his impact sending shants, tureens, and platters into the stratosphere that had disgorged him. With a single blow Andrew was knocked to the earth. "To be more precise," Sherlock Holmes's strident tones rang throughout the tavern. As a man, the wave of filthy humanity that had been poised to crash on the tableau stopped at the bizarre sight.

Holmes's grey eyes glittered like unholy pearls as he dropped into a boxer's stance. "Mr. Lestrade is a *Breton* – from a fine and unique province unequaled in the world. They are English to the eyes of the French, and French to the English, although they are quite neither. They have been staunchly Celtic since the 5th century, have endured waves of invasion from everyone, and thus can fight any which way they so choose."

Holmes had ripped his coat off and insultingly tossed it over the face of the ineffectual barkeep. "As would anyone in a truly inspiring fight."

Lestrade panted, getting to his feet. "Right now I can think of worse things than being rescued by an amateur detective."

"Rescue? My dear Lestrade, we're simply ensuring the fight is fair." Holmes somehow dissuaded the truth of that by the way his lips were coiling up at the edges.

Lestrade thought Goliath must have seen a similar smile on a shepherd named David. "Well, then!" he crowed with his fist up and parallel. "Who is next?"

Cutler and Wallace (as expected), ran for Lestrade simultaneously. They fell short of the mark when their heads impacted neatly as a ball against a cricket bat by two very large, dark brown hands. Lestrade wondered if he could be any more surprised when the "twins" sagged down to reveal a smug Watson from the back. Then he took in the sight of the doctor, who was as black-skinned as a full-term sailor, adorned in battered sailing togs, a large, crusted scar over his throat like a second mouth, and on his face . . . .

"My God, that's a wonderful tattoo," Lestrade breathed.

Watson grinned, nearly giving the little detective a heart attack at the skillfully applied job of rotting teeth.

"You're working, aren't you?" Lestrade muttered to Holmes. "I understand that would be a cavil at this point. Thank you for coming."

"You'll have to forgive Watson," Holmes murmured back. "He was rendered mute from a glancing blow off a naval saber during the Canal Labor Dispute." Holmes's lightning smile flared and subsided to its usual low embers. "Although I confess, it has damaged his ability to express himself not at all," the detective admired. "He has unexplored possibilities in the stage."

One might say that about you, Lestrade thought. He ducked a flying tin cup.

"Five down," Holmes gloated as Bartram staggered to his feet, his face the shade of raw beef. "I suggest from the perspective of a humble observer that this fracas be resolved between the instigator and the attacked."

Myron had not moved since his initial retreat against the wall when the spoil had first erupted.

"I'm staying clear of this," he grunted.

"Myron, you coward!" Bartram seethed, saliva flying from his mouth.

"You seem big enough to deal with him." Myron retorted. The comment sliced like a scythe.

Bartram purpled. He rose up like a stone giant. "Right, then," he spat. "Boxing and wrestling. Fair enough."

"Hardly," Holmes drawled. "But we shall see who will win – wrestler or savatier."

"So long as he doesn't get his hands on me," Lestrade muttered, and slipped into position. "Cheatham. Whenever you're ready."

NOTES

1. Thin bubbly ice. Usually only strong enough to bear up the weight of a cat. Crane still has some West Somerset words in his vocabulary.
2. Drachm = 1/8th of an ounce.
3. Ale and gin mixture.

Chapter XI

One should never count on getting full satisfaction for a long-term humiliation. It is statistically impossible. Weeks of piled-upon aggravation weren't going to be addressed by a few kicks, however well placed they might be. On the other hand, Bartram Cheatham was confident (or angry) enough to just go for Lestrade with all pistons.

Lestrade's choices were made simple when he realised his opponent had thrown caution to the winds and was just aiming to wrap his big hands about his neck.

From his viewpoint, Watson didn't have the best show in the house, but he did see the reactions of half the tavern at the sight – and sound – of the little man's spinning kick snap into Cheatham's shin. Lestrade looked as though he had tried to kick a tree – and a petrified one at that – but Cheatham's shin-bone came out the poorer. The sound of a fracture more than proved. The doctor winced, knowing full well that Cheatham was about to have a brief but blessed moment of battle-fueled painlessness, and then . . . .

Cheatham roared.

The sound promised pain and revenge and everything else imagination could conjure. Watson thought of a bull crocodile that was the terror of his Australian childhood. Holmes quickly spun to suss the spectators, his left fist poised for mayhem. Two unknown youngsters promptly jumped him.

The fight, alas, was celebrated by more fights erupting in satellite explosions throughout the tavern. Eventually it came to the point where even the chucker-outs could not ignore the property damage. Lestrade, Holmes, and Watson carried themselves out of the premises barely a step ahead of the third wave of seizures. Lestrade and Holmes were laughing.

Watson, still in character, was shaking silently. They stumbled to a stop at the edge of the canal and sank down on the stone wall while lantern-beriggged fishermen in search of misdirected eels and flotsam floated by with bewildered expressions.

"A tavern full of cloggers, and we survived without a broken bone." Watson was rightfully amazed.

"Good Lord." Lestrade lifted his bruised face to the moon-banked clouds. The cold air felt shamefully good on his injuries. "I haven't done a *coup-de-vache* in years. Good thing I still know how."

"That would be the kick that broke Mr. Cheatham's shin?" Holmes glanced at Watson. "That is commonly known as the 'cow-kick', Watson, and I assure you, it is not a thing to be forgotten."

"I doubt I will. I saw some things that reminded me of the Highlander kick in a fight . . . but the English mindset against using anything but one's fists is threatening the form." (This observation was separate from the good, solid blood-sports of the working-man.) The doctor pulled a clean handkerchief out of his sleeve and began wiping his face. "May I please take this scar off, Holmes?"

"Be my guest."

Lestrade retched as Watson peeled the horrible thing off his neck. The doctor regarded it a moment and flipped it into the canal. "No one will find that but the eels," the little detective remarked. "How is it your tattoo isn't running from sweat?"

"Holmes painted me with a dye and henna mixture. I won't look myself again until I steam in the Turkish baths every day for a week." Watson sounded put out – possibly from the future damage to his bank account.

"If I forgot to mention it before, Lestrade, congratulations. Chausson should be mandatory for Scotland Yard – For your information, Watson, fewer people are harmed in the sport than any other. There's also the benefit that if one confines the blows to their feet, they spare their hands for report-writing."

"That's encouraging," Watson commented ruefully. "But Mr. Cheatham can hardly say that." He suddenly laughed, very softly. Amusement at someone's pain was so unlike him the others stared. "Five men versed in Lancashire wrestling, considered the most damaging style on the island, appear to be a poor match against French boxing, English boxing, and good Scottish rugby."

Lestrade laughed until he felt ill. "It was worth it to see the look on their faces when you hung Andrew on those antlers. They've been terrified at the quality of my company – Now that they've met me, I'm sure their fears are justified."

"I confess I don't understand what exactly instigated the fisticuffs," Holmes mused. "But it was clear Bartram meant to create that reaction from you."

Watson cleared his throat and pointed to the remains of the pie, which Lestrade was still wearing on his left sleeve.

"Potato?" Holmes inquired blankly.

"It's a Lancashire dish," Lestrade said darkly. "Meatless. It's commonly known as 'Fatherless Pie'." He gritted his teeth. "Someone told him I was disowned."

"Ah," Holmes sniffed. "Quimper, no doubt."

"Wait a – ! Is that what you were doing in there? Looking for that greasy fox?" Lestrade blinked as the puzzle-pieces finally fell in place.

"I suppose this was Mr. Cheatham's attempt at being clever – a first attempt, I would hope. There is much room for improvement."

"All the room in the world," Watson said darkly, conjuring a smile from his companions. "What say you we find a more sedate establishment and have a glass to celebrate? I hear The Malmsey Keg has a new run on black ciders." [1]

"Now that appeals." Lestrade climbed to his feet wearily. They fell into step by the canal, the carnivale sounds of the tavern fading in the distance. The fishermen seemed glad of their departure.

"Chausson remains one of my favorite spectator sports." Holmes paused to yawn – a motion that made his fresh bruises stretch in the moonlight. Watson openly shuddered. "Not that I have the skill for it. Singlestick is my closest analogy. But I am surprised, Lestrade. If a renowned wrestler seeks to add you to his list of enemies, surely he would have done well to investigate the colour of your gloves." Holmes slipped a look to Watson. "He has worn the golden for five years."

"He's smart, but not bright," Lestrade said curtly. "To be blunt, it may be a consequence of his career." He wearily began dusting the worst remains of the tavern off his hat. "But I'm sure that will remain a mystery."

Holmes saw Watson make a gesture behind Lestrade. Holmes's eyes lit up. "I see. Lestrade, could Mr. Cheatham's damaged brain possibly be under the impression that you would have attentions directed at his sister?"

Lestrade prayed for strength even as he winced. "A policemen and a Mill Heiress?" He retorted with just a bit too much heat. "That would be a fine thing, now, wouldn't it?" And despite his scorn, a part of him was relieved. No power in London would encourage their acquaintance now. It scalded, but nothing would have come out of it anyway. Her family was against even their platonic friendship.

He was shocked when Holmes made no contemptuous response to that, but merely looked curious. "If she is an heiress, why would she be operating that establishment?"

Lestrade looked at Holmes as if he had lost as many brain-cells as Cheatham. "She's an independent woman, and not about to sit idle."

"I understood she is a *former* heiress," Watson mused.

"It is close enough for the paint." Lestrade's hat would have to do. He jammed it on his head. "Social works are all fine if one wants to whittle their time away while waiting for a husband to come along and provide for her for the rest of her life, but that's a mystery I've never fathomed. She wants to work, and these aren't the mill-towns where a lady can work and still be respected."

"I don't think anyone has ever fathomed that puzzle of society," Watson commented. "It's easier to view everyone in the same light. At least, it is for me." He grinned. His amusement at life was Gaelic as opposed to Lestrade's Gallic, but they understood each other. "My people served the nobility. That doesn't mean we fathomed them. We just had a developed instinct on what was required."

"I wondered how you could bear Mr. Holmes." Lestrade jabbed, eliciting a pleased laugh from the detective. He must be taking the drug again. Watson's expression confirmed it.

"You are in rare form, Inspector. Do not stop on my part." Holmes's teeth gleamed in the lamplight, although he was far from predatory. The only part of the man that struck Lestrade as primitive was his strange relish for the facets of life no one else found digestible.

"Yes, Doctor. I have noticed that while you perform the same amount of respect to everyone, your friend gives the courtesy of universal irreverence," Lestrade grinned.

Holmes naturally took that as a compliment. As it led to his largess in purchasing the first three rounds of drinks, Lestrade could hardly fault it.

Shouting and pounding sent Clea out of bed, into her dressing-gown and flying down the stairs. Her father was already stepping into the drawing room similarly attired. Children and wives of the Cheatham sept bustled in from every available doorway.

"Bartram!" someone cried. The big wrestler was red-faced and squirming on his canvas stretcher. Myron and Robert looked worse for the wear for bearing his weight, but that was little enough compared to Andrew, Cutler, and Wallace. "What happened to you?"

"That little detective of yours is what did it." Andrew turned and gave a hateful look such as Clea had never seen, not ever from her kin. "He's broken his shinbone! He won't be fighting again for a good long time!"

Clea remembered little of what happened after that. With Andrew's words, a universal censure struck. With Bartram's sudden lack of income, a great deal of financial stability had left the House. Even Robert's wife looked horrified at her.

Charles Cheatham pressed for details. They were grudgingly supplied, but the old fighter was experienced in tomfoolery. He wrung out the details as he produced a salve of his own blend that smelled like a Christmas tree combined with mint. Bartram took the application of the stuff and the plaster bandaged without complaint. The slug of whisky put him out for the remainder of the night.

". . . Well, if Quimper is involved in it even indirectly, you might as well say he's planned the whole sorry mess." Lestrade gave up on his collar. He pulled it off and stuffed it in the one coat pocket that wasn't ripped open. The euphoria of finally doing something was starting to dull under the knowledge that there would be no more visits to The Rose.

Best to spare her that humiliation.

"He is clever." Holmes paused to knock a rock out of his shoe. As the shoe had a hole in the sole for the sake of disguise, he was often stopping. "But he thinks too highly of himself. I would give much to find his superiors."

"No doubt someone with a completely respectable façade," Watson pointed out. Of the three, he looked the least off for the fight. Lestrade thought it might have something to do with his approach. He preferred to toss his opponents as far away as possible, thus avoiding any chance for further unwanted contact. When Cutler and Wallace had tried for another round, Watson had merely tipped the table over their bodies, pinning them to the floor. *Would a term at Blackheath count as professional training?* thought Lestrade He would have to ask Bradstreet the next time he saw him.

"Bloody 'ell in a steam engine!"

A knot of sober, well-dressed men were coming out of their own choice of establishment just as they were walking by. Lestrade noted belatedly the wooden sign above the door: The Elegant Barley. Ah, well.

"Geoffrey?" Inspector Bradstreet led the frozen gapes.

Lestrade sighed and stopped in the street. He lifted his hands and spun on one foot so they could take in the full panorama of what had been his next-best suit and coat only five hours ago. At least the ciders numbed the bruises. He was starting to feel ready for another go if the Cheathams came back.

Bradstreet had trouble finding his voice. He took in the fact that his best friend bore a close resemblance to a County Cork scarecrow during the Famine. He put his hand to his head and began to shake it. Lestrade smirked. Bradstreet glared. "Geoffrey Lestrade," he whined like an old woman, "you went to a fight without me!"

The Yarders collapsed into histrionics. Even Gregson. Ah, the Brotherhood.

"I would have invited you, Roger, honestly, but I thought you were still out."

"I did. At least, I still did this morning. A few nips of *How-come-you-so*, and right as rain by suppertime." Bradstreet bowed slightly as if a close brush with Death's Angel was no more than a small inconvenience to his constitution.

"You look like you fell asleep in front of a Clyde Engine," Gregson said with his usual tact. He looked past Lestrade. "Who're your friends, Ratty?"

"Gregson, you either have partaken too much or not enough." Sherlock Holmes's voice vibrated the air, and Lestrade relished the newly-widened eyes. "Or perhaps you need glasses."

"I'll be – is that Watson in the back?" MacDonald's jaw slacked open. "Where the deevil were you? Is tha' a real tattoo – Watson, what happened to your teeth?"

"Watson and I were conducting an investigation at The Bronze Farthing when we ran afoul of a Cheatham plot against your comrade," Holmes answered grandly. "Did you know Bartram of Lancashire was unaware Mr. Lestrade is a golden gloves fighter?"

Gregson threw back his head and roared. He leaned on to Bradstreet and Youghal for support. "So there is a patron saint of Scotland Yard!"

"I told you we've got two," Youghal protested. "The Archangel Michael, and Saint Sebastian – but save him for when you're workin' the beat during epidemics."

Bradstreet gave them all a bad look. "I can't believe I missed this. You owe me, sir," he said frostily. "I'd have crawled out of my own coffin to see that."

"What, you would have missed your own funeral?" Lestrade grinned.

Bradstreet snorted. "Can't have a funeral without the guest of honour, you pancake-eater. It'd just be postponed."

MacDonald peered Watson up and down, studying the makeup. "I'd swear that was woad." He scowled. "Holmes, how did you get that crack een the canine?"

"And he's off again," Gregson sighed. "I'd say goodbye, but he won't even notice. Mr. Holmes, have you ever thought of pin-money teaching the C.I.D. a thing or two about your ghastly makeup skills?"

"Some of them are medically hazardous, Gregson," Holmes protested. He caught Watson's expression. "Within reason," he added. Watson did not look fooled. "And expensive," he finished. "But I would be interested in sharing."

"Well, come on." Bradstreet stepped backwards and held the door open. "You need to tell us all about it. Make it a good enough story, Geoffrey, and I'll chip a downer [2] for your laundry bill." He smirked. "You too, Mr. Holmes."

"Oh, but I couldn't – "

"We can always ask the doctor what it was you did," Bradstreet said sweetly.

Gregson's face lit up like a Roman candle at the thought. He turned an angelic beam to the amused doctor. Holmes openly squashed a look of horror.

"Oh, I don't know, he's not talking too much tonight." Lestrade led the way with good-natured resignation. "He was rendered mute by a naval saber during the last Canal Labor Dispute, you know. Which reminds me, Roger: Does rugby qualify as professional combat?"

"It is if you're facing down an Irish charge . . . ."

"Clea?"

Solitude and a knitted throw made a better companion than the silent anger of the Cheathams. Clea had fled to the isolation of the drawing room. She looked up from her teary study of the fireplace.

"Clea." Myron shifted his weight. "We're coming in to talk." He produced his big arm and their father joined his side. The three passed a tight, uneasy silence while the fire did all the talking. Clea could not bear to look at either of them.

Myron spoke first. "What happened was Bartram's fault," he began slowly. He was the most intelligent brother, but he had ironically had the fewest opportunities for his brain. Times had been poorer in his youth. He was not comfortable with displaying his brains. "He provoked the fight. I don't know what got into him. He never used to be this way."

"No." Clea agreed thinly. "Not before we moved here."

"Would Mr. Quimper be able to talk to him?" their father asked, but he sounded as if he already knew the answer that was coming.

"Mr. Quimper is behind all this," Clea said bitterly. "Look at him! Bartram can't or won't do anything without his consent!"

160

Myron rubbed his square cheeks. "He has us over a barrel, Clea." He said it as gently as possible to his sister, but the words were for Charles. "He knows too much about our family transactions. Bartram was working illegal fights. That's where a lot of that money was coming in. One word to the police and Bartram will be wearing the broad arrow."

Clea felt bile rise in her throat. "Is that why he pays court?" she hissed. "Because he knows we have little enough to offer him?"

"We have plenty to offer Mr. Quimper," Myron said heavily. "We have a respectable name. He would like to hide behind it, conduct his own activities." His gloomy face was even more so in the flicker of firelight. "I blame myself for not paying attention. He's my brother."

"I must take the blame." Charles said harshly. "I tried to impress on him the honour of my art. But there is only one Charles Cheatham . . . and many Quimpers." The old man lowered his head. "How much trouble is he in?" he asked heavily.

"I'm not certain." Myron was actually disturbed enough to rise to his feet. He was thicker than Bartram. When he moved he gave the impression of a boulder, rolling with imperfect grace. "At first the advice he gave us was sound. Shares in businesses. Investments in a bank here and there. Then he gave us more lists of investments. I thought at the time the handwriting was similar because he had a secretary. I didn't think that he would be a secret owner in so many . . . ." Myron hesitated. "Varied interests."

"What dust mean, varied?" Charles asked sharply.

"Well, you know how you and Mum invested in the Mill when you were young?" Myron began. "And how you also invested in the companies that made the carding, and the dyes, and the guilds? It made sense to have ownership in some aspect of every part of the Mill." Charles and Clea nodded. "It looks like Mr. Quimper is doing the same thing, only he isn't focusing on one thing like a little Mill." Myron gave up all pretense of being calm and went to the brandy on the table. "He's working on all parts of London that are affected by the water trade." He sipped slowly. "It's easier to smuggle something by water than it is by rail. It's quiet and not restricted to public schedule."

"I think I see," Charles answered heavily.

"The Americans have a phrase, Father." Myron rubbed his graying temples. "They would call Mr. Quimper 'a big fish in a small pond'." I think he's a very clever man who serves a larger master. Someone has to be funding his interests, after all." He passed off that worrisome pronouncement flatly. "I never caught on until a few days ago, yet I waited like a dunce, looking for proof." He breathed out. "Stockbrokers talk. Bankers talk. Investors talk. I went to our solicitors and found many of his

161

partners have . . . dealt with the law in the past. Smuggling. Theft. A suspicion of forgery. He has never been touched, but if you look at the records, he seems to make poor choices in his employees." Myron looked down, twisting his tie-pin. "His employees see prison or swing."

"Like Mr. Lestrade's brothers," Clea whispered.

"He's got Bartram convinced that he must be made happy at all costs. That our entire family fortune rides on his forbearance."

"Does it?" Charles asked sharply.

Myron did not reply at first. Clea felt sick.

"Father . . . he could hurt us very badly. He has the means. He's proven he has the nerve. He as good as pushed Bartram into that fight with the inspector. If things had gone the way Quimper planned, I truly think we'd have a policeman's blood on our conscience." Myron took another drink. "Bartram would be at the mercy of the courts, and we do not have the means to hire proper legal advice."

"But Mr. Quimper does."

"But Mr. Quimper does."

Clea had enough. She rose and poured drinks for herself and Charles. "T'would be simple for someone of his intelligence to plant evidence, make us culpable of some terrible crime. He could easily use us as a figurehead for his business goals, and then allow us to fall when the evidence tracks to us."

"We've never refused a fight." Charles protested. "Not ever. Hold What is Yours," he quoted the family motto.

"In order to fight, we need an opponent." Myron spoke sharply. "Quimper has taken that from us. He owns the wrestling-mat, father. What will he do when he learns his best wrestler is invalided out?" He sank back down to the sofa. "The only place where he seems human is where Clea is concerned."

Clea's hand went to her mouth. "I'll have nothing to do with him!" she protested.

"Nor would we have you." Charles answered sadly. "I wanted the best for you, dear, but the best does not mean this." He leaned forward, hands over his blind eyes. "Our name and reputation . . . ." he muttered over and over. Clea didn't know what was worse: Her father facing the total destruction of the name he had worked for, or the utter helpless fear on Myron's.

NOTES

1. Reference to Cadbury apple ciders. As soon as the cider is drawn, the drink turns black.
2. Sixpence.

Chapter XII

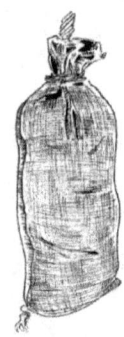

221b Baker Street:

"**W**atson!"

Sherlock Holmes was normally quite careful in rousing a veteran. When they had first roomed together, the detective had learned that the doctor would wake up by degrees simply by the weight of being watched. While Watson had thankfully passed beyond that stage of nerve, it was still not advisable to give him any more shocks than absolutely necessary.

Holmes knew full well he had the most patient of companions. That only extended to indignities he could not control, like his habitual amnesia of manners, meals, and troublesome chemical experiments.

No one deliberately deprived an ex-soldier of sleep without a very good cause.

Watson snapped upright in bed, eyes wide. "Holmes! What is it?"

"Watson, grab your coat. We need to get to Scotland Yard as soon as possible."

"Is it the case?" Watson yanked for his clean change of clothes – already lain out for unpredictable needs such as this one and the hour was late enough to be early for the next.

"This is a strange case," Holmes answered indirectly. His long fingers tapped metronomic emotions against his forearm as he stared out Watson's small window. "I nearly fell for the most typical of mistakes in investigations, my dear fellow. I made an assumption."

An ordinary person would have pressed for further details. Watson knew better. He kept his mouth shut as his fingers flew over his collar and cravat. Holmes pulled his shoes out and held them up. "It will not take long to discern this," he admitted, "but time is of the essence and I would dislike sullying my reputation at the Yard."

"A failure or two would only prove you're human. I doubt the most jealous policeman would grudge you a human moment."

"I refer to how I see my reputation at the Yard, Watson. How another sees me is inconsequential!"

That would be pure arrogance, Watson thought, if it wasn't very true.

"Inspector Gregson, do you have an updated list of the businesses our Jethro Quimper is suspected of influencing?"

" Of course." Gregson pulled the list out of his drawer without a blink. Holmes scanned the paper, eyes taut. "That's not a complete list, though. It's missing a few taverns."

"Such as The Bronze Farthing," Holmes scolded.

"And The Kelpie." Gregson pinked slightly, no doubt thinking of the rescued and elderly owners. "We need proof, y' know."

Holmes sighed through his nose but held back his lecture for another day. "The drowning was at the canals by Little Venice. The stolen flour barrels were emptied in Little Venice. Bartram of Cheatham, Watson tells me, was likely the man who put Lestrade out of work twice. He has a Little Venice address, and he works for Quimper's interests. Where does this all fit in with missing lead and missing seamen?"

"We figured out the missing seamen all right," Gregson protested. "The Norway-Sumatra Line wasn't asking questions about the men they were collecting."

"There are twenty seamen missing, Inspector! Twenty! That is too high a number to attribute to a single company line!" Holmes snapped. "Look beyond the first facts and see into the true facts! You told me yourself that the men arrested at The Kelpie refused to talk! That has Quimper's stamp on it. He is a genius for recruiting people against their will, and controlling them without their knowledge! Now, we have fourteen surviving and six dead men – Would they have any relationship whatsoever with the twenty men who are missing?"

"Tie-mates," Watson blurted. Gregson and Holmes turned to him. Watson flushed. "What if they're tie-mates?"

"Don't know what that would be, Doctor," Gregson condescended, but Holmes's face was already sharpening.

"Co-workers. Mates. Men who serve together on the same ship. They're two halves of a team." The coastal-raised Watson would never understand how anyone could live so close to the sea and be ignorant.

"Tie-mates serve together through thick and thin. If one can't make it, the other won't." Watson shrugged. "I'm not saying it is the explanation."

"You don't have to," Holmes murmured. "Gregson? We are looking for a large structure along the waterfront. Thames-close, but not too close to the canals. The structure would have to provide docking for a twenty-man ship. Be suited for storing large amounts of goods, but well-built enough to keep people. And it would have to be fortified well enough to bar inquisitive detectives and informers from noticing men are being held against their will. It would preferably be settled on the original lands of the city, which puts it just barely out of the jurisdiction of the River Police and into yours."

Gregson swore. "Only Quimper would . . . ." He stamped to his desk and yanked maps. On the third one his thick finger stabbed down. "Here. It has to be the Limehouse Warehouse, named after the Lime Oast of the Thames. Its goods-payable office rests a whole quarter-mile downcurrent on the south shore! Privately owned by The Father Thames Company. Suspected of Quimper's partial ownership. True owners supposed to live somewhere off Venice – the actual Venice, that is. Hard to contact." He scowled. "Goods in metal, gunsmithing, and basic trade . . . ." He gaped for a moment. "Gunsmithing," he repeated.

"*Lead,*" Holmes said succinctly. "Watson, if you would accompany me, please, I believe Inspector Gregson needs to prepare for a rather innovative siege."

"Holmes, wait a moment!"

The detective stopped, whistling for a cab and held his stick up to hold the driver while Watson limped to the kerb.

"What exactly are we looking for?" the doctor demanded.

Holmes grinned. "My good fellow, I finally have a chance to unearth the odious Mr. Quimper's business partners. I've waited almost as long as Lestrade for this day!" He smacked the hansom's ceiling with his stick. "London Library!"

They piled into the cab. "Shouldn't we let Lestrade know?" Watson protested.

"My dear Watson, Lestrade is a professional man. He will not be concerned if I pursue this thread. He is far more worried about another matter close to home."

Watson goggled. "Are you admitting, to me, that you pay enough attention to the softer emotions to realise Lestrade is – ?" He couldn't finish the thought.

166

Holmes chuckled. The sound spread and grew louder. "I hope that your friend Lomax is on duty today," he noted. "Did you bring your revolver?"

"We'll need a revolver at a library?"

"I sincerely hope not. I was thinking about after."

"Are you going to tell me what this is about?" Watson asked with very little hope.

Holmes leaned back in his bench. "Insurance," he said obscurely. "The only legally sanctioned form of blackmail."

"Mr. Lestrade!"

Lestrade's first reaction was to put his back against the nearest wall. He watched as Myron Cheatham lifted both hands in a peace sign, puffing his way through the crowd.

"Inspector," Mr. Cheatham gasped, "you were the closest authority. I couldn't find a constable anywhere. They seem to have vanished off the map!"

The old chestnut held that one never saw a Bobby when they needed one. They were only seen four times in one hour when they patrolled their beat. "I assure you they're working," he said curtly. As battered as he still was from the fight, it was easier to keep it simple. "What can I do for you, sir?"

"I need to speak with you!" Myron insisted. High spots of pink brushed across his face. "Inspector, it is important!"

"I never said it wasn't," Lestrade protested. "What is happening?"

"Clea didn't come home last night." Myron wheezed. "Mr. Quimper phrased his intentions to her yesterday when he came to see Bartram."

Lestrade paled. "Mr. Cheatham," he said slowly, "tell me everything that happened."

"Mr. Quimper showed up right after dinner." Myron Cheatham started. "We were having our drinks in the parlour . . . and . . . he knocked on the door himself." Distress watered the other man's eyes. "We had to let him in!"

Lestrade wouldn't have. Bloody social climbers. He kept his mouth shut and waited. Myron continued . . . .

Clea had not been paying attention to much of anything. Her thoughts had wrapped in herself and in a rare moment of self-pity – she did not understand or recognise depression – she took to bed where no one would bother her.

167

She admitted she was surprised to fall asleep for hours past her usual time. When she awoke it was approaching supper, and she told herself it was all about the drinks she'd had in the drawing room the night before.

Bartram had been moved to the couch, his leg wrapped in thick bandages soaked in plaster. She watched him carefully. He watched her. Neither actually spoke. Clea worried over the bowls of stew and bread bought from the nearest bake-oven. She was grateful that a broken shin did nothing to Bartram's appetite.

"Stop looking like that," her father had murmured into her ear.

Clea forgot herself. "How dust know what I'm up to?"

Charles Cheatham turned his blind eyes Heaven-ward. "I'm blind, not silly-pated, my dear girl," he pointed out. "Nor have I lived to the days of my forgetfulness."

Bartram dozed much of the evening, floating on the release of drugs. Clea had no faith that would last. She had endured broken bones too, and the opium fruits lasted but a brief time before they played havoc on the dreams. She preferred a clear mind.

In deference to Bartram and the strain on the family, the drinks were excavated early. They were gathered around the first round when Mr. Quimper paid an unexpected call.

"He proposed to her." Myron choked. "He bowed like he was some high gentleman, and he owned as to how he would be deeply honoured for the privilege of our name to his."

He had brought a bottle of wine for Bartram as a convalescence-gift, made Robert and Myron's children laugh with a few droll anecdotes about traveling in cold weather, and assured the family that Bartram's finances would not be harmed. It was a poor agent who did not account for emergencies. Charles Cheatham nearly sagged with relief. Clea dropped her eyes to the floor.

And then, when the time for brandy and cigars emerged, and Clea was all too glad to leave with the rest of the women, Jethro Quimper had most respectfully inquired if she had any suitors. Charles Cheatham, of course, had to say she had none. It was the first time the Cheathams had ever been faced with the consequences of keeping interests away from their sister. Quimper looked as though he knew full well they had learned to be afraid of him, for he smiled often over his cigar, and when he asked if he might pay court to Miss Clea, there was no polite way to refuse.

"And then what happened?" Lestrade fairly shouted. "What did you say to that tripe?" Myron's red-faced silence told all: The Cheatham power and authority was easily cowed in the presence of the real thing. Lestrade

168

managed not to strike him. "What?" he demanded, forcing the man to confess.

"We didn't say anything. We didn't know what to say!" Myron protested. At Lestrade's face he futilely defended himself. "No one's ever paid court to her before! What were we supposed to say?"

"She's your only sister, you jackanape!" Lestrade did shake him then, and quite hard. He was less than half Myron's size, but he did it. "What the Bloody Hell were you thinking? Did you think this would never happen? Did you reaming kanurds [1] think your muscles could keep her from the world's Quimpers?" Lestrade was about to hit the poor bastard. He punched his gloved fist into his palm instead.

"They had a conversation," Myron swallowed thickly. "Alone, by the hot-house window." He caught Lestrade's astonishment. "We can't afford the glass tax," he explained. 'It came with the house and we're boarding it over – but Clea was growing her cooking-things in it, and that's where she really feels . . . safe. I told her to take him there." Myron breathed in as Lestrade grudgingly gave him a point for having one clever thought. "He . . . returned as if nothing at all had happened. Stayed to his usual time, shared his cigars . . . and he promised to visit again at the next opportunity."

"I have a feeling she felt differently?" Lestrade offered coldly.

"She spoke to me, afterwards." Myron's face remained the colour of beef brisket. He stared at his feet, his embarrassment spreading all the way to his ears.

"He didn't term it as marriage, as such." She'd swallowed, pale at the memory. "He said . . . if it made it easier to think about, it would be an excellent business merger." Her throat worked as if words were sticking inside. As Myron watched, she picked up a pot of ginger and brushed the dust off the leaves. "He said we had something he wanted, a fine reputation. And he had something we needed . . . money."

Lestrade pressed his teeth together. Myron finished quickly.

"She went to her shop as usual, but when closing-time came, I went to get her . . . The tweeny said Mr. Quimper had just came and offered to escort her home."

Lestrade did not hit the wall. That would have been stupid. He leaned on it instead and rubbed his throbbing eyes.

"She's been gone a night," Myron choked. "Her reputation . . . ."

"Oh, for the love of – Mr. Cheatham, for what it's worth, Jethro Quimper won't lay a single finger on your sister." Lestrade wondered if it were possible to feel any worse at this moment. "He'll return her today or

169

tomorrow with charm and assurances, and he'll have some flyaway excuse for holding on to her the way he did . . . and then he'll offer to marry her to preserve her good name and avoid a scandal."

"He kidnapped her so he could marry her?" Myron's eyes were enormous. "Why?"

Oh, you fool. "This happens more often than you might think, Mr. Cheatham. Some couples even kidnap themselves to force angry parents' permission to marry." Lestrade knew he didn't have to say the next part, but Myron needed to hear it. "And Quimper's father tried to do that very thing with a woman, years ago. She still refused him for another, I'm pleased to say." *And he never forgave my father.*

"He did . . . " Myron breathed. He gulped hard.

"Quimper has half-a dozen houses in London that I know of." The detective forced the man's mind back on the track. "Do you know where he's living now?"

"He . . . he doesn't stay more than one night in any of his houses." Myron tried to think. "Says he's never satisfied."

"Yes, that would make it difficult to arrest him or write out a search warrant." Lestrade chewed on his lip. "Listen. The evidence we collect should give us all we need to legally search everything that has his name on it, but you must keep quiet about this while we work. We can't let word get out. Do you understand?" Myron nodded and looked happier. "Can you go to the station and tell them what you've told me? I'll tell Mr. Gregson – he's in charge of this case – and we'll start looking as soon as we get there." Lestrade sighed and clapped the big man's shoulder, although he really wanted to do something more violent. "Hurry, now. Get a cab."

Bradstreet took it all with a whistle. Gregson was more creative.

"That tears it," the tow-headed man said coolly. "Anyone happens on him tonight. I'm going to write it in as an Act of God. I've had it."

"At least we know he wouldn't keep her here," Bradstreet said, trying to be helpful. "He's too fastidious to even set foot in a place like this."

They all regarded the warehouse in concern. The fading light of evening made the massive square over the Thames look like a large safe.

Lestrade had to agree with Bradstreet. For all his work in water-crimes, Quimper was un-attached to things that smelt of the ocean or a strong river. He studied the quick pencil sketch made of the property to put his mind to use. What he wanted to do was lead some addlepated charge of rescue, but he knew full well how foolish he – and his men – and his Chief – would look. Notices and alerts had been quietly posted for the on-duty Bobbies to watch for any sign of the agent and his men – and Clea.

If this place doesn't tell us where to look, I don't know what will.

Arrogant men were careless men. Quimper had won many a round against the police before, but he had never been so full of brass. This would be his undoing. It had to be.

He won't kill her, he repeated to himself.

"He won't put a finger on her."

Lestrade nearly jumped out of his skin at Bradstreet's low voice right in his ear – close enough that the moustache tickled his neck.

"Wh – ?" He panted, completely out of sorts but keeping his voice down to a squeak.

"He doesn't dare touch her, Geoffrey." Bradstreet's deep eyes bored into his friend's. "Remember that."

"How can you be so sure?" Lestrade wanted to believe him, but he needed reason to believe him.

"He wants her family's good will, and those bruisers aren't the brightest lot, are they?"

"Umm . . . no . . . " Lestrade winced. "What does that have to do with it?"

"You can reason with smart men," Bradstreet reminded him. "Would you trust them not to be rash and do something very stupid?"

"I'd trust them to do something stupid, once they recovered."

"There you go. Also," Bradstreet nodded, "he wants Clea's head for numbers, correct?"

"Yes. What of it?"

"If he needs her head for numbers," Bradstreet explained patiently, "that means he isn't as smart as she is with 'em, correct?"

"I'm not following you – " Lestrade's eyes went wide.

Bradstreet waited.

"Oh," the little Yarder said in a tiny voice. "You think she'd sabotage him."

"Smart brains can hide anything with the right numbers. He can't risk it."

Lestrade's face twisted up bitterly. "Trust him to be merciful because it just happens to be less trouble for him."

Thirty men can take up a lot of space, but Gregson had learned from the mistakes of The Kelpie. All the men had done at least two jobs with the C.I.D. beforehand. Youghal had tracked the three escaped sailors from The Kelpie – the fourth being Bartram Cheatham – and they were perfectly willing to trade time in gaol to help rescue their missing friends. They were very angry.

They hovered now, sullen and gnawing cheap quids, glowering with much anger and no fear at all at the large building that had come to represent a large predator of their ilk. The plain-clothed police wore the darkest clothing they could find. Lestrade had on his pea-jacket and was grateful for its shield against the crisp wind cutting up the way.

"Place is big enough to hide a few river-boats inside it!" PC Harkness supplied. He was on specific loan from the Water Police while his usual mates manned the river. "Built like a brick privy. Privately owned like you said. Took a look in there once on other business." He spread his hands in a diagonal. "There's a rail staircase that runs up the western wall. Leads to a catwalk. There are large sandbags hanging from pulleys to counterweight the lifting of large goods."

"Sandbags, eh? Everybody remember to duck, please," Gregson growled. "Bad enough we'll be facing death by lead poisoning. Now we have to think of death by great bloody canvas hammers."

The cold was blowing over the Thames-tide. It thickened the very air about London and did much to take away the first festive attempts of Christmas along the waterfront.

Lestrade winced, feeling the air-pressure build in his ears as Bradstreet dispensed hot cups of broth and brick-hard bread to sop. The dusk that sheltered them would soon turn into a liability.

"Tide won't be exactly in our full favour, lads," he grumbled. "Best we get something in before the fight."

"I don't have faith about this." Gregson stared into his own mug and dunked the day-old bread to soften. "Too many variables." He passed his gaze over Lestrade, but the other man was sipping his drink with utmost concentration. Gregson looked at Bradstreet, who dropped his body by him. "A quick raid. That's all we need," he said casually. "Wind's on our side. Tide's at past-four, and we've been having bloody abnormally high tides all year thanks to the weather.

"Cloud cover's making it turn dark sooner. It won't be easy for anyone trying a quick run to sea, and we'll hit 'em with the search warrant before the tide goes out." He passed out eyepatches with cold efficiency. Lestrade put his over the right eye.

"By the by, t'whom do we owe this device?" Jones wondered. "This is like something that Holmes character would come up with."

"It's an old trick," Bradstreet explained. "Soon as we're in that dark room, you flip that eyepatch up and close the eye you were using. You'll focus the faster and live the longer!"

Lestrade grumbled something sour into his cup that sounded suspiciously like a line from Gilbert and Sullivan.

"The lads are in!" Gregson hissed. "Everyone, time to go!"

The first of Quimper's men at the dock stopped long enough to draw their weapons – long foreign blades, but the leader had a small gun. At first it looked as though he would start firing, but Gregson barked his address and they realised they were against the Metro. Even that wouldn't have necessarily stopped them, but there were many men. The constables piled on them before they could run off. Two more, much harder and seasoned-looking than the sentries, emerged armed and prepared for a rival gang-war. When they ignored Gregson's bellow of desist, he put a requisitioned bullet into each one's leg. The sight of armed policemen was usually enough to demoralise any foe and panic spread amongst the lot. Nearly every soul in England believed policemen were never allowed firearms. But when they were, the guilty had reason to fly.

Everyone operated under Gregson's plan. They stampeded as into the warehouse with no expectations of anything but disaster. The first shot from the opposition lit up from the dark corners and one of the constables pitched forward with a choked gasp. Youghal paused to grab him up. The poor man bled freely from his upper arm, dangerously close to the large artery. He stopped on the spot and began ripping up a tourniquet, freeing the rest of the men for the invasion.

"Prepare for anything" rarely fit the occasion that demanded a full contingent of Yarders on a case.

Constable Rance, one of the old-timers from the Lauriston Gardens case, [2] stopped in his tracks and gagged. The foul stench drifted over the rest of the men a bare moment later. Lestrade stopped breathing. *Gangrene? Rot?* He frantically racked his brains for the cause of the smell. Diptheria was sweet. Sometimes tuberculosis like beer . . . .

Jones flipped up the panel of his dark lantern to spill light over a cluster of huddled figures at their feet against a row of yellow hogsheads.

"I think these are the meessing seamen." MacDonald whispered.

"Too right, sir," Constable Crane whispered back. The men were clad in filthy rags and surrounded by scraps of garbage. They numbered at least twenty and were chained together, three men to each length. The ends bolted into the wall. He lifted his bull's-eye up, though the dull fire in the back cast a bit of light over them. "Why aren't they moving, sir?"

Gregson knelt to the nearest man, shook him slightly and sniffed his breath. "They've been grogged stupid," he said in disgust. "They're sick as dogs and drugged them too! Don't even know if we're here or not!"

"That . . . bug-hunting demander!" [3] Bradstreet swore under his breath. "That Haymarket Hec! I feel like giving his moronic brains a drag!" [4]

"You never talk like this while we're in the Yard," Lestrade muttered.

"That's like cursing in church."

173

"Look out!" Crane screeched. "They set fire to the barrels!"

Gregson took off running to the side. "King! Harkness! Send for the fire-trucks!"

Bradstreet ran to the nearest sailor. He swore again in Border Gaelic and tugged at the chain furiously. MacDonald was at his side in a heartbeat. He bent, hefted up a heavy iron bar off the floor and swung. An eye-bolt holding a string of chain burst out of the wall.

"They're too sick to run!" He snapped. "Start lifting!" He swung again. Another bolt snapped.

"How? They're all chained together!"

"We all start lifting!" Gregson picked a likely man covered in navy togs and powder-scars. "Brown! Forbes! Get over here right now!"

Lestrade stuffed his revolver back in his pocket and grunted as he pulled a lithe-looking ropewalker stupidly to his feet. The little Yarder merely folded the man over his shoulders, the chain hanging at his feet, hoping his strength was up to this. The other men followed suit, but the prisoners' confinement forced them all to step at what felt like a snail's pace. It was like the nightmares where one felt the terror of something hunting after them, yet they were unable to run from it. Death reeked. Poison cloyed their nostrils in the dark and behind them, a crackle of fire and scorching salt-wood.

Behind them a barrel went whump as air compressed into flame. They could feel the heat of it on their backs.

No one had ever seen a barrel catch ablaze like that. It burned with a hellish light and no sound. The heat roiled across the room and slapped their faces in a taunt.

"Hot as coal . . . " Gregson gulped. "They weren't joking. These barrels are bombs!"

"It's going to catch against the wall before we finish getting them all out!" Bradstreet panted. Jones and Lanner fell in to assist. Half the police had stayed outside with the sailors to conduct a hard discipline on the unruly gang but it was starting to look like they needed to drop all and just run.

"Lestrade, can you get up what's left of that staircase?" Gregson peered frantically against the corner. "If someone could drop those sand-bags, it might slow down the burn . . . ."

Lestrade strained up under his load with the eye kept in darkness. Gregson was pointing to a scrap of dismantled staircase that led to a no-longer functioning second story and a rickety catwalk. He looked further up, his heart sinking.

Whoever had taken out the stairs and floor had rigged large sand-bags on bound pulleys to control the placement of heavy goods like the hogsheads. There was no room for a man Gregson's size, and barely space for a small one.

"Just keep moving," he said curtly. As soon as they were outside he dropped his man and started running, reaching for his pocketknife as he ran.

"Don't get killed, you dupe!" Gregson shouted after him. He caught Bradstreet's quick gallows-grin as they went back into the building for the next batch of hostages. "Don't give me that look. You know what the paperwork is like!"

NOTES

1. Drunks.
2. *A Study in Scarlet.*
3. A drunk-cheating robber who gains money through menace.
4. I'll throw his brains away for a full a drag (Three-month goal time).

Chapter XIII

Two of Quimper's men must have been trapped in the back after lighting the barrels. They shot at the constables trying to put out the fire, but the aim was wild in the mad light of the fire. Several of the volunteer sailors detached and fired back to protect the constables – proving they had smuggled weapons in with them. Gregson swore loudly enough to be heard over the chaos: This would threaten his badge. Someone screamed from pain or fear or outrage. It was impossible to tell which.

Lestrade scarpered up the ruined stairs as fast as he could manage. If he stopped to think about what he was doing, he was sure to freeze up and fall through the battered planks. As it was, he didn't know how he could get back down.

Worry about "down" when it happens! his uncles chided when they taught him to scale the rope ladders on their boats.

They're all dead now. Lestrade hated how his mind liked to point out these things when he needed to work.

The thread of walkway lurched under his weight in the murky firelight. The sand-bags were much of the strain on the structure. He held his breath and began sawing. It seemed to take forever. The rope was thick hemp, and the sailors were being filed out with agonizing slowness.

The rope snapped under its weight. He watched, sweating, as it struck the floor with an explosion of silica dust and shingle. The flames leaned backwards, but there was still plenty of wood exposed to the air, and that wood was thick with the salts and metals of the Thames. He gritted his teeth and cut at the next rope in line.

Boom!

A barrel collapsed inward, flames spreading across the planks less than a yard from a drugged Negro in a red billy. [1] Youghal yelped and dropped the man he was hauling to pull that one away from certain death.

Another sand bag burst behind the flames. Lestrade was buying them time but nothing more. The warehouse was catching tinder faster than they could stop it.

The constables had better protection. Their heavy coats and cork helmets might look silly but they were designed for punishment. Harry Murcher, another whom Gregson hadn't seen since Lauriston Gardens, simply ran, dragging a chain of limp seamen across the floor with supernatural strength. Smoke curled from his coat as embers sputtered against the thick wool. Three grown men slid on the boards in his wake. Their mates grabbed them up at the doorway and kept running.

It was finally down to the seventh and last chain of men. Gregson and Bradstreet ran for them at the same time, and hauled. Not enough time to spare broken bones or sprains. Flames exploded up a seam of tar against the wall. Salted wood popped and snapped fountains of green sparks.

"Lestrade!" Bradstreet roared, his big voice echoing through the burning warehouse. "Where are you?"

"I'm back here!" Lestrade shouted, but the wall of fire blocked the sound. He gagged on a plume of smoke and cast about frantically for a way out. This part of the warehouse was nothing more than a roasting-box. Fire burst out of the boards under his feet, and then he was crashing through and into the Thames.

Bradstreet screamed as Lestrade vanished in the flames. Gregson latched on to him with strength unknown to either man. "Let go, Toby!"

"You can't help him!" Gregson shouted back in that cold, hateful voice everyone despised at the station. "Get back! The whole thing is collapsing! Get back!" Bradstreet was still pulling against him. Gregson hit him in the back of the head with his truncheon and the big man went limp. It was the quickest way to save both their lives.

Lestrade gulped for air – sooty and thick with flying ash, it was better than breathing the Thames. Icy water lapped at his head. His heavy jacket was pulling him down. His fingers, already numb inside their gloves, touched the withered oak of the dock-timber and fought for purchase.

Everything he thought he'd known about the Thames was horribly wrong. He didn't know this frozen wilderness of dark and water. Nothing was familiar. He didn't know where he was and he couldn't look, just stay above the waves and fight the suck tugging him down.

The current pulled against his intentions, pressing against him as he gathered his bearings. A burning splinter landed on his shoulder and sizzled out.

He couldn't clue how to crawl out of the water, or even swim without help. The coat was thirty-ounce wool and sodden. It had protected him from the fire but was now killing him. He couldn't unbutton it one-handed.

He needed help but he didn't know who could be trusted. His eyes and ears were clogged with dirty water. Black outlines of blurry men running back and forth could be anyone and the current pulled greedily. It was all he could do to hold fast.

Smoke choked his breath. He hung on for dear life and hoped no more of the building would fall down above him. Fire-bells clanged up the street. A brass sound over civilian shrieks.

Something gently bumped his side. Lestrade blinked seawater out of his eyes to stare into the white face of a dead man. One of Quimper's dockhands.

The body floated awkwardly, its arm draped accidentally over the scorched timber that gave it loft. The detective watched numbly as it gently spun in the current, half of the head caved in from a blow pressing the eyeballs out of its sockets. It drifted away from him and with increasing speed with the current. Soon it would wash up against the Lime Oast of the Thames.

His left arm wasn't working like it should. Lestrade puzzled that over for a moment, still foggy. He couldn't examine it by hand without letting go of his moor. Yet if he stayed in place, he would be pulled under. Finally, he held his breath, aimed, and let go of the pier. The current washed him up against the stone wall of the Thames in a sudden lift and slap.

The Thames roared. The tide was swollen with the weight of the winds and shifting: Five hours to come in. Seven hours to come out. The wind was pushing up against the flow of the current, making the drain even slower and colder. If he didn't get out, the Old Man would pull him down as easily as any relic.

Lestrade did not want to be another relic of history to wash ashore the next day. He most especially wanted to live long enough to see the look on Quimper's face when Clea was out of his cold grip. He struck out, favoring his better arm, and found the luck of a floating timber. He held on for all he was worth. The current dashed him back against the wall, hard, and he lost his grip for a moment as the timber struck his ribs. He went under and the flames of the warehouse dissolved in moonless dark.

Bradstreet's face was raw from close exposure to the fire. Scotland Yard had given up. They simply watched, far from the wall of heat as steam-pumps pulled water out of the Thames and into the warehouse. War-like clouds billowed up, mixing with the soot-soaked natural clouds and returning fine black rain upon the men.

"It's Dante's Inferno," Gregson said in wonder. "It started with the barrels and whatever they were holding in them, caught on the tar they'd puttied between the planks of the building itself . . . ."

"They were going to wait until a high tide," Bradstreet spoke slowly, thinking hard. "Put some of those barrels into whatever ship they were insuring, stock it with the crew . . . start an accidental fire, and just . . . just watch the flames jump from the warehouse to the ship. It would burn as the tide pulled it out. Yank all the evidence straight into the ocean where no one could investigate it without a team of divers and the current would pull the loose portions to bits and scatter 'em all over creation. The lead in the barrels would have helped sink it to the bottom . . . "

". . . there would be enough bodies to pass as crew and burnt past recognition. Who would know their real identities?"

". . . spent months collecting the materials for this job, tiny bits at a time. We wouldn't have noticed! No one would have noticed except for Holmes. The ship would have burnt down . . . ."

"And Quimper collects a tight sum on insurance . . . ." Gregson quietly pulled out his penny smokes.

Neither man spoke for several breaths, each one waiting for the other to say it.

"There's no sign of him." Gregson did it first. He might have felt a little bad for hitting Bradstreet in the head.

"There won't be any sign of him either, not if he's in that," Bradstreet said bitterly. His moustache dripped black water down his chin.

"He knows how to swim," Gregson pointed out. "Man, have some faith in the facts."

"What Bloody Hell facts are you talking about?" Bradstreet snapped.

"No body, no evidence."

Bradstreet gulped hard, overcome in the face of Gregson's cool sense.

Gregson nodded at the flurry of fire-fighters. "The Water Police are looking for him and anyone else that might have gotten wet. We can't do much more than hope for now – and get these poor bastards to the hospital. Someone will have to take their statements as soon as they pull out of whatever's in their blood."

Bradstreet sighed. "If it's all the same to you, I'd rather stay here."

Gregson grunted. "Let's take a walk."

Lestrade was flopped over the frozen rocks without a single scrap of memory to explain his escape from a watery grave. A large timber was floating down to the land-spit. Was that how he survived? He stared, eyes glazed as it slowly spun in a circle with the eddying current. *Current.* This was the Lime Oast of the Thames.

It was now the dead of night. When he blinked silt out of his eyes, the orange glow of the Krakatoan sunset turned into the lit roar of the upstream warehouse.

179

The reek of sea and death and forgotten things filled his lungs. Gulls screamed complaints. Rats washed down from the warehouse ran over his body in their haste for land. He shuddered at the light touch of their feet and stood on instinct to feel the universe spin in circles. Blood loss and shock lightened his head. He stopped and sank to his knees, putting his head down as he braced his gloved hands on the ice-covered rocks.

By degrees he felt his heavy body equalizing, taking the strain off his heart. Thank God for C.I.D. training, he thought hazily. More rats squeaked by, fat and sleek. After a moment he felt ready to keep going. He could hear shouting as civilians ran about on the higher ground, moving closer to the free show. There would be pickpockets in that crowd, taking advantage of the excitement. Rat-catchers would be out, adding to their collection of prey for the gaming dens or for tricking tomorrow's customers. Someone might see him despite his dark clothing, but they would most likely retreat at the sight of a copper if they didn't feel the urge to stick his ribs. He was wearing a suit of good wool and that would keep him from freezing, but it also made him a mark for the snatchers. And he had a good coat too. A winter coat was worth a man's life in London. Sailors drowned drunks in these docks for income.

The warehouse was a giant fireball dominating the black sky. He noted that without being able to fully prioritize the fact. Report location, he knew the procedure by heart. Gregson's case. Stand by for Gregson. Find out what happens next . . . .

Barefooted urchins swarmed like the rats themselves, picking over the drift against the mudlarks fighting for their rightful territory. A small blond boy stood at the top of the rubble shoring up the water. Toby Irish? Lestrade didn't see how that could be. His head buzzed like a toy steam engine. The child had a burlap sack in one hand. Crude iron tongs in the other. The bag was squirming. Oh, no, no, no. Don't you be baiting rats for the pits, Toby . . . .

"Toby?" He tried, but his voice strangled, filling his eyes with tears that finally washed the dross out. When he blinked them free again, he could see, but the boy was gone and it was just the mudlarks. Just imagined it . . . .

It wasn't the finest place to call for help, but it was good enough for what had happened. He stumbled, nearly mindless from shock to the heavy door that connected the stone building to the sentry's post inside. Deserted? No, he had to be imagining things. These buildings were never deserted. Too many victims washed ashore here. *It's just your punch-drunk, roasted, frozen mind talking . . . .*

"Hoy!" he rasped with a throat that felt as though he had gulped splinters. The door fell open at his knock. "Hoy there." Who'd be on duty?

He tried to remember. The protocols. Night-watchman? A PC paid to watch? "Is anyone there?" he whispered in the door. Sagged against it and stared at the beautiful sight of the lonely Morse key sitting on top of the desk. A lamp burnt expensive oil. Someone was inside.

"Call the Yard!" Lestrade tried to shout, but his Thames-swollen throat was thick. He coughed. "Inspector Gregson . . . needs help."

"I'm sorry, Lestrade," a terribly familiar voice rippled in the darkness. "But we aren't accepting or transmitting wires at this time."

A pale blue figure rose from its seat at the north-facing window for the Thames and stepped forward, heavy bronze-headed walking stick clicking like a third leg.

"Quimper," Lestrade breathed.

"Amazing what gets rejected by the Thames these days," the agent commented in mild surprise. "Considering you, that should be almost a compliment." He shook his head with a *tsk*'ing noise.

"Where is everyone?" Lestrade demanded with what little authority he could pull from his throat.

"Oh, we're closed for business. Everyone's gone home. Safety inspection tomorrow. Everyone ought to look their best . . . Well, 'tomorrow' meaning seven-sharp." Quimper pulled out his white-gold watch and looked at the time. "Three hours from now, almost to the dot." He snapped the time-piece shut. "Couldn't risk an unknown being on duty while something from my warehouse could float down here, you know. Case in point!" He laughed out loud.

"Jethro Quimper, you are under arrest and while you do not have to say anything, it . . . ."

Lestrade's full recitation of the rights was easily ignored by Quimper, who laughed the whole time he was being given it.

"And what would the charge be, Oh, Inspector Plod?" The tall man paused to make a show of wiping a stray tear from his eye.

"Miss Cheatham's family reported . . . you kidnapped her today," Lestrade snapped. "They know what your intentions are, Quimper . . . Where is she?"

"Oh, calm down. What do you take me for? A peasant?" Quimper drawled. "Some long-in-the-memory peasant with more grudge than sense? She's perfectly safe. A guest at a friend's house . . . ." He chuckled at the look on Lestrade's face. "Well, I couldn't take her to any of *my* houses. That wouldn't be proper, would it?" His thumb rubbed circles on the smooth watch-metal as he spoke. "I don't repeat my father's mistakes . . . that was how the police found your mother, wasn't it? But I'm sure you know all about that story." That last was a taunt.

"So you're adding to the family legacy?" Lestrade was stunned at the level of hatred building inside him just by facing the man for the first time in years. Neither man resembled what they had been back then. Quimper had risen even further in his fortunes, outstripping the wealth and influence of his father while the constable was now a detective. Older and wearing down from duty. "Not . . . like you, Quimper. I thought you were a bit . . . neater than that."

"Kind of you to say so." Quimper turned with a smile on his handsome face. With his side to the warehouse inferno, he looked exactly like Lestrade's concept of the devil: A heartbreakingly beautiful man with a hollow for a heart. The firelight bounced off his pale eyes like lantern-mirrors, adding to the horror. "But as to *neater* . . . one might say the same of you. Look at you, Erminig, [2] bleeding on the floor. The Lestrade I remember was always so particular about his wardrobe."

Quimper was right. Small sluggish drops of blood had soaked down Lestrade's worthless arm and onto the floor. Dark venal blood, not the bright red of arterial loss. What happened? He couldn't remember.

Quimper was shaking his head sadly from side to side. "Jafrez," he began regretfully, using Lestrade's long-ago boyhood name before he was called *Geoffrey*, "you really have caused my people a great deal of trouble." He held up his stick parallel in his hands and began walking forward. Lestrade could see every detail, every cut of the *fleur-de-lis* cut in the metal. "My clients prefer results, you know." The stick looked to weigh half-a-stone with its bronze head. It spun a wheel in his gloved hand.

"Really," Lestrade panted. "I'd be flattered if you made more sense, Quimper."

Quimper paused. The iris paused. "I do beg your pardon?"

"What was Armoricus to you, Quimper?" Lestrade held his breath and leaned against the wall to stand, clutching at his arm. Iron gone. Truncheon gone. Pocket-knife gone. Odds . . . gone. "He was a smart man, but he wasn't a genius like you. He was just good at following orders."

Quimper sniffed. "He was a good man in my army," he retorted with a voice of melting ice. "You couldn't understand that. He followed my orders because he believed in me. Just like poor Paul." The stick flashed out, no more than a controlled tap, and the floor rose up to slap the inspector. "The way Bartram believed in me. A general needs his sergeants!"

Distaste warped the handsome face as Quimper stepped over him. The tip of the stick pressed directly above Lestrade's heart – Lestrade wouldn't be surprised if a spring-loaded knife was hiding in the bottom. "I spent three-and-twenty (*prod*) excruciating (*prod*) years, you fool!" Quimper snarled. "You were his brother," he pointed out coldly. "You

182

were supposed to protect him, yet you put the rope around his neck yourself and I lost decades!"

"And if I hadn't?" Lestrade shouted with what little breath he had left. "What would you have done to the rest of them, Quimper! Do you think I didn't see the future?"

"Future?" Quimper twisted in a skull's grin, all handsome features suddenly rotted out. "You don't even know the past, Lestrade. How would you divine the future?" The stick moved, struck down on his shoulder.

"Now you're babbling," Lestrade gasped through a world of pain. "I knew it would happen sooner or later."

"Carnival dwarf." Quimper grabbed a handful of the inspector's coatfront and slammed him upwards into the wall as if a twelvestone man was nothing. "You were supposed to protect your flesh and blood!" He pulled Lestrade back, and slammed him into the wall again. The air left his lungs and did not return. "Armoricus was my sergeant! You were to cover for him and Paul!"

"That would have looked good in my . . . annual review!" Lestrade gasped as he grabbed at Quimper's wrist. It was like holding on to an iron pipe. "You corrupted them, Quimper! I wasn't going to let you do the same to me!"

"That was the whole point!" Quimper struck harder. Stars burst behind the back of his head and in front of his face. "You fool! You could have been working for me the whole time. I would have let them step down. You could have saved their lives!"

And it was all horribly clear.

Good enough to have a dedicated, obedient pair of men in your illegal army.

Better still if their brother was secretly working for you within the law.

Quimper had been planning this as soon as he saw Armoricus' younger brother wanted to wear the badge. A new man. Working on the inside from the very beginning. A blind eye to a job here and there, a growing culpability . . . perhaps rising through the ranks on the gratuity of Quimper's other secret partners, becoming respectable and high-ranking, but through it all his puppet. A respectable, admired, law-abiding spy and puppet for Quimper's criminal empire.

Lestrade needed half-a-second to see the yawning, elegant pitfall Quimper had set for him . . . and how it had enraged the hunter for his quarry to completely miss it.

"You are a dead man," he said through his teeth.

"After you." Quimper grinned back. He lifted the stick again. A bolt of lightning shaped like a French iris cracked across Lestrade's face before the complete abyss.

NOTE

1. Handkerchief, usually silk.
2. Breton for stoat.

Chapter XIV

Jethro Quimper kept his smile while Lestrade collapsed across the planks, just to make sure the detective wouldn't miss a moment of it – and then let it drop off his face. Much as he'd like to, there would be no sense in leaving him there to be found. Dumping him out the window would accomplish nothing. The tide would simply lash the body back up against the rocks where the police surgeons could investigate the evidence. He gritted his teeth at the inconvenience and hauled him over his shoulder. His face warped again at the contact of a cold, sopping-wet, smoke-scorched, and bleeding detective contaminating his blue coat.

Outside, it was but a few steps behind the building to the waiting carriage. No one noticed over the excitement of the fire across the river, nor did he expect them to. He whistled once and his dogsbody appeared from behind the horses.

"Make ready, Mr. Craddock," he said curtly. Craddock opened the door and he tossed Lestrade in without preamble. He stepped on him on the way to his usual spot, but that was only justice for the stain on his shoulder. "Home, then."

Craddock signaled their driver, and they took off.

Quimper watched the smudge of fire burn against the black London sky. Sometimes it was just unbelievable that anyone would notice one more source of smoke in this wretched ton. He muttered a loose string of syllables from several different languages and leaned on his stick. He glared down at the unconscious detective, wondering where in the world they could drop him that wouldn't be tied to him. His best options depended on time, which he did not have.

Time.

Quimper growled to himself. His heart tapped from unexpected exertion and excitement. It surprised him just how much he enjoyed hitting the other man. Not a professional attitude, to be sure, but things were not very professional tonight.

The warehouse was going up in flames too far ahead of schedule to commit the damage Quimper's employers needed. The ship was supposed to dock first. The crew was supposed to be placed aboard and then the false cargo would have lit from within the hold. The insurance on the cargo would have been collected in one night, with thirty-per-cent to Quimper's superiors. All for naught.

It would be difficult to salvage this loss. It would be even more difficult to explain himself. For years he had been permitted leeway and privilege because his methods garnered results. And now . . . this was not the result anyone needed. Bad enough the little tramp had ruined a half-decade of plans just by being himself. That was the worst part. Quimper took pride in his ability to recruit the un-recruitable, but this had been his worst failure.

Bad enough the rivalry between the Lestrades and Quimpers hadn't ended with a Quimper victory. Bad enough Lestrade had survived unbroken to continue his plodding campaign of harassment against everything illegal in London. If it were only possible to kill the wretched dog more than once!

Quimper stopped his angry musings for a moment. In the distance the fire-bells and shouts underscored the last of the warehouse going up in very hot flames. At least there would be little to trace.

Kill him more than once – ?

Quimper absorbed a possibility or three in his mind. His lips curved as he looked down at his insensate rival. Perhaps he could salvage something after all. Peace of mind was a wonderful thing . . . .

Quimper felt his tension bleed out the further they rode from the waterfront. The Thames followed them by his window. As he watched the river smooth out and narrow a bit, and then they followed the Kensington Canal from the river to Chelsea Creek. It was a minor canal, plagued by eternal problems of silt, but profitable enough for the gas-works to keep its interests. Quimper had always liked that area because here it was possible to forget one was close to the stinking Thames.

He wasn't foolish enough to actually live there. Even he could be traced. Quimper did not want to have to explain to his superiors that he had made a mistake from arrogance. They were not forgiving of errors, and much less when the errors were born of flaws in the pride.

186

The West London Extension Railway rattled ballast under hooves and wheels, partially jostling his thoughts to another subject. Quimper sighed in his distaste. They were nearly at the estate.

Good of Beckett to let him use his home *in absentina*. It had turned out to be far more useful than he had dreamed thanks to its proximity to the water, the respectable façade of the district, the convenience of the trainline . . .

. . . and of course, the goldfish pond . . . .

Nearly time. Quimper knelt in the bottom of the carriage and rolled the inspector on his back inside the narrow space. Just like that lead-thief they'd dropped in Little Venice. Quimper had made careful mental notes for improvement that first time, but overall he'd been satisfied at the way things had worked out. There was nothing quite like a public execution to bring about a proper sense of morale among one's army.

Of course business first, then pleasure. This wasn't going to be a public execution, but it would give him the chance to iron out his new technique.

Cold air whistled down Lestrade's exposed throat, pulling him out of a void. He had no sense of up or down at first. Or why Quimper would want to do something with his collar and cravat. The tall man rolled him to his front and pinned him to the floor with one knee on his back, using the cravat to bind his wrists together.

"Destroy that," Quimper held up his collar. "He won't need it." Craddock stuffed it in his pocket quickly as he saw to the horses. "Oh, good." Quimper smiled cheerfully. "You're waking up. Just in time."

Lestrade wasn't completely sure if he was awake or not. His eyes burned from the Thames, his ribs felt the collision with the timber, and his head felt as though Quimper's stick was still in his forehead. He had no clue on their location except it was a small country estate. Just walking on grass was enough of a marvel in London.

"As I said, a friend's place." Quimper's good humour remained as he propelled the two of them across a strip of dead grass and onto a stone tile patio. If anyone saw them, Quimper would appear to be nothing more than a considerate friend helping a tired man walk to the house. "He has excellent taste, really, but a bit on the impractical side. Insists on growing tender perennials, so every spring he has to replant half of what he bought the year before! I'll allow it is stunning in bloom, but honestly . . . Some people can't be trusted with their own finances . . . ." He sighed sadly. "I like him very much, but he does possess a few strange qualities . . . not the least being the type of parties he likes to host. Not fit for anyone of a respectable reputation. Not at all . . . ."

187

Quimper turned them until they were underneath a large open-air porch. The worst of the winter wind was blocked by a hollow chest-high stone wall ringing the porch, its top disgorging strangely shaped dead vines and shrubs. In the middle of the porch and only a few steps from the door rested a long oblong pool. Where its surface should have been smooth and clean ice, it was a rough, uneven and scarred-over sculpture. The surface had been broken up once before, and the loose cakes of ice had re-sealed clumsily in the chill air.

Lestrade realised what exactly he was looking at. His heart lurched in his chest. Sheer instinct drove the strength out of his mind for a moment. He almost stumbled but Quimper held him upright with a chuckle.

"But he does have the sense for fish," Quimper admitted. He pushed Lestrade to his knees at the side of the pond. Lestrade swallowed against the rising pulse in his throat. "Mr. Craddock, if you would be so kind . . . ?" The big man silently went to the side of the wall where an assortment of lawn chairs rested and hefted a large splitting maul. He struck the edge of the ice. Blue-white cracks opened.

"Mr. Craddock, be careful now, don't scar up the stonework . . . " Quimper cautioned. "As I was saying, he has the taste for unusual colours and breeds. It's a pleasant thing having a fish pond . . . I always prefer to have things that aren't specialised. Something should have more than one use, you know." Quimper patted him on the back. Lestrade recoiled and the other man laughed in an awful way. Craddock had finished smashing the ice. Cakes shifted and rolled against each other. Craddock pushed some of the cakes atop each other, making a clear space.

"That should be good enough, thank you. Why don't you see how our guest is faring? Come here when you're finished." Quimper smiled as the door shut after the big man. "Not a conversationalist, not at all. But a good listener."

"So now what?" Lestrade asked through his teeth – a perverse facet that didn't want to continue this conversation if it meant enduring the man's insufferable arrogance. "You drown me. Throw me into one of the canals with lead in my pockets?"

"Oh, perhaps not." Quimper stood up to push his stick down into Lestrade's aching shoulder. "And I doubt I'll have to put anything in your pockets at all. You are aware. It can take as long as twenty days for a drowning victim to wash up at the Office?"

He propped his boot against the detective's ribs and pushed. Lestrade's eyes went wide and he had time to breathe in once as the edge of the water rushed up to meet him. Quimper pressed the tip of his stick against his ribs and pressed gently. He watched as the infuriating man went under the water with a satisfying splash.

This was how that poor lead-thief at the canals had drowned. Lestrade saw nothing but water, felt nothing but the smooth polished surface of the marble pond at his back and the pressure of the damned stick holding him down less than a yard under the water of a fish pond. The water was clean and clear. Through floating cakes of ice he could see Quimper's blurred form, holding him down by the sternum. Only a little pressure was enough. Not enough to bruise through the layers of wool. His gloved hands would leave no damning marks because they were tied with his own soft cravat. Who would think to notice if a corpse still had its tie on if it was missing its collar? Tearing the collar off was as sure a sign of suffocation as shredding one's shirt. Through the curtain of water, he saw his killer pull out his pocket-watch and look down in consultation.

He's *timing me*? Lestrade realised. His blood pounded in his ears as the need to breathe overwhelmed his brain. Quimper suddenly lifted the pressure off his chest and he wrenched to the surface with a gasp.

"One minute," Quimper commented. "Not bad at all, considering this is not your first dunking tonight." He watched as the detective choked up water and went limp against the side of the pond. "Well, we can work on that, can't we?" He mused. The tip of the stick found its spot. Quimper smiled into Lestrade's grim face as he pushed him back down.

The door flung open. Quimper had the presence of mind to turn but remained cool. Clea Cheatham ran outside in her day-dress, Mr. Craddock a step behind her. Quimper was privately amused. He should have warned about the woman's spirit.

She stopped upright, lapis eyes wide and round as she took in his presence, and slowly, what he was doing.

"I do beg your pardon, Miss Cheatham," Quimper lifted his hat calmly. "You surprised me at my work."

"Stop it!" Clea screamed. Her hands covered her mouth. "You're killing him!"

"My goodness, Miss Cheatham," Quimper said gently. "That is the point." He paused to take in her white face. "My dear, please don't be so alarmed. Drowning is the least painful way one can meet his Maker. Trust me, I've investigated." He smiled. "Just because I'm a good businessman doesn't mean I inflict any more pain than necessary." But he let up the pressure and watched as the detective leaned forward on his knees, choking out the water between gasps for air.

Clea was choking back her own breath. "Mr. Quimper, please," she pled brokenly. "There's no need to do any of this!"

"I fear I must disagree." Quimper decided Lestrade had given his lungs enough oxygen and pushed him back under the water again. He leaned slightly on the weight of his stick, and patted his pockets down for a cigarette.

Right, Lestrade thought as consciousness blurred. *Keep smoking that vile leaf, you Mandrake toff. When Sherlock Holmes investigates my corpse, your perfumed ashes will lead him right to your cursed doorstep.* It wasn't much satisfaction, but by God it would have to do.

Clea tried too hard to break free from Craddock's grip. She cried out at a sudden stab of pain in her wrists.

"Craddock," Quimper chided. "Mind your manners to our guest." He glanced down at the water, read his watch to time Lestrade's frantic struggles.

Craddock put both his hands on her shoulders, pressing her down into the lawn chair set away from the pond. In the cold air her teeth chattered, or was it only just the cold? Quimper considered possibilities in his mind.

"Miss Cheatham, do forgive me. I didn't inquire if you wished to watch this." Quimper let up on the pressure. "We can take you to another part of the house, or at least offer you a coat," he offered grandly as Lestrade sagged against the edge of the pond. "This could go on for hours, and this sort of weather would hardly benefit you." The detective doubled over barely above the surface of the pond and vomited clear water.

"Please!" Her eyes were streaming icy tears, but inwardly Clea was promising a fate to Quimper far worse than anything he could imagine on Lestrade. "Mr. Quimper, let him go! Whatever you want! Just . . . let him go!"

Lestrade wasted his first breath of air: "Clea, shut up!"

"Manners." Quimper scolded and pushed him back under the pond. He puffed calmly on his cigarette. Clea watched in pounding horror through the tears in her eyes. Lestrade was getting weaker with each submersion.

She couldn't say how much longer Quimper would keep doing this, but she had an awful feeling he would keep it up as long as he could.

"Mr. Quimper, I mean it." Clea gulped loudly. She was close to becoming violently ill at the thought, but witnessing Lestrade's slow murder was far worse. "Whatever you want. I'll talk to my family. We'll do whatever you want."

Quimper allowed distaste to flick over his face. "My good woman, if this is your response to my proposal, I'm not in favor of coercion when it comes to a lady."

Clea forced down a ball of white-hot rage. "T'isn't coercion, Mr. Quimper," she said with a control that would pride her father. "You have something I want. I have something you want."

Quimper slowly smiled around his wreath of smoke. "This is true," he conceded. "This is true." He looked pleased. "Your father spoke of your business acumen." He paused and let Lestrade up for air. "Strange how your life keeps circling around mine, Lestrade. You wouldn't work for me, even at the cost of the ones you loved. And now, it seems Miss Cheatham cares enough for you to make a different choice."

I'll kill him! Lestrade thought through a blind curtain of hacking coughs. *I swear, I'll find a way to kill him legally.*

"Don't – !" he tried to say, but Quimper's stick pushed him back under in warning. Just a dunk this time. "What did I tell you about manners?" he murmured. "Let the lady speak."

"Stop it, both of you!" Clea rose to her feet. She kept her hands to her side, and they stared at her, waiting. For a moment, uncertainty crossed her features and she wrenched her hands into her apron, as if embarrassed. "I'm not a proper lady," she began slowly, her eyes gleaming with tears, "but I'll do what I see is right." She glared down at Lestrade, and then met Quimper's mildly surprised blue eyes. "And with that, I will properly say goodbye to you, Inspector, and the next time we see each other again, it will be inside our own lines of duty."

Quimper was smiling from ear to ear. His night was turning out to be splendid beyond his dreams. "Well said, my dear." He took a polite step to the side. "By all means, bid your farewells."

Clea held her breath and slid to one knee. She wanted to start screaming every imprecation she had learned from the mill-women. She forced herself to put her hands on Lestrade's wet shoulders instead. "I expect you to stay away from us," she said evenly. "Stay away from all of us. I won't ask if you care a bit for your own life, Mr. Lestrade. If you can't remember to step out with a starched collar, I doubt you'd remember something like breathing. But for my sake, stay away."

"I hear you," he breathed. It was like cutting his own arm off, but he got it out somehow. Rage burnt the frost right out of his blood. It steamed through his skin and stole what little breath he had left. But he had no riposte against the look in her eyes. *He'll put his hands on her just because he knows what it will do to both of us. He'll smile at me the whole time, and it won't matter to him what she feels. My God, does he really hate me that much?*

She nodded, and rose to her feet. "Mr. Quimper," she nodded coolly. "I shall return to my rooms now. Have the fire built up." She turned her back on them all. Craddock started, and hurried to catch up. She ignored his hand on her arm as they left the patio.

Quimper finished his smoke regretfully. "Interesting . . . " he commented. "Lestrade, are you up on your French? I'm brought in mind

191

of the late Amiel's work: '*Women wish to be loved not because they are pretty, or good, or well bred, or graceful, or intelligent, but because they are themselves.*' He chuckled to himself.

"Quimper, if you're going to throw quotes while you're drowning me, I'd like you to just skip over that part and finish up – a last request, as it were." Lestrade managed to talk through his gnashed teeth. If he kept them closed tightly enough they wouldn't chatter.

Quimper beamed. "Drown you? I dealt with Miss Cheatham, Inspector."

"And you fully intend to go through with it," Lestrade scoffed. His brown eyes were nothing but pools of lava behind the wet hair falling down his face. It wasn't easy keeping control while slowly drowning in a frozen fishpond. Quimper admitted to a grudging respect for the man. Stubborn just wasn't enough of a word for him.

"Of course I fully intend to go through with it." Quimper tapped his shoulder with the stick, warning, still smiling. "Watching you live with this decision from day to day? Watching you pretend you're still an upstanding member of the law you love? Knowing your priceless sense of the law has been besmirched?" He laughed out loud. "All these years, Lestrade, I have finally managed to contaminate you. It wasn't from someone you loved, but from someone who loved you. I adore irony.

"However," Quimper pressed the inspector backwards into the water with sadistic slowness. Instinctive panic returned into his quarry's eyes as he tried to fight the press downward, "for the sake of our story to Scotland Yard, we will have to make certain you're unconscious. You'll forgive me if I choose that particular moment." The agent's eyes glittered feverishly against his pleasant tone. "I look forward to spending the rest of your life watching you tread water."

Chapter XV

Clea Cheatham stopped in front of her room's doors and turned to look up at her large dogsbody. He looked confused. Clea's estimation of Quimper made a comforting decrease in the face of his employment. "I'll need a fire built if I am going to endure another night in this house, Mr. Craddock," she snapped at him as if she were speaking to a sulky nephew.

"I'll see what I can do, Miss Cheatham." Craddock responded. As soon as he turned his head to the side, breaking his direct view of her hands, Clea moved. She was small, but wrestling had been designed for small fighters, and she was a Cheatham from Lancashire. The carpet muffled his fall.

Quimper examined his watch. Lestrade had stopped struggling. *Pity, really.* He would have been satisfied with spending the rest of the night on this, but business was a higher duty. Knowing he had finally won over the little beggar helped his magnanimous state. He snapped his watch shut and reached down, hauling the smaller man above the water. Lestrade began to breathe in great, shuddering jerks and gasps as a thin layer of ice formed over his coat, but was otherwise unresponsive. Quimper thought he might possibly die of exposure before they could deliver him to the Bobbies and sighed in exasperation. There was always a wrinkle in every plan.

"'*The hour is come, but not the man* . . .'" he leaned down and quoted. "Up you go, Jafrez my lad . . . ." Quimper went so far as to haul him completely to the patio stones. "Don't go anywhere just yet, now . . . ." He chuckled to himself and stepped to the hanging bell-pull by the door. "Belkin, Thomas . . . Ah, there you are. Would you be so kind as to get the cab ready for our guest? Don't dawdle, now. We have to prepare for a wedding." He stepped aside and reached for another cigarette, glad to be away from the chill of ice.

Clea's heart nearly stopped for the fifth time that night as she closed the door. Moving Craddock had not been a simple matter, but she was used to hauling her own weight plus-some. The blood pounded in her ears and she waited, listening for others. Time ticked in her mind as she calculated. She knew she had to hurry. She took off running. Silly rich men and their pretensions had to put carpet on every floor. All the better for being quiet.

Quimper caught a flicker of movement. Lestrade was regaining consciousness. Well, what of it? He wouldn't be in any fit shape for much tonight. And it would be impolite not to bid a guest farewell. He pulled out another cigarette and nipped it into the silver holder as he knelt by his side. "Awake so soon, Lestrade? You had me fooled there. Acting in the blood and all that? You should change your name to something more suitable, such as . . . *Bouledogue*. Yes, '*bulldog*' is fitting."

He dropped ash on the inspector's white face. "You should get your rest. You'll be needed at Scotland Yard tomorrow, helping write all those reports." He slapped Lestrade's icy jaw until the man's eyes fluttered open. "Many, many reports that make me look in the best possible light." He smiled. "No one will believe it unless you write it, you know. Half of London knows just how badly you hate me." Quimper was thoroughly enjoying himself as he watched Lestrade's face settle to stone. "But times change, don't they? Our families were friends, once upon a time. They can be again." Lestrade looked ill. He turned his head to the side to look at anything else but Quimper. "*Tsk*." Quimper turned his face until they were looking eye to eye. "Feuds often end at weddings," he pointed out. "You simply must attend. We wouldn't think of having it without you."

And then at that point, Quimper stopped moving. He stopped breathing.

He stopped doing anything.

Lestrade's eyes were black as caverns from long years of collected rage and he shook from cold but his hand was steady as he held Clea's small apron-knife against Quimper's throat.

She dropped it into the pond when she held his shoulders, Quimper realised. He had no choice but to admire the presence of the woman's mind. She had faith his fingers would find it while he was being drowned in the water. What an Amazon.

Clea swung the door open with both hands and instinctively stopped, checking the lay of the land. "Mr. Lestrade!" Clea gasped with relief. "Thank God!"

"Maybe . . . you should . . . tie him up," Lestrade strangled. "Before my hand slips." It was a grim situation, but he relished the flash of horror on Quimper's face. Neither man moved, locked in their gaze until Clea finished it by running inside, running back out, and dropping a Chinese vase on Quimper's head. The tall man folded up over Lestrade's chest without a protest.

"Not sure th-that was – Oh, never mind . . . ." Lestrade had the presence of mind to hand her the knife back. "Could you . . . help me up? He's got to . . . have an ars – senal in his p-pockets . . . somewhere."

"Here's one." Clea fished out a small flask and yanked at the cap. "No protests. You're white as winter."

"Wasn't . . . 'bout t' . . . " Lestrade took the flask down and gasped for breath. It hit worse than Bradstreet's poteen. (It crossed Lestrade's mind to wonder how that was even possible.) In the meantime, Clea was pulling him to his feet and pushing Quimper's small revolver into his hand. He was so cold he could barely pull the trigger, but he worked the catch off in case he was forced to use it.

"We need to get you warm and dry," she announced. "And we have to get out of here quickly!"

"Yes, I know," he managed through a throat that, thawed with Quimper's expensive turpentine, was letting him feel just how raw it was.

"No, I mean, we have to get out of here quickly." Clea stared him in the face.

Lestrade stared back. "Miss Cheatham, what did you do?"

"I set the upstairs on fire. It should bring help rather quickly."

"Yes, let's do go," Lestrade groaned. "But tomorrow when you're giving your story to Gregson, please forget to remember that part of it."

Clea guided him into the lawn chair Craddock had kept her in and Lestrade watched with an exhausted smile as she trussed Quimper up with a bell-cord harvest from the inside rooms. "Normally I use this knot when I'm on a rack of lamb." Clea sniffed. "It seems to work as well on a pig." She grinned at Lestrade's snort and helped him up again. "I like him like this. He looks good like this, dust tha' think?"

"I'm thinking he should have known it's unlucky to view the bride before the wedding." They smiled at each other for the first time. Lestrade remembered himself and looked away. His gaze fell to the unconscious agent on the way out. "*Kenavo*," he muttered.

Clea kept her mouth shut while they staggered across the lawn. Holding on for her support, Lestrade was silent too. She doubted he had it in him to talk anyway. Smoke leaked out the rooftops and the men Quimper had sent for the cab ran right past them in their haste to find water. After this night, it was wonderful to be ignored. They stopped for a

195

moment, swaying in the middle of the greensward as he tried to recover his breath.

His log-bruised ribs throbbed with each step, each breath, each blink.

"What did you say to him when we left?" she asked at last. He was shivering violently. She didn't like the night air either, but he was soaking wet.

"What – *kenavo*?" He blinked wearily. A skin of ice fell off his sleeve. "Means . . . *goodbye*."

"It sounded Cornish."

"Cornwall . . . Brittany . . . We're c-cousins." Lestrade caught a gust of wind and began shivering in earnest. "Some of us had b-better sense and moved to France . . . ."

"Let's get you out of this." Clea caught his look and admitted she deserved it. "Let's get us both out of this," she corrected, "My God, dust know of that?"

"Mnm?" Lestrade looked down. "I . . . forgot," he said groggily. The scratch had opened up again.

"Holy Saint John Rigby," Clea exclaimed. "I might imagine you'd forget about something like bleeding while you drowned." She thought about shaking him but that would have to wait. "Stop . . . ." She swore under her breath.

Lestrade collapsed at her direction, which was at the remains of an old gazebo. He watched as she went inside and yanked out an old traveller's blanket from behind a seat. "Nothing like wool," she decided, and threw the whole thing over their shoulders. "Might as well wait for the rescue," she shivered. "I couldn't go much further." Under the musty blanket she was ripping cloth. "Mr. Lestrade, can you reach over and hand me that stick on the ground? You need a tourniquet."

Lestrade complied by inches. "Not bad," he decided. "I can only wonder at the amount of practice you've had . . . ."

"It isn't easy being a wrestler, but 'tis harder to have one in the family." Clea said wearily. "And I have more than one."

"Oh."

A taut, uncomfortable silence followed. Alarms were making their way to the estate. More people were running around.

"What will happen to Bartram?" Clea whispered.

"Precious little now that the truth is out. You needn't worry."

She sagged against him in relief. He still didn't smell like pig. "Thank you," she sniffed. Nearly another minute passed while she tried to hang on to her composure.

"You know, you could cry it all out," Lestrade pointed out reasonably. The usual platitudes didn't fit this lady. "Pretend you're having a weak moment and all that."

Clea's stumble of amusement caught in her tears. "I could at that," she acknowledged.

It hurt like the devil, but he pulled his arm around her. The blanket began to store up their combined warmth. Very gradually, Lestrade's breath began to steam in the air as his core temperature rose to something like normal.

"Well," Clea cleared her throat. The fit of weeping had passed. It had mostly been from relief. "Say something."

Lestrade's mind slowly processed. "What?" He mumbled.

"Stay awake. Talk." She poked him. "Say something."

"I understand, but you're going to have to give me something to talk about," he answered wearily. "I can't rub two thoughts together."

"Say something Breton."

"I don't speak it much. I understand it better than I speak it."

"Well, I don't speak it at all. Anything would be better than nothing."

Lestrade shuffled around in his mind. "*Nedeleg laouen* . . . Happy Christmas."

She repeated it slowly. "I'm almost surprised Christmas hasn't passed these past few nights," she whispered.

"Still has eleven more days," Lestrade agreed with her by the tone of his voice. "Then it's . . . *bloavezh mat*. Happy New Year. *Mat*. Good . . . *Bihan*. Small." Fatigue was clawing at his chest, pulling his eyes shut. "*Karout . . . a ran ac'hanout*."

"Yes, I know," she said quietly.

It took a moment for her words to soak in. "I didn't tell you what that meant," he mumbled.

"Dust have to?" Clea smiled, and a tiny spark of that the old, smug little devil was gleaming in her eyes again. "I saw what it meant." *I love you*, he'd said, and she knew. She leaned her head against his shoulder and they watched the first of the fire-pumps gallop up the drive.

Clea took over. A soft haze settled over Lestrade and he simply let her do all the talking. It wasn't as if she didn't know how. By degrees he slid sideways on the gazebo bench until he was lying full out. Someone shook him gingerly, then everything went away for a bit. He came to himself to realise two familiar voices were holding council over him.

"Looks like him," Bradstreet was saying. "I dunno. Aren't we supposed to be looking for him in the Thames?"

"That's what I thought," Gregson's smug voice was weirdly ineffectual to Lestrade's tired psyche. "Maybe we should give the river another go. Make sure he's not still there."

"You . . . you copper-bottomed pigs-for-brains!" Clea shrieked. Her rage went through Lestrade, but he had no ability to react to it. There was a sound like a fist striking a wet bag of sand, and a Gregson-like grunt. "You mumpers! You're getting him into the back of that ambulance right now, dust hear me? Right now!" Lestrade was just aware enough to be glad he was not the unfortunate Gregson at that moment.

"Mr. Lestrade?" Clea's voice had gone soft. He felt her hand on his forehead, pushing back his wet hair. "They're going to take us home now." Silence. "Dust hear me?" He heard her pull in her breath. "*Karout a ran ac'hanout.*"

"Good . . . job . . ." Lestrade heard himself say, and then, thank God, the doors shut on the ambulance.

Bradstreet and Gregson watched the ambulance wheel away. "Did she just call him a running carrot?" the Runner wondered.

"I don't keep track of your barbaric Celt tongues," Gregson snorted. He found a match and cupped his hands against the wind to light up a much-deserved smoke. "My cold Anglo-Saxon language is quite enough." His pale eyes lit up with delight at something across the lawn. He waved at Jethro Quimper being herded into the Black Mariah by a small regiment of very happy constables.

"Bretons were at peace with Vikings, you know," Bradstreet warned. "So you can't use that argument."

"Vikings were never at peace with anybody," Gregson snipped loftily. He passed over his cigarette-case to Bradstreet. The big man took one gratefully. "They just had a very large list of those they fought with at the time."

"Hmm." Bradstreet fixed himself a smoke. "That and a bawbie will buy you a bannock." The two stood in silence for a few minutes while the fire was contained on the roof. "Wouldn't you love to be a fly on the wall," he smiled, "when Miss Cheatham is returned to her family?"

Gregson tried his best not to snicker, but it was impossible. "Well, at least it answers your question, Roger."

"Hmm? What question?"

"Oh, an idle comment you made some years back. I'm not surprised you don't recall . . . You never had a head for details . . . ."

"Tobias . . . ."

Gregson struck a Bradstreet-like pose. "'*God almighty.*'" He made a very poor mid-country burr. "'*What kind of woman for Geoffrey?*'"

198

"She wrestles, she punches, she carries a knife," Bradstreet ticked points off his fingers, "and she can do all three with her tongue!" They started laughing. It felt grand. Several constables gawped as they hustled by. Making it all the funnier. Bradstreet, atypically, sobered first. "But she's not quite our kind," he said quietly. "Rules are different in the country than they are here."

Gregson conceded that with a shrug, but he took another smoke before he responded. "If it's up to him, it'll make the difference . . . But we'll see what happens, won't we. I have a feeling we haven't heard the last of Miss Cheatham."

Bradstreet cheerfully waved to the furious white face on the other side of the barred Black Maria. "I daresay not . . . I look forward to hearing her statement tomorrow against Mr. Quimper."

Watson was never idle in the dangerous moments between night and day. He was either asleep or alert. Dusk was a strange era for soldiers and warriors, for the timid lighting threatened and hid in equal measure: The mongers and buskers packed up their wares for the day even as their calls redoubled in effort, for they were reluctant to miss a chance for one last penny. In their wake slipped the denizens of the night: Those who plied the night-trades, and the tougher, hardier lot who were willing to wrest an honest wage in the dangerous hours among dangerous men. The young man's senses were a live tuning-fork in this atmosphere. He had walked too many nights as a physician on this very street, and he would never do so without his stick at hand.

The doctor's flesh tingled with the familiar old song of combat. Against the anarchy of London's night he had to strain to catch what impressions he had, and he did not like the little scraps and dottles he got. Warnings sang in his ears like sand-demons, a natural phenomenon from the temperature shifts in dry Afghanistan.

One moment John Watson was walking alongside his friend in a congested London street as a gust of wind pressed their backs. The next he was dragging his companion through the crook of his arm until their forms were completely drowned in the dark pools between the street-lamps.

The two men waited in the darkness. They breathed and listened to their hearts beat underneath the rattle of the traps and waggons, but otherwise did nothing.

A cluster of blind children walked by, single-file, hands on shoulders while the leader cried for alms. Watson's medical eye recognized retinal detachment, measles, and pox. The leader was almost blind herself from strabismus.

Sherlock Holmes watched his friend's hand slide slowly, almost painstakingly, down to the coat-pocket where his revolver rested.

Then – *footsteps*.

Quick, shambling, uneven gait and the heavy hoof-sound of wooden shoes. Watson tensed like a drumskin and pressed Holmes backwards into the darkness. His pocket bulged as his thumb curled upon the safety latch.

Loud, gasping breathing met their ears seconds before the owner burst into view: A rough-looking lout with smallpox scars over his face and hands and a nose badly shortened by a blade to the left. Instead of the slum's usual battered hat, he wore a tatty seaman's knit cap yanked almost over his eyes – a sore attempt to hide his bulbous forehead. Watson, who had placed himself between the alley-way and Holmes, saw the flash of a strange, coiling tattoo upon the back of the man's right paw, and then he was still galloping, heavy brogans going clop-clop-clop as he kept running.

Holmes's lips twisted in a faint smile and he bent to whisper in his friend's ear: "Well done, Watson."

Watson smiled at the praise, but his brown eyes glinted as he whispered back, "He won't be fooled long."

"Ah, but I know another route." With an imp in his grin, Holmes nimbled around Watson and leaped on his long legs almost straight up an ancient stone flight. From the ground, Watson could see the steps were uneven from age and untold feet. They were also well-greased with London condensation and dirt. He winced and followed at a far more cautious pace. Gravity and its consequence was yet another Law to which Holmes had but a thin comprehension. There were times when his friend recalled the sort of childhood compatriot that survives innumerable mishaps for no real reason outside of mythology, or the belief in guardian angels.

The doctor was healthier than his first arrival upon London, and he had even gained some long-overdue mass. He did not want to reverse his slim fortunes by a mis-step. One hand stroked the uneven brickwork of the building as he stepped up. The other kept his walking stick close to his side. Just ahead of his gaze he could see Holmes's spats and collar peeping white glints in the dark, going up, and up, until he nipped sharply to the right and vanished altogether.

Watson found a large opening in the bricks. He stepped in with his better foot first and blinked flying strands of web out of his face. Holmes had stopped and was resting (for lack of any other word) precariously close to a steep drop into an unfathomable darkness.

"Holmes?"

"*Shhh . . . .*" Holmes's pale skin reflected the barest scraps of light from the outside illumination sliding through the gaps and cracks in the broken building. Boards creaked, shifting and swelling as the Tide turned and damp sank around them.

No sand-demons here. No dry wind, no sand. The city was warning her travellers, and they could feel her groan and rumble and sigh with weight, and then more weight, of the heavy fogs that tried to settle in the low places.

Watson's senses had saved them from their unwashed pursuer. Now Holmes was sparing them another sort of threat.

The doctor waited, knowing not to ask his commander in the field about his thoughts.

Holmes listened with every sharp, needling sense attuned out, his grey eyes like metal as he waited for something that only he could hear. Watson had been exposed to this fey talent of Holmes before, and he knew better than to doubt it.

For a few minutes, Watson thought his eyes were adjusting to the poor light. Then as his friend grew in outline and definition, he blinked.

Sherlock Holmes stepped closer, a dull, dirty orange glow just barely showing his face. His black brows pressed together in surprise and just as quickly sprang apart.

"Well, well," he murmured softly. "It would appear some fortune is on our side."

Watson twisted to look through the splintered cracks in the weathered wall-boards. A fireball lit the underbellies of black cloud over the Thames, and when he strained he could just barely make the fire-bells.

"'Fortune'?"

"That is along the Estuary. I wager all businessmen – and in particular the dishonest ones – are running to secure their goods now. And that would include the friends of the fellow we are about to visit."

"Should we call for the Yard?"

"The less they know – and they know precious little indeed – the better until we collect our data." Holmes's teeth gleamed, something like the Cheshire Cat, and he lifted a stout whistle in his free hand. "But if we do need assistance, we can always call."

Watson edged forward until he was nearly wrapped within the shadows. "This is not a part of London where one may confidently call for help."

"We may hope help is not needed," was the calm rejoinder. "Are you rested?"

"Somewhat." Watson bent and straightened his leg and rolled his stiff shoulder.

"We are nearly at our journey's end. Should there be no further surprises with unexpected friends, we may finish the matter and be home before dawn."

Watson had to wonder why Holmes was being so confident of success, but he knew better than to ask. If Holmes wanted him to know, he would tell him.

He nodded, and Holmes's supernaturally-sharp vision caught the movement. There was another quick flash of teeth at a quick smile and the Detective was turning, walking quickly to a rusted-rail and stone steps on the opposite side of the empty building. He might have been an acrobat about to leap into a fathomless space.

And Watson would follow him.

The story continues in:
Test of the Professionals:
The Peaceful Night Poisonings

MX Publishing

MX Publishing is the world's largest specialist Sherlock Holmes publisher, with over six-hundred titles and over two-hundred authors creating the latest in Sherlock Holmes fiction and non-fiction

The catalogue includes several award winning books, and over four-hundred-and-fifty have been converted into audio.

MX Publishing also has one of the largest communities of Holmes fans on Facebook, with regular contributions from dozens of authors.

www.mxpublishing.com

@mxpublishing on Facebook, Twitter, and Instagram